Honor O'Flynn

A Search for the True
Will of God

by
James Bailey

Advance Praise

It's my privilege to have read the first novel, Bailey's Blood, and to have called Jim Bailey a friend. I was his pastor and he shared with me the vision and some of the stories he had compiled and to be sure they are the stuff upon from which great novels, spell-binding come. I've also read some of this new novel and it, too, has the quality of greatness associated with it. Thanks Jim for continuing to use your God given talents productively.

~ *Dr Robert Orr*, Vice President, Academic Development at California State Christian University

Honor O'Flynn by James Bailey portrays a young lass who undergoes a life-long transformation. Dr. Bailey uses his gift of intricately weaving events of the era into actions and dialogue that allows the reader to feel a part of the action. The girl, Honor, is faced with issues ingrained from her Catholic upbringing that complicate her maturing in America. Does she honor her early pledge to become a nun or does she capitulate and become a child bride to a purchaser in the New World? This fast-paced novel holds the reader's interest as one internalizes sociological mores of an earlier era through dialogue and subtle humor that denotes Dr. Bailey's writings.

~ *T. Robert Stearns*, EdS, Public Education

Poignant romance and a deep spiritual growth are not to be outshined by the interesting depth of humor provided throughout this fast-paced, easy and fun to read Christian romance by James Bailey. Beautiful imagery enhances a writing style that is sure to be enjoyed by young and old alike - keeping the reader fully immersed in the somewhat troublesome journey of Honor O'Flynn. It is easy to relate to the characters and feel the emotions of young Honor as she seeks to keep true to the commitment of her youth - while being faced with the reality of the life she may really be intended to live. Knowing this work is a fictionalized history only serves to increase the rich experience of understanding another culture and an America of another time.

~ *Anna Weber,* Literary Strategist, Voices in Print, Arizona

Dedication

It seems reasonable to dedicate this story to all the descendents of Honor O'Flynn and William Logsdon of which there are a great many. But especially, I dedicate the novel to: Hannah, Morgan, Laurel, Carrick and Katherine Montague, my grandchildren and the ninth great grandchildren to these two American colonists.

Preface

Honora O'Flynn is one of my ancestors, and with the novel that bears her Americanized name, I want to tell her story, but there is a religious motivation for the novel as well. In my 70 years, I have met people who in their youth fell in love with the very idea of serving God in some important way.

... Perhaps they admired the esteem in which a special pastor was held;

... Perhaps they loved the story of some reporting missionary;

... Perhaps the enthusiasm that many feel when first coming to faith energized them as nothing had previously done.

So, instead of waiting to see where God will lead them they set about driving their lives toward their perceived goal. Then when older they become frustrated with the reality of their service or they find themselves ungifted for the challenge. They become relatively unproductive in that service.

I have a different view based on Henry Blackaby's book, *Experiencing God*. Instead of asking God to help attain our perceived goals we simply ask him to take control of our lives and open the doors needed to take us where He wants us to go. From that time forward we need only enjoy the adventures that come our way, giving Him the glory for whatever He achieves through our efforts. We should never confuse our own ambitions with His will, because that is the root cause of our failure to be in His will.

So, let me ask: Did God really have Honor kidnapped to a strange new land, or was her experience caused by circumstances of the day? For most of the seventeenth century, England faced three major problems: The crown had opposed Catholicism in all of Britain, leaving many of its people eager for revolution; rival nations were colonizing the New World, threatening England's standing as a world power; and the population in Britain was growing and taxing the food supply. To remain unified and strong, the crown needed a way to neutralize dissident Catholics and move many of its people to North America.

Ship captains were chartered to take England's down-trodden men and women to America. Many men and boys paid for their passage by selling themselves as indentured servants to mid-America plantation owners. This practice led to a 10 to 1 male to female population ratio in those colonies. So the captains were chartered to also take poor and imprisoned women who would pay for their transportation by agreeing to become brides.

Often, the transported individuals or their parents signed transportation contracts with ship representatives. It was typical for those representatives to prowl the poorer parts of town looking for drunk and starving men and women who sign in exchange for whiskey or food. The jails were emptied of capital criminals including people who were convicted of petty thievery. If a ship's space could hold a few more people, unscrupulous captains often kidnapped young men and women to increase their profits. A ship could make good money bringing people here and returning with a hold full of produce, mainly tobacco. In addition, the ship captains received grants for up to 50 acres of land for every individual who arrived in good health.

The first documented indentured male and female servants arrived in the colonies in 1619, and by the mid-17th century, nearly two-thirds of the arriving European immigrants were indentured. They came for several reasons. In middle-colonies like Virginia and Maryland, tobacco was a profitable but labor intensive crop. The large demand for both laborers and brides made transporting them profitable.

The voyage to America took between eight and twelve weeks. Food was scarce. In one reported case each person was given three biscuits and 3/5 of a pint of water daily. Many died of starvation or disease.

Tobacco brides were typically auctioned for 150 pounds of tobacco leaves. That's only about three cubic feet of leaves. At auction, the women usually had the right to refuse the highest bid but if unsold they would, like the men, be sold as indentured house servants. The service periods were for between four and seven years after which they were given provisions and land to start their freeman's lives.

I hope you enjoy this Christian Romance story about discerning between God's will and one's own desires as it unfolds against the backdrop of the difficulties faced by many immigrants to America.

Acknowledgements

I wish to acknowledge the great help offered during the writing of the novel. First, to Laura Osrini and my wife Petra who edited the manuscript. Second, to Christian Kapahnke who designed the cover. Also to Amanda Applegate who sat for the picture which graces the cover. Lastly I acknowledge my writer's critique group for their efforts: Winifred Doane, Richard Jacobs, Harvey Smith, Linda Stryker, Santos Vega.

Chapter One

Fourteen-year-old Honor O'Flynn's story began in April 1701 in County Kerry, Ireland. Folks in the tiny village of Dingle, where Honor lived with her family, described it as a wee bit o' heaven that had slipped through the fingers of the Almighty. Peaceful and pastoral, Dingle rested atop rolling green hills overlooking a quiet cove behind a limestone peninsula with a hill called Ballymacadoyl. It was the perfect place for a pious Catholic girl to live out her life in service to her Lord. But the Lord had other plans — Dingle, you see, was the village closest to the American colonies.

The cool, salty-sweet smells of the village wafted, as the sea breeze blended with the scent of heather and hawkweed. Generally more quiet than not, the occasional lowing cows could be heard beyond the chirping birds, and, on the hour, gongs from St. James' church bell.

Dingle's houses were built in shallow bowls dug out of the rocky soil, encircled with mounds of dirt to keep out the wind. The walls were erected from flat stones piled five feet high and plastered in mud; the roofs from saplings covered with dirt, and grass. Most of the houses had no windows, but all had wood doors, dirt floors, and stone fireplaces. Most homes had gardens protected by stick-and-waddle fences which grew lush with vegetables. A typical Dingle family might keep a cow for milk and raise a few sheep for wool.

Narrow pathways fanned out from Dingle's central square where folks came to draw water and celebrate Mass. Across from St. James Catholic Church was the pub where tired men gathered each evening for the almost religious ritual of discussing village gossip and tipping a frothy pint. the white Church had a tall bell tower, around whose clanging bell the people of Dingle, and those who farmed along its pathways, organized their days. All who attended St. James were considered townsmen.

Everyone in Dingle expected the fishermen to visit St. James each morning to pray for a good catch and a safe trip home. The farmers were expected to be there, as well, praying for good weather and abundant crops. Saturday was the day for confessions, in preparation for Sunday's Mass. On Tuesdays and Thursdays, the children took schooling and Catholic instruction in the room next to the sanctuary. Be it for sure, even with the Anglican King James on the throne of England, Dingle remained very much a predictable Catholic community.

●●●

Honor's mother, Caitlin, loved to comb her daughter's hair and braid it into pigtails that sprang out like spouts of water from each side of the girl's freckled face. "God bless ye, child," Caitlin said, tying a yellow ribbon to the first braid. "And may the sons of Ireland be smilin' on ye all this very day."

Honor found comfort in taking after both of her parents, possessing her mother's easy charm and her father's strength of purpose. A bit more than five feet tall, she weighed all of seven stones.

"Aye darlin', but yer becoming a handsome young woman. May God bless yer heart and bless all yer other parts as well."

In her own way, Honor also resisted growing up. "Oh Ma, I'm not like you yet. I'm still just a wee girl who sucks her thumb at night."

"Nae, girl, that's not what Father Hannigan tells me. He says all the boys run to sit with you in catechism, especially Sean."

"Oh Ma," Honor dropped her head. "Sean just wants to hold my hand. He told me he wants to go to Killarney and find work as a carpenter's apprentice. He said the houses there have wooden floors and glass windows. Surely, you're nae wantin' Sean to be takin' me away?"

"Nae, not for a minute. Do you know who's buried on the hill above the Church?" Caitlin asked, beginning the other braid.

"Aye, you told me, all the people of Dingle rest there in peace."

"Don't ye be forgettin', child, all the people of Dingle, not those who move away. We quickly forget about the ones who leave. I can't remember a one of them. But you'll soon be findin' a fine young lad in the village to wed."

"Ma, what if God wants something else for me?"

"Just last week, Father told me, 'God must be lovin' your Honor special, for He's blessed her with a smile that sparkles and dimples that delight. All the boys will fall for her darlin' green eyes and her bright red hair. What do ye suppose Father might be meanin' by that?"

"Aye, Ma. Father Hannigan loves me, true, and I love him as well." The braiding was finished, and Honor stood up. "But he sure is full of the blarney."

Caitlin took hold of Honor's head and looked into her eyes, smiling, "I'm not so sure. Maybe he knows that God made you very beautiful for some good lad."

Honor changed the subject. "I told Father that God wants me to be a nun, to teach the children in our village. That's what I'm goin' to be... a nun."

"Bless me, and what did Father say to that?"

"He said that the children need a good teacher."

"That they do, darlin', but yer a wee bit young to be knowin' what God wants of thee. My prayer is that you get all your wishes but one. Then, don't ye know, you'll always have something to strive for."

Her hair finished, Honor completed her chores and hurried through breakfast. Then she and her nine-year-old brother, Donovan, ran to the barn to give their father his expected hug. An imposing figure and a good father, Cillian was a farmer who did double duty as the mayor of Dingle. As he did every morning, Cillian shook Donny's hand and admonished him, "Stand tall lad, and take care of yer sister." Then Cillian wrapped his strong arms about Honor and kissed the top of her

3

bright red hair, "Ye be careful now, darlin'. They say the English are prowling about."

"We'll be careful, Da." She stepped back, blowing her father a kiss, and ran off with Donny, who was no taller than four feet and a bit chunky at five stones. She smiled as he pranced ahead of her, like a knight on a steed in search of a great adventure.

●●●

Donny shouted, "Hurrah to me." He leapt high in the air. "I'll be beatin' you to the water for sure." Honor reveled in his little-boy competitive nature and excitement. Digging sticks in one hand and wicker baskets in the other, each raced toward the cleft in the rocks that led to the sea.

Earlier that morning, the fishermen had gone beyond the peninsula to Dingle Bay, in search of a good day's catch. The only boat in sight was a merchant ship resting at anchor a mile or so from the town's dock, its British flag unfurled.

Honor and her brother ran across the wet, sandy tidal bed, excited about the clam-harvesting challenge that awaited them. She noticed a dinghy that sat empty where the sand fell away and the deep water began, but ignored it. By half past nine, Honor and Donny had reached the clam beds that held the sweet, juicy mollusks. They added the big ones to their baskets, leaving the smaller ones for another day. Two dozen of the tasty creatures would be enough to supplement the family's supper of cabbage soup and bread. The morning's adventure enveloped them both.

"I've found another big one," Donovan pulled out his stick to reveal a sandy lump with clamshell sides.

Honor turned to look at him. "That be but three for thee, Donny, and four for me," Honor shouted. The tide had not fully ebbed, and Honor stood barefoot in a six-inch-deep pool, occupying a shallow depression in the tidal bed.

"I be tellin' ye true, I've got the most and I'm the best." Honor challenged her brother.

"Nae, thee might be faster, but I'm the boy and I'm stronger."

"Here's another big one. 'Tis five for me," Honor dragged her stick through the bed and uncovered another clammy lump of sand.

Suddenly, the gulls which had been feasting on fingerlings took flight. They began to screech as they circled overhead. Honor looked up to see a youth of perhaps nineteen or twenty springing toward her like a hungry tiger. His blue tunic and knee pants identified him as a British merchant ensign, the dreaded enemy of all Irish mothers who cherished their innocent daughters. Immediately, she sensed great danger.

"Run, Donny, run," she screamed, taking flight across the sand with the ensign close at her heels. Honor raced toward the shore, knowing the older and faster ensign would have no trouble closing the yards that separated them.

She dropped her stick, pulling up the front of her skirt to free her legs, her strides as long and rapid as possible. Her mouth gaped wide and her heart pounded loudly, delivering extra oxygen to her muscles. Discovering too soon that she could not win the race, Honor turned and threw her basket of clams at the enemy.

The ensign flew past her, slapping at her shoulder to push her down on the wet sand. Splash! Then he returned to subdue his catch.

Honor tried to crawl away, rise, and run again, but the ensign stepped on her leg and then planted both feet on either side of her. He turned her on her back, dropped to his knees, and sat on her belly, roaring like a wild animal.

"Mother of God," she screamed in her highest pitched voice. "Let me go!" She wriggled and kicked and tried to scratch his face.

The ensign grabbed her arms and spread them out against the sand. "Why would I let you go, wench?" he spit, licking his hungry lips with a sneer. "Why would I catch you and then let you go?"

"Don't touch me, ye devil," Honor hissed with desperation. "If ye hurt me, I'll scratch yer eyes out."

With all her strength, she tried to kick and twist herself free of his grip, but nothing worked. Her heart thumped like a drum, and her body shook to its beat. Awful thoughts flashed through her mind as she struggled to free herself. *Da told me, but I wasn't careful. I shouldn't have come here with an English ship in the harbor. I should have seen him comin'. If he kills me, it'll be all my sin. It's my own fault.*

"No, God. No!" She yelled a loud prayer as her enemy rose to his knees and pressed his weight down on her outstretched arms. The sides of his filthy tunic hung open to reveal an even dirtier ruffled blouse. "Ye can't do that to me!" she bellowed.

"I can do as I please. You're mine now, wench."

Donovan finally caught up to her, running to her aide and jumping on the ensign's shoulders, grabbing at his head. But the sailor reached around and easily pulled the small boy off his back, flinging Donny across the watery sand. Honor screamed again as the ensign pulled his short sword from its scabbard. *My God, he's goin' to kill Donny*, she thought.

She saw Donovan stand up for another attack, but the ensign swung the sword shouting, "Stand away, boy, or I'll cut your head off and eat you for supper."

Honor screamed, "Donny, go get Da. Run quick, lad. Get Da." Donovan ran off as she resumed her struggle.

"Help!" She gritted her teeth and scratched his face with her free hand. Using her legs, she reared up as high as she could.

The ensign rode her bucking belly like a horseman atop an unwilling filly. "Jump all you want, wench. I like my whores feisty."

Saints above, he's going to rape me. Panic rushed through her like a mighty river washing away its constraining levee. He replaced his sword and smirked with lecherous glee. Like a dirty, old man, he grinned through rotting teeth, a monster prepared to lay waste her childhood. His face brought the vilest of images to mind as Honor remembered her mother telling her what English boys want.

"Don't do this! I'm still a virgin. I'm just twelve," Honor repeated the lie her mother had told the smallish girl to use if she ever found herself in just this situation. With a loud cry, she pleaded, "I want to be a nun. Please, don't do this." The eyes of her soul stared into the pits of the devil's own blackness.

He bent close to her face, his breath reeking and his body smelling of stale sweat. His matted hair hung down either side of his face, inches from her mouth. She turned her head to the side but continued to stare at him.

He grinned again. "I can do whatever I want. You're naught but a papist whore. Lucky for you, the captain likes skinny, young virgins. He'll pay a great sum when he sees this red hair and learns you ain't yet been done."

"Ye won't be havin' me, and neither will yer captain. Let me go!"

He grabbed her free hand and pushed it back into the sand.

"Help!" she cried again. "Someone help me!" She looked toward the docks, but they were too far away for anyone to hear her fear-weakened voice.

"No one's gonna help you, wench," he smirked. "And neither will I let you go. You're to be taken to the Americas and sold as a bride." With Donovan halfway up the cliff, the ensign stood and pulled Honor up with him. He twisted her arms behind her and tied them at the elbows with a length of cord. He looked at the back of her sand-encrusted dress and splashed water on her, as if to clean it. "If you come along smartly, I'll not be sporting with you."

With staccato thoughts, Honor began to consider the worst. I'll be a soiled woman. I'll be sold to a fat, ugly man. I'll nae see home again. I'll nae be a nun. Da and Ma will forget about me. A savage will kill me. Her thoughts shifted to one of salvation: God will have to save me if He wants me to teach the children.

The ensign relaxed his grip to turn her around, and Honor fled. With her hands tied behind her back, though, she couldn't match his speed. He caught up to her easily and pushed her down to the sand again. Then he picked her up and slapped her hard across the face. He grabbed her arm as he stalked toward the drop-off and the dinghy, yanking her arm to hasten her along.

"Whatever you wanted to be wench, say goodbye to it forever. You belong to the British Merchant Marine now, and you'll soon belong to some lonely, old man in the colonies."

For Honor, the well-defined world of Dingle had vanished, and she was on her own. Minutes passed like hours as the dinghy moved away from the sand bar. Honor suddenly saw her father run across the sandy shallows of Dingle Bay. By then, though, she could only squirm inside the small boat as the ensign rowed it into ever deeper water.

"Honor," she heard Cillian shout as he ran, "Jump into the water!" But the ensign had seated her in the boat and tied her to an iron loop mounted in the transom.

She kicked at the lad as he pulled on the oars, but it did little good. Honor shouted to her father, "Da, he's tied me to the boat. Come an' save me! I'm nae wantin' to go with him. Hurry, Da! Hurry!"

Her father ran as fast as he could, a pitchfork in his hand. Her fears grew as the water deepened, and her father's approach became more labored. By the time Cillian stopped running, the dinghy had a hundred-foot head start in the race to the British merchantman.

"Bring my daughter back," Cillian shouted between gasps for air. "I'll pay thee twice what she's worth in the colonies." The ensign didn't stop rowing. "She'll never let thee sell her. She'll vex thee more than she's worth." Cillian threw the pitchfork as far as he could, his face awash in fear. "She's been given to God, and the children need her. If ye take her, the saints will curse thee and all yer family. Bring her back!"

Honor tried to kick the ensign again, but he sat too far away for her to land a strong blow. "Da," she shouted, "he won't stop!" Reality tightened its fearful grip. Between heart-pounding gasps for air, Honor whispered a tearful prayer. "Mother of God … please come and help me … I'm terrible afraid." She watched Cillian wade out deeper, but with every pull on the oars, the very core of her world slipped farther and farther away.

Cillian shouted again, "Honor, darlin', I'm not able. It's too deep. Send a letter and I'll come to fetch thee. Please, darlin', don't let them take yer soul."

"I'll not forget, Da. I'll be escapin' and writin' thee as soon as I'm able." Her fate was clear — she would have to find her own way home. "With God as my witness, Da," she shouted, "I promise to come back. I promise, Da. I promise."

Chapter Two

At about the same time, across the Atlantic Ocean in eastern Maryland, William Logsdon was working his land with a field servant named Isaac. William was thirty-seven years old, a big man, and a devout Anglican. Twenty-seven years earlier, in 1673, his parents had given him to an English ship's Captain to be taken to America and sold as an indentured servant. Young William was the second son and would inherit nothing but poverty if he stayed in England. After working for six years, William was awarded twenty acres of land, a musket, a plow, and a sack of tobacco seeds. By April 1701, he had grown his holdings into a three-hundred-acre plantation named *Brotherly Love*. Yet, in spite of his worldly success, he was alone, childless, and unfulfilled.

Little more than twelve feet wide and a foot deep, the Gwynn Falls Creek meandered along one side of the *Brotherly Love* plantation. The creek flowed over rocks and sandbars, its sides overgrown with trees, shrubs, and grass. An abundance of animals drank from the spot where the water ran swift and the trout grew fat. Maples, oaks, and other trees along its banks supported a variety of songbirds. In places, the tree branches grew together over the creek to form a peaceful shaded tunnel.

Should a tree fall into the water and block the passage of carts, the local settlers would have to remove it before commerce could continue. Such clearings made it easy to discern where the settled areas ended and Indian country began. European culture ended where fallen logs cluttered the creeks and blocked the way of the white man's two-wheeled carts. Four wheels didn't ride well along the rocky riverbeds, and a heavily loaded wagon was likely to break an axle. Even two wheels made for a rocky ride, and cargo had to be transported in baskets or tied to the cart bed. Backcountry creek beds and game trails

— the common routes between most places — became the spots men claimed as their land and built their plantations.

●●●

"Have you heard the chopping upriver?" William asked Isaac. "I believe we have new neighbors. We should go help them clear their land." Early the next day, the two men loaded their cart with tools and began their trek westward. Isaac drove. "It ain't like plowing, Isaac. Don't try to tell the horse where to go. Just point her up river and let her work out how to get there. Tie the reins off and let the mare have her head, so you can watch for deer."

A half-mile upriver, they heard people at work off to one side. "Look, there's the trail through the trees," said Isaac, pulling the horse to a halt. Settlers on the frontier had to hack out tillable land from an old-growth forest where trees grew large and far apart, with ferns and small bushes growing between the tree stumps. That morning, the cleared land looked like an overgrown pile of fresh-cut branches.

"They got near an acre cleared already," said William, "but they have a lot of stumps to pull out and burn." In addition to the stumps, rocks had to be dug up and set aside for a fireplace and fences. The work of clearing just one acre of new farmland could take several men and strong horses a week of long days. In William's mind, there were six good days for work, but on the seventh, the animals and men should rest.

As they entered the small clearing, William and Isaac watched as a large man swung an axe and two boys harnessed horses to a stump. Three piles of tree branches burned near a small tent set off to the side.

"Sir," said William, addressing the apparent landowner. The new neighbor walked toward the cart. "My name is William Logsdon. I live a short piece down river." William put his hand on Isaac's shoulder. "And this strong fellow is my servant, Isaac." Isaac lifted his tri-cornered hat and smiled.

In broken English, the new neighbor introduced himself. "*Guten tag,* Wilhelm. I am Walter Rusch, new neighbor for you."

"Good day to you, as well. My ears tell me that you are German," William stepped off the cart and reached out his hand.

"*Ja.* I come from *München* in Bavaria and have for three months been here."

"Welcome to Maryland. I see you have two lads with you."

"These are *meine Kinder,* Christian *und* Hans. *Und* I have also two daughters name Petra and Annesliase. They are *mit meinem Bruder* in Annapolis. We are five." The two boys shook William's and Isaac's hands.

"And does your wife stay with your brother as well?"

"*Nein. Meine frau ist* no more. She got the fever in München one year ago last October."

"My sympathy for your loss," William said. "Isaac and I have come to help you clear your land and build a cabin. We have axes and wedges, and we brought two strong horses with harnesses to help pull stumps. Can you use some help?"

"This *ist* very kind, *und* I would be much happy for help. How long you can stay?"

"We can stay as long as you need us. And since we live but a short distance away, we offer my cabin and barn for you to use until your cabin is ready."

●●●

After three hours of work, the crew sat down for a meal. William went to his cart and returned with a bundle in his arms. "We brought some smoked venison, carrots, and blueberries."

"*Und* we have hard bread, potatoes, and cheese," Walter added.

As they shared their meal, Walter continued his story. "I come to make a better life for *meine Kinder.* Too many people have no land to farm in my country."

William looked at the two boys and Isaac, who sat on stumps and ate with hungry attention. "Your boys seem like strong, hard workers. How old are they?"

"Christian, he *ist* fourteen and Hans *ist* eleven. *Meine* daughters are fifteen and nine. Do you have children, *Herr* Logsdon?"

"No, that is a problem. I'm not yet wedded," answered William. "My greatest desire is to wed soon and start a family. I'm thirty-seven years old and have lived in this country since I was ten. It is time to find a wife."

"*Ja*, I understand. *Meine* Frieda ist not two years gone and already I feel alone. *Und meine Kinder* miss their *Mutter*. So, I will to wed again myself."

William folded his arms in the make-believe hug of an imaginary woman. He said, "I dream often of someone warm at night and of children's laughter and play."

"*Ja, eine gute frau ist wunderbar*. A man alone *ist* but half a family." Walter set his food down. "*Herr* Logsdon, Anneliese, *meine* first daughter, *ist* of age to wed. Perhaps you should meet her when she comes to my new farm?"

"Oh no, I think it wrong for a man of thirty-seven to wed a woman of fifteen. People would think I'm her father, and when they learned the truth, they might consider me dishonorable."

"*Nein*, many good men lose wife *und* wed again to young *Fräulein*. Fifteen *ist* old enough."

William pointed his finger upward like a preacher about to deliver a deep Biblical truth. "No. I hope to purchase a widow near my own age, perhaps a woman with small children already. In that way, I would satisfy my need and help another family at the same time. I also plan to purchase another servant as soon my tobacco is cured and ready to sell."

Surprise flashed across Walter's face. "In Maryland, how does one purchase a *frau*?"

"It's quite easy." William took his store-bought pipe from his pocket and packed it with homegrown tobacco. He stood, stepped over to one of the tree stump fires and, with a stick, lit the pipe. "Every few weeks, a ship arrives from England. The ships often have people who have paid for their passage with a contract to become servants or brides. Some ships carry but a few people, while others carry many. This summer, I'll go to Annapolis and wait for a ship. If there are good people on board, I will buy the contracts of a young lad and an older woman."

Walter's eyes showed astonishment at the idea of a purchased bride, because in his native Europe, the bride's family would bring the dowry. "This *ist* very different. How much costs a bride?"

"That would depend on the woman. I guess the younger women are more expensive, as are the healthier ones." William nodded, "Isaac over there cost me two hundred pounds of tobacco leaves."

"You can purchase a *frau und* a son *mit* tobacco leaves?" asked Walter. "This would never be in Bavaria."

"No," answered William. "You don't actually purchase people. You pay the cost of their sea voyage to get here. In exchange, the servant agrees to work for three to seven years. The longer the service, the more you must pay."

Walter pushed out his lips, wagging his head from side to side. "*Ach*, this cannot be so. Why would you purchase a wife for only a few years?"

William laughed. "No, that's for the lads who are indentured. You can also purchase a maid-servant for a number of years, but you purchase tobacco brides for life. That is why marriageable women are more expensive."

"It *ist* a new world, this Maryland, I can say that." Walter laughed. He slapped his knee. "I must learn more about it." Then he changed the subject. "Wilhelm, this meat *ist sehr gut. Was ist das?*"

"It is very good indeed, smoked venison. Game is plentiful here. We kill a deer every few weeks and smoke it so it won't spoil. Until you can build your own smokehouse, you can use mine. I trust you have a musket to hunt with."

"*Ja*, I have a musket and have seen the wild animals. But I am not so *gut* at hunting. Perhaps you can teach me this, as well? In *München* I am carpenter."

William stood up. "Perhaps Isaac and your two boys can hunt deer on Sunday. They can kill a deer, butcher it, and smoke it for you. That will give you meat enough for several weeks."

"*Gut*, then we will hunt on *Sonntag*. How can I ever to repay all this kindness?" asked Walter.

"Many years ago, when I began to clear my first twenty acres, two neighbors rode over to help me fell the trees and build a cabin. They helped me for three weeks. That taught me that neighbor helping neighbor is the only way folks can survive in the backcountry."

"Das ist gut way."

"Neighbors helped me when I cleared my land, and I repay them by helping you. When another neighbor settles nearby, you will repay me by helping them get settled. That is the way things are done here."

"*Und* what *ist* your land called?" asked Walter

"*Brotherly Love*, after the place where I grew up in England.

"I will name my land *Grosser Gott*," said Walter. "This means for you, God is great." William smiled. "This is a good name, *ja*?"

Walter rose and called to his boys. "For now, we cut down more trees." The five of them cut three more trees that afternoon and pulled out the stumps. By the end of the day, they had cleared almost a quarter of an acre and made room for a small cabin. As dusk approached, the day's work came to a halt. The boys walked the horses to the river to let them drink their fill. Then, all five stripped off their clothes and sat down in the cold water to bathe.

"Here, I have some soap brought." Walter handed two bars of lye soap to William and Isaac. The soap did wonders washing off the dirt and sweat they had all accumulated. When they finished bathing, the men and boys pulled fern fronds, dried themselves, and dressed. Then they harnessed the horse to William's cart. Walter's two horses and William's second horse were tied to the rear of the cart, and the five rode off toward *Brotherly Love*.

William and Walter continued to get acquainted. "Where from come you, *und* why come you to Maryland?" asked Walter.

"I am English, and my father made ropes, but he wanted me to own my own land and have a better life. He indentured me to a Captain Smith, who brought me here years ago. There were eight boys on our ship. Six of us were sold in Annapolis, and the other two went on to Virginia with Captain Smith."

William continued, "My master's name is Frederick Kruger. He owned a plantation east of here. He went to Church every Sunday, and taught me how to grow tobacco and other crops. His wife taught me to read English, so that I might be able to read the Bible. She also taught me to speak a little Algonquin."

"*Herr* Kruger *ist ein goot deutscher* name. You should have learned some of my language."

"She taught me a little."

"What is this Algonquin?" asked Walter.

"Those are the Indian people here in Maryland. There is a Powhatan village to the south and a Susquehanna village not far to the north. Both speak Algonquin.

"So *Frau* Kruger taught you to speak *mit* the Indians."

"Yes. I stayed with the Krugers for six years. When I left, I had all the tools I needed to start my own plantation. The Colonial government gave me a warrant for land, so I bought a plantation where I have added to and worked my own land ever since."

"That *ist* another reason to get a *frau* for me," Walter inserted. "I will find an English woman. My land *ist* fifty acres. I bought it from Maryland for sixty-five English pounds, but it *ist nicht gut* to be without a woman. It would be a *gut* life for the English woman."

"I agree — your soil looks good," William commented. "My soil is good, as well. *Brotherly Love* has grown to three hundred acres, with almost forty cleared. After I purchase another field servant, I hope to expand to sixty acres of crops."

●●●

They rode on for another ten minutes before arriving at the cultivated field along the creek that held William's plantation. "We're here," said William to his new neighbor. By the moonlight, he pointed out the cabin, horse barn, smokehouse, vegetable barn, and chicken coop. The two barns had been built close to the small cabin, making the fifteen by fifteen foot cabin look much larger. Two roofs connected the living quarters to the barns. The front door of the cabin faced the animal barn, and the rear door looked out on the vegetable barn. The side facing the creek included a shuttered window. A tiny smokehouse and small chicken coop stood behind the two barns.

All the buildings had been constructed with mud-caulked logs and had split-log roofs covered with animal skins that were held in place with rocks. The space between the cabin and each barn had been roofed over to provide storage space for some of William's tools. The distance from the creek to the cabin, about fifty feet, was covered with grass and wild flowers. The front yard also served as a pasture for the cows and horses. A fresh country aroma emanating from the pile of cow and horse fertilizer overwhelmed the scent of the abundant wildflowers. A garden of about a quarter acre had been fenced off behind the cabin and vegetable barn to keep out the deer and other large animals. Squash, beans, carrots, and other vegetables grew, with the hope that the rabbits and squirrels wouldn't eat too much. A tobacco field stretched off into the darkness, planted to the left of the structures. On the other side were fields with other cash crops, all in their spring awakening.

William's chest puffed in pride over the wealth he had accumulated since becoming a freeman. His plantation appeared as though lifted out of Eden before Adam and Eve encountered the Tree of Knowledge. He had all a man could want, save the love of a good woman and the joy of little children running to greet their father.

When the cart stopped before the cabin, the drowsy youths unhitched the horses, tying them to short logs, which allowed them to graze. William and Walter went inside to rebuild the fire and prepare supper.

Helping clear Walter Rusch's land took several weeks, but in the end, five and a half acres were cleared and a small cabin erected. Two other neighbors brought their wives and children to help with the forest clearing. The children piled up a great many stones from the river, which, before winter would be made into a stone fireplace and walls to shore up the cabin. Until then, the roof would have a smoke-hole and a fire pit in the center of the floor. Many of the tree limbs that had gone unused for the cabin were cut into appropriate lengths, split, and stacked up against the north wall to fuel the fire and add insulation from the winter winds.

"*Das ist wunderbar*," said Walter. "I forever am to each of you grateful. We will make a celebration. I go to Annapolis and return *mit meinen* daughters, *meinem Bruder* and his family. We make a feast for you and your families one week from today."

Chapter Three

When Honor and her captor reached the Blissful Lady, a sailor dropped a rope ladder to greet them. Plunk! The rope hit the dinghy as the ensign pulled in the oars, the waves rubbing the small craft against the ship's hull. Honor remained silent, but she couldn't stop shivering as the cold North Sea wind penetrated her wet cotton dress. She looked toward Dingle's boat dock but saw no boat coming to her rescue.

I don't think I can swim that far, she thought. She closed her eyes and prayed silently, *Holy Mother, help me.*

Honor began to devise a new escape plan for the moment the ensign untied her. I could rock the dinghy and dump him into the water. Then I'll hit him on the head with an oars and row back home.

Honor watched as the ensign tied the dinghy off and shouted to the sailor above, "Throw down the hoist rope." The sailor tossed a heavy rope. Slap! The rope struck Honor across the back. The ensign knelt in front of her and untied her from the transom, but left her arms lashed behind her back. He spun her around and forced her to kneel. When she tried to break free he slapped the back of her head. "Stop that," he demanded, and knelt with his full weight on the back of her legs. As Honor screamed, the ensign's weight portended the inevitability of her painful situation. He grabbed the hoist rope, the dinghy rocking from side to side as he passed the rope under her arms and around her torso. Tying a knot behind her neck, he sat back. "Hoist her up, swab."

The pain in Honor's knees subsided as the ache under her armpits increased. She felt like a pig hung by a butcher, its neck about to be slit. *Maybe*, she thought, *he'll be untyin' me when we're on the ship. Then I'll run to the other side of the boat, jump into the water, and swim to Ballymacadoyl.*

On deck, Honor's arms remained tied. She bit her lip to hold back her tears of fear and frustration, as she looked around for an opportunity for escape. Thinking the old, gray *Blissful Lady* looked quite small, Honor noticed that it smelled of rotting wood and decay. The sails of the ship's three masts were gathered and tied haphazardly along horizontal yardarms. The Lady's forecastle and quarterdeck rose high, like a proud warship. She had the appearance of an undisciplined, old merchant vessel useful for nothing important. Ladder-like steps descended from the center deck through doorways into the ship's bowels. Ropes hung everywhere and wooden barrels were scattered about the deck. A few sailors stood about watching the arrival of the new passenger. Dirty and scraggly, the men all looked as unkempt as the ship they served. They leered and grinned at Honor; one man grabbed himself and blew a kiss in her direction. She noticed an older officer standing on the quarterdeck. He wore a rumpled blue uniform, and like the ship, he looked old and worn out.

When the ensign came aboard, he untied the hoist rope and spun Honor around. Her arms still tethered, she almost fell.

"Stop it." She shouted. "I am the mayor's daughter. Untie me this instant!"

The ensign pushed her up the stairs, ignoring her protests, and took her to the quarterdeck where the older officer waited. "I caught me a beauty, sir, and she says she's a virgin. I want to register her as a contract bride."

"Kind sir," Honor began, hoping a refined demeanor would ease the situation with the officer.

The officer scowled contemptuously as he grabbed her hair and pulled her closer. She tried to pull away, but the officer slapped her across the face. He clamped his hand on her jaw and forced her mouth open so he could look at her teeth.

He looked her body up and down, as though to estimate her market appeal. "Skinny wench, what's your name?"

Honor lifted her head. "Honor O'Flynn, I'm a very important person and ye must let me go." She drew a deep breath. "Me da is the Mayor of Dingle, and he'll pay thee well if ye let me go. I've given myself to the Holy Catholic Church. Have ye no fear of God?"

"How old be you, papist whore?"

She stiffened her lips and set her jaw, but her fears had returned in earnest.

The officer was about to slap her again when the ensign spoke up. "She said she's twelve. With her red hair and virginity, she should sell for a tidy sum and earn me a two pound capture fee."

"Put her below and come to my cabin at six bells. I'll have a contract for you to sign, and the reward will be yours."

The ensign grabbed Honor by the arm and walked her to the hatchway that led below. Honor balked, and he pushed her. She stumbled, falling down the first ten steps and landing on her rump. The ensign stepped down and picked her up, taking a whale-oil lantern from a hook. Then he pushed her down another ladder to the lowest deck. She kept her footing but had to hold her breath to avoid the stench of human excrement.

The middle-deck appeared almost bright and cheery, compared to the bowels that would be Honor's new home, with nary a porthole to let in a breeze to freshen the air. Except for the tiny flames from two lanterns, the "passenger" hold was dark and smelled worse than a privy in the heat of summer. Putrid water sloshed across the floor.

Honor could make out two aisles and three rows of wooden shelves aligned toward the rear of the ship. The aisles could not have been more than two feet wide and twenty-five feet long. The shelves on either side of the aisles were stacked two high — to form spaces where people were stowed. A bucket sat at the head of each aisle. The low ceiling required the ensign to lower his head as he stood beside her. Men and women lay on the upper and lower shelves. With no head room to sit up, each person's space looked to be little more than two feet wide and five feet long. The bottom shelf rested on boards about a foot off the deck's water-covered floor.

My God, thought Honor. Her jaw began to quiver as she prayed aloud, "Mother of God, help me in my hour of despair."

"Speak not, wench," the ensign said. He held the dim lantern ahead and pulled Honor to the left. Barefoot, she made her way down an aisle. She could barely see the raised heads and silent eyes, as they examined the new arrival. A weak male voice cried out for water. The wails continued as they walked sideways down a narrow aisle toward the stern. "Sweet Mother of God," she pleaded with the ensign. "Have mercy and give that poor soul some water."

The ensign cupped his hand over her mouth. "I told you to say nothing," he spat. "That one's too weak. We're but two weeks at sea, and already he cries like a baby. For him, water is a waste. He'll die soon anyway."

Honor could feel drums pounding in her ears as she gasped for air, breathing in the foul stench of excrement and vomit.

"Help me," cried another voice, as a hand reached out and grabbed her skirt.

Honor jumped back and shrieked. The ensign grabbed the offender's arm, slamming it down on the wooden shelf. Then he shook Honor hard and pushed her deeper into the beast's belly.

A woman shouted, "I'm hungry." The ensign pushed Honor forward again, so that she bumped into one of the wooden stanchions holding up the shelves. The ensign turned her sideways and wedged her between two of the wooden pillars.

He untied her hands and spun her around to face him. "Just do as you're told, and you'll live to see America."

Her defiance spent and her eyes full of tears, Honor's whole body began to tremble. "Please don't be doin' this. I nae want to go to America."

All the top shelf spaces were occupied, so the ensign grabbed her hair and pushed her, head first, into a lower space.

The sailors had orders to put men only on the top shelf and women only on the bottom, so there would be no fraternizing among the "passengers." Honor's face made contact with a damp rag. She started as a hand pushed her away. "Don't touch me," its owner said.

From the other side, two hands grasped her shoulders, pulling her deeper into the space. She struggled to get away, but the hands wouldn't let go. She heard "Shush," as the hands turned into arms that enfolded her. Then the ensign grabbed the rope that hung from the stanchion, put it through a hole in the cargo storage shelf, and tied it around Honor's ankles. He pulled the rope tight. Her whole body convulsed in fear, and she wet herself.

Honor continued to tremble as the ensign walked away. She gasped again for air, and folded her arms tight, so as not to touch whoever was next to her.

"Don't be afraid, little one," said a voice that sounded like an English woman.

Honor watched the ensign climb out of the hold, taking the oil lamp with him and leaving the frightened girl in complete darkness. The woman reached out and stroked Honor's hair. "How old are you, child? I think my daughter is about your age. Would you like me to hold you?" In desperate need of comfort in the face of what might have been the very essence of hell, Honor reluctantly slid over and allowed herself to be gathered in. The woman seems old, Honor thought as she nestled her head into the softness of the large breasts. Honor felt a kiss on her forehead and heard the whispered words, "I love you, Rose."

They lay together for some time, the woman rocking and the child sobbing. Eventually, Honor's heartbeat slowed and her crying turned to occasional hiccups. She began to pull herself together, finally forming a few words. "I'm Honor. They stole me from the beach. I shouldn't be here."

"I'm Ann Smyth. My friends call me Comfort. I have three children: Rose, Tommy, and little Samuel. Rose is about your age." Comfort pulled Honor's head back into her warmth and started to hum a lullaby. After several minutes, she said, "You have a beautiful name. May I call you Honor?"

Comfort smiled and kissed Honor's red hair. "I'm no devil. I'm just a mother, but I do come from England. You may call me Comfort if you like." Then the woman took a small rag doll from her pocket and gave it to Honor. "I made this for Rose. It's the thing I look at to remind me of my babies — my most precious possessions."

Honor said, "My dearest thing is the Holy Mother. She's my dearest friend and I want to be like her." Honor thought for a few seconds, "Are ye a heathen? Da says all the English are heathens."

"Well, I believe in God, and I pray each day. While my husband lived, he read the Bible to me often, and we went to Church every week." Honor snuggled back into Comfort's bosom, and the older woman kissed her again. "Thank you, Lord," said Comfort as she rocked back and forth.

Honor whispered, "I'm thankin' the saints that the English boy didn't rob me. But he called me a papist whore. He must be a heathen."

"I know," Comfort replied. "The English think the Irish are all papists and the Pope is the antichrist. Pay no heed to talk like that. I've been poor all my life and I know all about foolish insults. My master often called me a whore. And whenever any of his children came into my presence, I had to walk to a wall and put my nose up against it. He said I was not worthy to look upon his children and should never speak to them. I've learned to let go of insults and think about more important things, like my children."

Sometime later, the ship's bell clanged twice. Honor jerked her head around. "What's that?"

"That's how we tell time. It's twelve-thirty. Sailors divide the day into six watches, and each watch has four hours. The bells clang every half hour, first one clang then two, all the way to eight clangs. Then they start over. Two bells on the afternoon watch mean that it's twelve-thirty. We go on deck twice a day, at six bells in the forenoon and evening watches. That's the time when we can relieve ourselves, eat something, and go up top to get a breath of fresh air."

Honor pulled herself back. Now that her eyes had become used to the darkness, she could see Comfort more clearly. In the dim light, the woman looked about the same age as Honor's mother, but heavier. Her eyes looked dark, and her thin lips had a permanent smile. Her plain dress opened at the top and her hair fell from what might have once been a white bonnet.

The gentleness of her new friend helped Honor regain her happier disposition. She smiled and said, "Will they be untyin' me when it's time to eat? Ma says when I'm hungry, I can eat more than she can cook."

"Yes, dear, then they'll untie you."

Honor whispered, "I have a plan. When they take us up to the top deck, I'm gonna jump into the water and swim home." She thought for a moment and added, "Ye can come with me if thee want. Let's just pee on their dumb old boat and jump into the water."

Smiling, Comfort said, "I'm sorry Honor, but the officers are afraid the new people might try to jump overboard when we're close to shore. Once we're out to sea, they'll untie you. Near the shore, they take us topside, one row at a time, but they watch us very closely. If they find you untied before we go to sea, they'll chain you down, and you will have to wait a whole day to relieve yourself." Comfort wriggled toward Honor's ankles and loosened the rope. "Maybe this will help."

"Aye, that feels a wee bit better," Honor said. "Did the sailors steal ye from England?"

"No. I'm here voluntarily," explained Comfort. "My husband died two years ago, and I had to leave my three children with my sister when I hired on as a house servant. Every month, I sent all my earnings to my sister to care for the children, but that left me with nothing. My employer, the one who told me to put my nose to the wall, offered me a one pound note if I would let him have his way." Her voice took an angry turn as she took in a deep breath. "When I refused, he had me arrested, saying I pilfered the linens. I swore my innocence, but the judge sentenced me to three years in the Old Bailey. Then, instead of prison, the judge offered me transport to the colonies."

The ship gave out a deep rumble. "What's that?" Honor asked.

"They're raising the anchor. The hold must be full, and the captain probably wants to get away from Ireland. It's best that you say goodbye, as you might never see your homeland again." Comfort paused for a moment, then said in a hushed voice, "Honor, sweetheart, I'm sorry you were kidnapped, but what did you mean that the sailor didn't rob you?"

"He didn't do what Ma says all English boys want." Honor rose up on her elbows and looked at Comfort. "But I don't want to go away. Why didn't the saints save me?"

"Look at me, little one. Tell me about your Da. He must be a good father."

Honor crawled back into Comfort's warmth, her eyes filled with tears again. "Oh, yes, he loves me very much. He says I'm as Irish as the shamrock. Did ye know that we have a farm and Da is the mayor of our village?"

"What's your da's name?"

"Cillian O'Flynn, and Ma is Caitlin. I have two brothers."

The anchor clunked as it came to rest on the ship's deck.

"It sounds as if you have a nice family," said Comfort, as she stroked Honor's hair, now dry but still encrusted with sand.

"I be almost fifteen. Donny came next — he be twelve. And then there's Michael. On account of her trouble, Ma can't have any more kids."

"What kind of trouble is that?" Comfort asked, to keep Honor talking.

"She won't tell me, but she said God decided that three children would be enough. Do ye think God decides those things?"

"Yes, child, I think God decides just about everything. Except, of course, when we do bad things. God doesn't make us sin."

Honor dwelled on Comfort's previous thought. "Why does God let bad people steal children? I'm thinkin' the sailor who stole me is a wicked person."

"Yes, I think he must be bad to have kidnapped you. How big is your farm?"

"Our farm is grand. It's high above the ocean on a flat place with lots of rocks and dirt. We're havin' lots of bushes too, but no trees, and sometimes it's very windy. On our farm, the grass is very green, and it's covered with yellow and orange flowers. We have a milk cow, and we grow lots of grass for our sheep to eat. The Dingle men make fences out of the rocks, so the sheep won't be runnin' away."

They could feel the ship start to move. Comfort held Honor tighter. "Your farm sounds wonderful," she said. "Do you help with the sheep?"

"Oh, no. That's Donny's job. But Ma has a big garden, and I be helpin' her with that. Every family in our village has a garden next to their cottage. Sometimes it rains hard and ye can nae work in the garden. I love runnin' in the grass when it rains, but I think I'm gettin' too old for such things."

The diversion worked. Honor looked up with a dimpled smile.

Comfort said, "Do you have a best friend you like to play with?"

"Aye, most of the children are too young, but I like Sean. He wants to hold my hand, but I don't let him."

"If you like him, why not hold his hand?"

"God wants me to be a virgin, so I can't be holdin' a boy's hand."

"I see. I'm sure that Sean is a nice lad. What does he look like?"

"He has blond hair, and he wears his hat on the back of his head. His curls come down on his forehead. All the girls like him, but he likes me best." They felt the ship lurch forward and start to roll with the waves.

"Are you glad that Sean likes you best?"

"Yes, but he's going to Killarney. He's taller than me and can run faster. Once he chased me home and grabbed my arm to pull me down into the grass. When I told the Father at confession, he laughed and said he would talk to Sean about it."

Comfort smiled. "Did you like it when Sean pulled you down?

"I wanted to hug him. I didn't tell Father that. Sometimes it's better not to tell the priest everything. I did sort of like it. That's why I had to go to confession. But, when he tried to kiss me, I slapped him hard."

"I'd guess that he's older than you?"

"Yes, he's almost sixteen. Did I tell ye he's very strong? None of the other boys will wrestle with him. Once he let me feel his arm, and I had to use two hands. I liked that a lot, but I didn't tell Father Hannigan."

"I think you're a bit devious when you like things you think might be wrong. Tell me more about Sean."

The ship started to sway as it surged toward the open sea. "He said he wants me to wed him. I told him, I can't, but if he stays in Dingle and becomes a priest, we could work together in the same parish. I could teach the children and he could say the Mass."

"I hope my Rose finds a nice boy and has many children. When a girl becomes fourteen, it's time to consider such things." Comfort rolled onto her back and stared teary-eyed up at an imaginary sky.

Honor rolled back as well and listened to the waves pass down the side of the ship. She asked quietly, "Do ye miss yer children?"

Comfort sniffled. "Right now, you're as close to a daughter as I have."

Chapter Four

A few hours later, the Blissful Lady rolled with the waves as the ship glided across the open ocean. Rolling and creaking, the ship's movement gave a nauseous inevitability to Honor's situation and made her sick to her stomach. She looked at Comfort with tear-filled eyes. "I don't want to go away. I want to go home."

"Little one, life is seldom what we want it to be, but don't be afraid. You'll be fifteen soon — old enough to start anew."

"But, I'm still needin' Da and Ma, and the children in our village need me. I don't understand why's God is allowin' this to happen. How will I teach the wee ones?"

"Honor, we've talked of this. God is not doing this to you. He's allowing this experience to strengthen you for the future. And children everywhere need teaching."

Honor pulled her knees up and curled into a fetal position. She felt Comfort's hand on her head as gentle, motherly fingers stroked her hair.

"Besides," said Comfort, "you still might find a way to get home."

Honor stayed curled up for a long time, and her thoughts turning once again to planning her escape. She'd escape and send a letter home to request money for her return voyage to Dingle.

After a while, she heard the crying sounds of a young boy on the shelf above her. The boy's crying shifted her thoughts from her own problems to his, and she smiled at Comfort. She looked toward the sound, rapping her knuckles on the board that separated her from the sobbing lad. "Were ye stolen by the sailors too? Are ye afraid?" She heard no answer. "I'll be escapin' when we get to America. Maybe we can escape together." Still, she heard no answer. "What's your name?"

"Obadiah."

Honor pulled herself toward Comfort. A new plan was taking shape. "Did ye hear him? Saints be praised, when we reach America, we can all run away and find help. If we run away at the same time, they won't be able to catch all of us."

"That sounds like a good plan, but where will we go to find help?"

"Any Catholic Church will help us. I'm Irish, and I'll be tellin' the priest that we're all stolen. I'll tell him that we want to go home."

"I see," said Comfort. "I'll think about your idea, but I doubt I can join you."

"I thought ye wanted to see yer children again. The boy up there and I will need yer help until Da sends money for our passages home."

"Little one, I've not been kidnapped. I want a better life. God willing, I'll be able to send for my babies one day. I don't want to escape. I want America to be my new home."

"But if ye help us, then Obadiah and I can escape together."

"I'll think about that, too, child. For now, I'd like to know about your village?"

The look on Honor's face changed from excitement to disappointment. Then, like a chastened child, she answered Comfort. "It's called Dingle. Everyone there works hard and prays to all the saints."

"It's a bit like that in England. We work hard and pray often."

"The English are evil. They send their soldiers to scare us and take our animals."

"I'm sorry. Sometimes the people who serve our King do terrible things. Is Dingle large?"

Joy return to her voice. "No, but it's a grand place with a beautiful church. Ye would love Dingle. There are many good houses on the paths that lead to the farms or down to the fishermen's dock. Our house is the third one on the path toward the dock."

"Tell me about your house."

"Ye should come and see it. It's made of rocks and has a grass roof," said Honor. "We don't have a wood floor, but the door is wood. The nicest part is the fireplace in the middle of the house. It's made of stones. Ma uses it to cook, and we keep a fire all winter."

"What do you burn in the fireplace?" Comfort asked. "In London we use coal if we can afford it."

"We don't have any coal. We have to burn peat. Donny and Michael dig it up. Sometimes Da makes tight bundles of the dead grass and twigs. We like to burn twigs because they smell much better than the peat, and they don't fill the house with so much smoke. My job is helpin' in the garden."

"And tell me, other than helping in the garden, what are your duties around the house?"

"I keep very busy. I make cheese and help Ma in the kitchen. Michael helps in the kitchen too. I spin wool into yarn that Ma makes into sweaters and shirts. Last winter, she knitted me a sweater. Ma made me this dress for my birthday from cloth that Da bought in Killarney," Honor motioning to her now filthy frock. "I have to wash the plates, knives, and forks three times a day, and I fetch water. I also go to school in the church twice a week. I can read very well."

"Oh, I'd love to eat your fresh cheese, but the poor in London can afford it only for holidays. You're lucky to live in the country. What kind of cheese do you make?"

"Yes, we have a cow in the pasture. I milk the cow every day and make cheese from the milk."

"Do you have a water pump, or does your water come from a fountain?"

"From the creek or from a fountain," Honor answered. "If ye live in town, ye can get water from the fountain where the footpaths come together." She added with a hint of pride, "I can write some too."

Comfort smiled at Honor's descriptions of her family. "Tell me about your brothers."

"Miss Comfort, you'd be lovin' them if ye met them. Donny is a little younger than myself, and I love him the most. He has brown hair like Da and a dimple in his chin. He used to go to school with me, but he didn't like it. After school, I make my chores into a game, so he likes to help me with them. I'm a wee bit bigger and faster than Donny, but he likes to race me wherever we go, always thinkin' he can beat me. Sometimes I let him beat me, and that makes him happy."

"I think all boys like to win."

"We were digging clams together when the sailor kidnapped me. Donny ran to get Da."

"What about Michael, what's he like?"

"Michael's the littlest. He helps me sometimes, but I always have to stop and show him how to do things. Ma says he's her wee devil with blond hair. Sometimes, when Ma takes him outside to give him a bath, she tickles him, and he pees on the grass and laughs. But when Ma swats him for it, she never hits him hard, so he doesn't cry."

"He must be all boy."

"Yes, and Michael likes to sleep next to me. He says I keep him warm in the winter. I think he loves me most when he snuggles up against my tummy at night. His hair tickles my nose and he snores, but that's okay."

"And where do you sleep?"

"We're very rich. We have two bedrooms in our house. Ma and Da get one, and we children get the other." Honor crawled back into Comfort's softness. The joy in her voice disappeared. "I want to go home," she sighed.

●●●

By seven o'clock that evening, the *Blissful Lady* began to roll. Honor sat up, as a topside bell clanged three sets of two. "Is it time to use the bucket? I have to go, bad."

"Yes, it's six bells, so now we get our thirty minutes' to use the bucket and go up to the top deck to see the sun. The officer will be by to untie you, but stay very still until he comes. Then run to the buckets and get in the shortest line."

Honor had used a bucket many times before, but not in a public place. As soon as the older boy in front of her finished, she stood astride the wooden receptacle, squatted down, and did the best she could, trying to keep her dress out of the bucket.

Once topside, Honor noticed a sailor staring at her. Standing behind a wooden plank, he had an iron pot in front of him and used a metal cup to scoop the yellow mush that filled the pot. He poured the thick yellow mush into a wooden bowl and handed it to the next person in line.

When Honor reached the serving station, the sailor leered at her. "The new red-haired wench, I see." He scooped out some mush, but let most of it slip back into the pot. She met his ogling eye, as he said, "If you want more lassie, come back so I can have a closer look at you." Then he dropped the ladle into the mush and reached toward her bodice with his filthy hand. She turned to the side, but not quickly enough. Catching the sleeve of her dress, he pulled her toward him and laughed. Then he blew a lurid kiss at her.

The older officer in the unkempt uniform walked over and grabbed the sailor by the scruff of his neck. He spun the sailor around and slapped him hard across the face. "Go to your hammock," he ordered. "I'll deal with you later." The officer pushed the sailor down and kicked him.

Honor watched as the frightened sailor crawled away and then ran toward the entrance to the hold. The officer pointed to another sailor, shouting, "Swab, serve the meal." The replacement sailor rushed to the plank and fished the ladle out of the mush. He grabbed Honor's bowl and ladled in a full scoop of mush.

Honor watched the others as they stood about, shoveling the yellow mush into their mouths with unwashed fingers.

Honor walked back to join Comfort. She felt safer, knowing Comfort was near.

Comfort said, "Eat, child. Don't wait for me."

The food consisted of corn meal mixed with sea-water, tiny pieces of onion, and salted horse meat. The ship had little room for firewood, so the mush was served cold. Honor forced herself to eat it.

As the motley group ate their simple meal, another sailor walked about with a bucket of water. He stopped at each person and poured a ladleful into their bowls. On reaching Honor, the sailor filled her ladle half full, spat into it, and poured the liquid into her bowl. Then he filled Comfort's bowl to the top. Honor looked at Comfort, unsure of the sailor's meaning.

"The sailor thinks it's your fault that his mate will be punished," said Comfort. "If the officers hear you talk to one of the sailors, they won't untie your ropes for the next free time. And, if they think a sailor seeks favors from you, they'll have him tied up and whipped."

"Why, for God's sake?"

"The captain doesn't want the sailors to get too close to female passengers, as it could cause what little discipline there is to vanish, and fights could erupt among the sailors. Stay close to me, Honor, and do as I do." Comfort gave the girl some of her own water. "Pay the sailors no mind. Think about your family. Think about Donny and Michael."

When both bowls were empty, Comfort took Honor's bowl and dropped it, along with her own, into a large barrel. Then Comfort accompanied Honor around the deck at a brisk pace. Honor noticed that most of the others were also walking briskly.

Comfort put her arm around Honor's right shoulder, and with her other hand, she brought Honor's fingers up to her mouth and kissed them. "Do you know what I think, child? We're God's gifts to each other. I think we can help each other while we're on this voyage." Honor looked up, put her arm around Comfort's waist, and smiled. For the moment, she felt safe.

A young lad in front of them turned around. "Good day," he said. "I'm Obadiah Green. May I walk with you?" He stepped toward Comfort's unoccupied left side, next to the rail. "Please mum, I'm alone."

The boy appeared to be Honor's age, but a little bigger in stature. He wore rather dirty knee-length trousers, with shoulder straps, and still shiny brass buttons. His shirt appeared stained but new, and his shoes looked sturdy. One black sock went up to his knees while the other gathered itself near his ankles. "We'd love to have you walk with us, Master Green," Comfort said as she reached out to accept him. "I've seen you before. Did you board the ship in England?"

Obadiah held onto Comfort's hand and with his other hand, took hold of her arm. "I didn't think I'd miss me Mum, but I do. I miss her a lot. I've never been away before."

"Why did you leave this time?" Honor asked.

"My dad was a carpenter in Chelmsford. He got sick and died. Mum can't afford to raise all five of us. Since I'm not the oldest, I decided to get a job in town. I wanted to stay near Chelmsford and send her money, but the sailors caught me stealing apples."

Honor butted in. "Then ye can escape with me, and we can go back together."

Obadiah answered both questions forcefully, "I'll not be escaping; I want to make my fortune in America."

"You sound grown up and determined," said Comfort. "That's good."

"But, I still miss me Mum."

Honor looked around from Comfort's other side and gave Obadiah a scowl. "If ye escape, ye can go back to help yer mum."

Obadiah ignored her and changed the subject, "I heard you come on board days ago. I'm on the upper shelf with the men."

Honor's ire grew at his comment, "All the men on top, and the women on the bottom? That's not fair."

"Life's not fair, little one," said Comfort. She pulled Honor in and gave her a little hug. "Perhaps the captain thinks men get sick more easily."

"All the more reason to hate the English captain," Honor grumbled.

A cool breeze blew, and the ship rose and fell with regularity. Honor's mind returned to the idea of escape. She turned to Obadiah. "Why don't you run away with me?"

He didn't answer.

Comfort asked Obadiah, "And why do you need a mum to hold your hand?"

Again, he didn't answer.

"Well," Honor interrupted. "If ye won't help me escape, then I won't help thee either. I'll run away by myself." She added smugly, "Besides, Comfort is my friend."

Comfort went on. "Lots of lads go to the American plantations to make their fortune. You may find that you are lucky to be here." She put her free arm around the boy's shoulder. "How old are you, Obadiah?"

"I'm almost fourteen."

"Then you're the same age as my Rose," Comfort said as she looked toward Honor and smiled. "Master Green, this is my new daughter, Honor O'Flynn." She turned back to Obadiah, "You two could be good friends, and I can be like a mum to you both."

Honor scowled at the boy again. She thought to herself, He should find another mum. We don't need him.

Chapter Five

When they returned to the hold, Obadiah sat on the edge of the lower bunk with Comfort, talking with her like the Mum he missed so much. Honor sat behind Comfort and Obadiah, her legs crossed and her arms wrapped around her knees. The hold was abuzz with voices, some in whispers while others were louder. For Honor, the chatter somehow made the vile nature of the hold almost cheery. The scary part was Obadiah; Honor needed a new plan.

She asked Comfort, "Why do they want to take us to America?"

"I suppose the King wants to own the Colonies, and he needs to have great numbers of his people living there before he can claim them."

"What about the people who are already there? Sean said they be savages who kill Europeans and steal things. Does the king want to own them too?"

Comfort said, "I guess they'll be our neighbors. Perhaps they'll become English subjects."

"Savages," Honor repeated. "I nae be wantin' neighbors who don't even wear clothes."

Obadiah spoke without turning to face Honor, "That's silly. Of course they wear clothes. When it gets cold, they would have to."

Honor went on, "Sean told me he heard from a sailor who's been there that they were naked. He said the savages paint their faces, don't wear clothes, and steal girls like me."

Comfort spoke up again, "Perhaps Sean wanted to scare you. They're probably not savages. They're people just like us."
"And the King of England would, of course, want such people

as subjects. All the more reason to hate the king," Honor continued.

This time Obadiah turned to look at Honor. "You don't know anything about the King!"

"I know a lot. He's the devil in England, and he takes priests away and steals girls like me and sends them away from their families."

Obadiah grew defensive, "The king isn't a devil. He's a good king and he doesn't take priests away! Besides, he's told the ship's captain to take boys like me to America. I'm gonna make my fortune there. If the Captain didn't take me, I'd never have anything."

"Ye know nothing about it. Ye are nae Irish. He told his soldiers to get rid of all the Catholics, and they have taken away the priests and burned the churches."

Comfort intervened, "Perhaps we need something different to talk about. Tell us about your family, Obadiah."

Intent to continue arguing, Honor said, "The king's nae carin' if the people they take to America want to go or not. Why should the King care who goes there?"

Comfort responded, "He doesn't want the Spanish and French to be able to claim the colonies as theirs."

Honor continued, "And why does he want me to live there? I'm not English."

Obadiah threw up his hands and sighed. "He's the King of England, Scotland, and Ireland. He's your King too, you know?"

"Nae, he's not my king. My King is in heaven," Honor said piously.

Comfort tried to stop the argument again by explaining what little she knew. "King James wants lots of men from Britain to build towns and make farms in America. And those men need wives so they can start families. I'm hoping to wed a landowner and give him children."

"Miss Comfort," said Honor, "I would burn in hell. I mean, if I had a baby."

"No, child, not if you're someone's wife. Then you can have lots of babies. If you're wedded, it's not a sin."

Obadiah spoke up, "I'm glad she won't be my wife. She argues too much."

"I don't want to talk about this anymore," Honor said, rolling over.

● ● ●

The next morning at six bells, the officers let the people in the hold go up for another meal and some water. No sailor stood by to scoop the mush. Breakfast consisted of two hard biscuits and a small square of cheese. The food lay on a bench in two separate piles, with a sailor at the watch so that no one could take a double portion.

Honor took one biscuit and one piece of cheese. She bit into the biscuit and said to Comfort, "It's hard to bite, but it doesn't taste as bad as the mush we ate for supper. What's it called?"

"Take two biscuits, little one. They're called hardtack. Poor people in London eat them all the time. We make them from flour and a little salt, mixed with water. After they're baked, they last a long time. The ship has lots of them. All our breakfast meals are hardtack with a bit of something else. Since I have been aboard, they have given us cheese, carrots, and apple butter. That's all we get until supper. Take two and eat them both."

As they circled the deck, Honor looked out to the horizon but could see no land. They were in the middle of a featureless expanse of water. *We're lost*, she thought as she began to grasp her new reality. *This horrible ship is all there is. If I fall into the water, I'll drown.* She skirted around Comfort to put the safety of Obadiah and the older woman between herself and the side rail. "We're all gonna die and be eaten by fish," she cried, grabbing Obadiah's arm.

The boy shook his arm loose and moved to the seaward side of Comfort.

Honor composed herself. "That's what happened to Jonah. A big fish swallowed him."

"Who's Jonah?" asked Obadiah

Honor peeked around Comfort's skirt. "He's a man in the Bible. He didn't do what God wanted and fell off a boat and was swallowed by a big fish."

"Little one, a fish can't swallow people. Fish aren't that big."

"Yes, they can. Father Hannigan told us all about it." Honor crossed herself. "I hope God doesn't get mad and allow a fish to swallow me."

"I don't know, child. Perhaps he already has."

Honor looked at Comfort, her eyes wide in surprise. "Do ye think I did a sin? Is that why they stole me and I have to live in the belly of this old ship?"

"I think she's gone batty," said Obadiah. Then he pointed toward the sailor who had grabbed at Honor's arm the day before. "Look."

The sailor stood, his arms tied above his head to one of the masts. With his knees buckled, torso shirtless, and head sagging backwards, he appeared almost unconscious. When Comfort looked up, she immediately noticed red welts across his back. She stopped. "See, Honor, what happened to that sailor because he touched you last night?"

Honor stared at the man in horror. "Why is he tied to the pole?"

"That's his punishment for touching you. He'll have to stand there for I don't know how long. The poor soul must be very thirsty."

"But he just grabbed my arm. That's nae so bad a thing."

"If they don't punish him for a small offense, he might try to climb into your space below. Imagine what would happen if the sailors thought they could do that. The officers can't afford to let them take too many liberties."

41

An officer walked up and threw a bucket of salt water on the man's red stripped back, causing the sailor to scream in agony.

The ensign who kidnapped Honor looked at her and spat in her direction, "Filthy whore."

Honor looked at Comfort. "My God, I'm sorry," cried Honor. "If what he did was so bad, it's part my fault for making that man sin."

"You didn't make him do anything," said Comfort. "He decided to touch you on his own."

"Do you know why nuns wear those long dresses and bonnets? So they don't have to worry about sinnin'. If I had let Sean kiss me, I might not be able to be a nun."

"Little one, you must learn that you're not responsible for what other people do."

"Nobody would want to kiss her anyway," said Obadiah.

Honor looked at him. "You don't know how hard it is to be like the Holy Mother. You're a boy."

When the mealtime ended and the passengers were sent below to their spaces, an ensign stood at the first ladder, counting the people. When it was Honor's turn to descend, the officer pushed her, and she fell all the way down to the first hold.

●●●

Later that day, when Honor and Comfort lay close to each other, Honor's thoughts turned dark again. She remembered Sean's harsh description of the New World. She asked Comfort, "Why, in the name of heaven, would ye want to be goin' to the Colonies by yerself? It seems so dangerous."

"It is dangerous, and many people are too fearful to venture there. I'm sure my new husband will protect me."

"But ye have no idea who ye will be wedded to. What if he's ugly and old? What if he beats you?"

"I don't know who he will be. I pray every night that he will be a good and kind man. He may be a farmer or a carpenter or who knows what. I hope he's a farmer. I'd like to live on a farm."

"It's not fair. I can't wed, so why am I here?" Honor pouted.

Comfort answered, "Little one, we spoke of this at breakfast. You are right. It's not fair, but I doubt that anyone cares what you want. Perhaps the ship's captain couldn't fill his quota with people from England, so he went to Ireland to kidnap more boys and girls."

"I'm afraid of the captain. I hate him because he sent that sailor to catch me.

"To hate the captain or fear him is a sin. When someone hurts you, just do your best to remain calm and think of things you like very much. You don't have to like the captain, but find a way to forgive him."

"And the boy who caught me, can I hate him?"

Comfort's face took on a look of disappointment. "What do you think a good Christian should do if she is kidnapped?"

Choosing not to hear, Honor went on, "What about the man who said ye stole the linens? Weren't you afraid of him? Don't you hate him?"

"Child, hating does no one any good."

"And the English King. He kidnapped our priests and our burned our churches. Good Christians should fight the people who do such evil things."

"That's not what my husband taught me. Christians hate the evil things, not the persons who do them." Comfort stroked Honor's hair and smiled. "What I think …"

Honor interrupted, "But why did God let the boy steal me from the beach? You and I are both good Christians, God should be protectin' us from such things. I don't hate God, but I'm a bit angry with Him."

"Why do you say 'I' so much? If you love God, then your life is not all about you. If God loves you, He'll let bad things happen so you can learn and grow. If someone does you evil, it may be hard to forgive him, but you must learn to do just that. Remember, your hatred hurts no one but you. If you want to be a nun, you must fear God, alone. When someone hurts you, try to think good thoughts about your blessings. I know that's not easy, but you have to try."

● ● ●

The next time an ensign came by to count heads, Honor asked him a question. "Please, sir, tell us where we're going?"

The young officer looked about to make sure no one would hear him as he talked to a woman. When he saw no other lanterns burning, he whispered, "We're bound for Maryland."

Comfort listened in.

"How long will it take to get there?" asked Honor.

"That depends on the weather. If we get good winds, we'll make Maryland in seven or eight weeks."

Honor's jaw dropped. "Pray God," she said loud enough for everyone to hear. "We can't be livin' that long in these small spaces. What did we do to deserve this?"

The ensign shrugged his shoulders. "If we come into a storm, it could take eight weeks just to make Nova Scotia and another two or three to sail down the coast. Believe me, wench, you should be prayin' that we don't come to foul weather."

"What will happen if we come to a storm?" Comfort asked in a whisper.

"I have been in a bad storm but once," he said. "We lost one in three of our cargo. We couldn't untie or feed the passengers for days. Enough die, even in good seas. If we come to bad weather, we could lose so many that not even the captain profits."

"Mother of God!" Honor cried out.

Chapter Six

For most of the voyage, Honor's health remained good. Toward the end of June, however, she became sick with diarrhea and soiled her already tattered clothes. The girl became so weak that Comfort had to help her topside when the bell rang six times. She set Honor on the deck against the side rail and brought her some food. "Here, little one, you have to eat something."

Honor held her stomach and groaned, laboring to shake her head no. Comfort prompted her again, "Just try." Honor did try, but her effort brought spasmodic vomiting. Her clothes became even more soiled, inside and out, and the odor began to sicken both Comfort and Obadiah.

"Honor," Comfort whispered. "I need to change your clothes. I'm going to ask an officer for a bucket of water so that I can wash you."

A different ensign than the one who had kidnapped Honor allowed the two women and Obadiah to remain on deck when the other passengers were marched below. Comfort reached down to pull Honor's dress up over her head. The girl's chemise protected what little modesty she had left, but it reeked from weeks of sweat and two days of diarrhea. It, too, had to come off, but to do so would leave the pious young woman naked for all to see.

"Please don't take all my clothes," cried Honor, though she was almost too weak to protest. "Don't let them see me," she whispered.

Comfort looked toward the ensign. "I have a brown dress in my space. Would you go and fetch it, please?" The ensign left and spoke to the sailor who had earlier been punished for touching Honor. The ensign descended to the lower deck.

"Obadiah," said Comfort. "Give me your blouse."

Honor watched as the lad took off his shirt and handed it to Comfort. Then the girl rolled onto her side and held her stomach. Comfort looked at Obadiah. "Now you must walk over there and turn your back while I clean her up."

Obadiah smiled at Honor. "I'm sorry that you're sick," he offered kindly.

Honor didn't smile but watched as Obadiah walked to the other side of the deck and looked into the wind as the ship's prow rose and dropped between the waves. She saw the second group of passengers come up from the ship's bowels. They stared at her in curiosity.

Comfort tried to cover Honor with Obadiah's blouse.

The sailor brought a bucket and a rag. He tied a rope to the bucket and scooped up some sea water while the ensign searched for the dress down below. When the sailor returned, he set the bucket down and just stood there. "Leave us now," said Comfort. "I need to change her dress, and she's very shy."

"Go away," shouted Honor, as Comfort reached under the blouse to remove her chemise. Honor grabbed Comfort's hands and pushed them away. "He can't be seein' me."

"I need to keep watch on the bucket," said the sailor firmly.

Comfort helped Honor up and looked at the sailor. "Go now, before the officer returns." She laid Honor's dress on the deck and poured water on the soiled parts. She scrubbed the material against itself and poured more water on it. Eventually, she rinsed the entire dress in the water and wrung out what water she could.

The sailor continued to watch, and Honor screamed at him. "Have ye no decency? Go away!"

With the dress a bit cleaner, Comfort pushed Obadiah's shirt under the chemise to cover at least the lower parts of the girl's body. She layered the wet dress over the shirt, covering Honor's entire body. The sailor just stood there, waiting.

Comfort looked at the young man and spoke sternly, "Don't you know that the officer will whip you again?" The sailor took several steps back, looked around for any officer who might be observing the scene, and then grinned at her through his rotten teeth.

Comfort moved and knelt down between Honor and the sailor. She began to remove Honor's chemise, a thin, soiled rag. Honor began to cry. She knew that Comfort would soon have to clean her bottom, the same way she had seen her Ma clean little Michael's many times.

Comfort rolled Honor onto her side, the woman's body and Obadiah's blouse shielding her middle, and the wet dress covering the top of her body. "I hate ye," Honor shouted at the sailor. "I hate all of ye!" She remembered Ma emphasizing that only sinful girls let boys look upon them. She turned toward the sailor, yelling, "Ye be makin' me sin, and God will be punishin' thee for that. I hope he makes thee fall overboard," she shrieked.

As the ensign came up from the stairwell, the sailor turned and walked away.

Comfort rolled Honor over and finished her motherly chore. Then she slipped the clean dress from the ensign over Honor's head. The girl cried painfully as Comfort sat her back up and kissed her forehead. "Don't cry, little one. We're almost finished."

As Honor looked up, the ensign smiled at her and said, "I'm sorry, wench."

"Sorry for what? Yer English friend stole me from the beach, and now thee have seen me."

"I didn't see anything. I looked away. And I'm sorry he kidnapped you."

Comfort looked at him and smiled. "Could you carry her to our place?" When the junior officer picked up the thin girl, she put her arm around his neck. Comfort followed them to the lowest deck, carrying the girl's dripping frock.

Honor spoke to the ensign, "That awful sailor brought me shame, and now I've done an evil thing. If I didn't get sick, he wouldn't have seen me naked."

"You've done no wrong, and no one has seen you naked. The sailor has brought shame to himself alone," the ensign said reassuringly.

Honor explained, "But he wouldn't go away until ye came. Please have him whipped again, hard."

Comfort put her other arm around Obadiah's neck and hugged him. When they reached Honor's place, Comfort slipped inside and used the now filthy water and rag to clean the shelf as best she could. She rolled Honor's wet dress into a ball and placed it at the foot of her sleeping space. The ensign sat Honor on the edge of her bunk and Comfort pulled her in. The ensign said, "Is there anything else I can do?"

"She will need lots of clean water to drink. Could you fetch us some every day for a while?"

He nodded.

"Thank you," said Comfort. "You're a good person."

He walked away. For the next few days, the ensign brought Honor clean water from the officer's supply.

One morning, Honor said to Comfort, "I'm just hatin' boys, all boys, except that good ensign, I don't hate him."

"I'm glad you said that, little one. I like him too. He wants to help." Comfort combed her fingers through Honor's hair.

"I'm sorry, but I wish ye wouldn't be likin' Obadiah so much," Honor whispered.

Frowning, Comfort changed the subject. "I know you'll be lost in my big, old dress, but it will cover you completely. When your dress is dry, you can put it back on." She changed her expression to that special smile mothers have. "Then, you'll be the pretty one again."

Honor did not think she could be pretty again. She believed her purity had been stolen and her dreams shattered. "I hate it when I sin."

"To be sick and seen indisposed is not a sin, but to hate another, for any reason, is. Did our Lord not say 'forgive them' when He hung on the cross? While the soldiers mocked him, did He not do something good? Don't let your anger take your good spirit from you. Jesus will not be pleased."

●●●

For the first five weeks of the journey, death visited the passengers four times. Honor watched as sailors carried the corpses from their bunks and tossed them over the side of the ship. On one occasion, she turned to Comfort with fear in her eyes. "Please don't let that happen to me." Honor prayed the Hail Mary for each deceased soul as the sailors carried their bodies to the ship's rail. She taught the prayer to Comfort, who recited it with her.

"Can you see how God uses you, even in this horrible place?" asked Comfort after one of the sea burials. Comfort continued, "Let me teach you another prayer. My husband taught it to me. He said it's a quote from the Bible. When you're a nun, you can pray them both." Comfort clasped Honor's hands in her own. "For I am persuaded that neither death, nor life, nor angels, nor principalities, nor powers, nor things present, nor things to come, nor height, nor depth, nor any other creature, shall be able to separate us from the love of God, which is in Christ Jesus, our Lord."

"I don't want to die. I hate this place."

"So does God."

Once, after praying for one of the departed souls, Honor and Comfort lay still in the darkness. Honor asked Comfort, "Do ye think Jesus loves us aboard this awful boat?"

"When my husband died, the parson told me that the Spirit of God is everywhere. He is always with us, even when we face the bad things. When you're poor like me, the love of God is sometimes the only good thing you have."

"Then, why isn't God savin' us? Doesn't He know how bad it is?"

"I don't know why He doesn't always answer our prayers the way we want them answered. I don't know why He allows us to suffer at others' evil hands. Maybe He wants to use bad experiences to teach us to trust Him, even when things are hard. Who knows, maybe He wants the bad people to change when they see that Christians forgive them."

"The English are supposed to be Christians. How can I be forgivin' them when they hurt Irish people on purpose?

"Let me tell you something else my husband taught me," Comfort offered. "You are responsible only for what you do, not for what others do. You don't have to like someone who hurts you and you don't have to be near them. But loving those people requires that you want the best for them. You might even want them to stop hurting others or to feel bad about what they did, and apologize and mean it. What you must do is pray for them whenever you're angry."

"That is nae easy for the Irish."

"It's not easy for any of us."

● ● ●

At the end of the sixth week, the *Blissful Lady* encountered one of the dreaded North Atlantic storms. The winds blew fifty to sixty miles per hour, and the waves reached a height of ten to fifteen feet.

At the breakfast meal on that awful day, Honor saw the black sky to the south, a clear omen of the tempest to come, and she wondered why the captain had given orders to turn the ship toward the storm. The wind and rain seemed to grow fiercer with every minute. The topside visit was cut short; the last two groups of passengers weren't allowed to go up at all. An ensign came down and told everyone to tie themselves to their spaces. Comfort tied Honor's ankle with the rope attached to a hole in the shelf board and then tied herself with a neighboring rope. Soon, Honor could hear the sailors slamming the hatches closed and watched as they stumbled down below and tied themselves to the bilge pumps. Above the roar of the storm, she could barely make out other sailors running on the two decks above her or the officers shouting orders. Soon, those sounds joined the cacophony of the rapidly mumbled prayers, uttered simultaneously through the bunks.

Three hours into the storm, a gust from the east turned the *Lady* sideways to the waves, putting her in extreme danger. The winds roared, pushing so hard against the ship that it listed to starboard and almost capsized. Screams for mercy filled the lower deck. The ship struggled as the captain tried in vain to turn her back into the wind, the waves effortlessly flipping the vessel sideways again.

When she came about, the *Blissful Lady* rose forty-five degrees at the bow, and then fell into the bottom of the next trough. Again and again, the ship rose and fell with petrifying predictability. Honor and Comfort held each other, arm in arm, praying that the Lord would once again still the waters.

Sick gray bodies slid right and left, constrained only by the tether that secured them to their spaces. Like a row of pendulums, the passengers swung in rhythm to the waves, crashing into each other as the ferocity of the storm attempted to beat out what little life they had left.

Honor heard the wind press hard against the masts as it tried to pry them from their wooden footings on the lower deck, the timbers creaking under enormous stress as the ship swayed from side to side. The roar of the gales grew unbearable, cries for help going unheard by even the closest neighbors who were themselves helpless. Terror, unfortunately, became Honor's constant companion.

Sailors stationed at the water pumps pushed and pulled at the handles in a feeble attempt to remove some of the sea water. But with every wave, water continued to pour down the passageway and through the cracks in the hull.

By the second day of the storm, the water rose to almost a foot deep, sloshing fore and aft as the ship rose and fell. Many passengers and sailors lost control of their stomachs and bowels, transforming the bilge water into a cesspool. While the storm blew and the ship rolled, the dead bodies were left to decompose in the rancid water, permeating the entire ship with the smell of death and decay. Honor tried pinching her nose and breathing through her mouth, but the foul smells were so intense that she could taste them. *He can't let me die,* she thought. *I will get home. I promised Da.*

After three days, the storm finally abated, leaving Honor weakened in body but fortified in determination. She cried from the depth of her Irish tenacity, "Mother of God, I will make my way home!"

●●●

As the waves calmed, the passengers were able to untie themselves. Several of the men climbed down to help the sailors pump out the putrid water. Others untied the bodies of the dead and carried them to the bottom of the stairs. From there, they would be taken topside to be heaved overboard.

Comfort turned away from the gruesome project to tend to a dying woman. The filthy sea water had caused the woman many problems. She had groaned continuously for the three days of the storm with severe stomach cramps, and her stool became yellowed with mucus and blackened with blood. Comfort tore pieces of cloth from her old brown dress, dipped them into the putrid water, and tried to keep the woman as clean as possible. When the woman died, it seemed that Comfort might have reached her limit. She cried uncontrollably and turned toward Honor, resting her head in the girl's lap. "I don't think I can go on," she sobbed.

Honor cared for her exhausted friend, empowered by the sense of being needed rather than being only indebted to the older woman. She recalled her happy days when had Ma entrusted Donovan to her care. Yet what she felt now seemed somehow different, a strangely energized sensation that she had never experienced in Ireland.

Honor patted Comfort's head and spoke hopeful words to cheer her. "I'm havin' a wonderful plan to tell thee of. We can escape together as soon as we reach Maryland." Comfort opened her eyes and smiled to acknowledge Honor's encouraging words. She rolled into the girl's bony body. Honor cradled Comfort, reciting to her an old Irish saying. "Me Da always says, 'When the winds come blowing, put yer face toward the sun and yer backside toward the storm.'"

●●●

Late one afternoon, the bell rang six times. Comfort opened her eyes and whispered to Honor, "Dear one, I shall love you forever, but I can't go on. You must go and get some food for yourself." Her eyes quickly closed again.

"And I'll be always lovin' thee, forever and ever." Honor tilted up Comfort's head and kissed her on the forehead. "Ye are the best friend I've ever had," she said softly, a tear trickling down her cheek.

Honor went topside at supper time and walked around the deck, sobbing quietly. She prayed aloud, perhaps for the first time directly to God himself, rather than through a saint or the Holy Mother. "Why are Ye doin' this to Comfort? Don't Ye know she loves me?" She thought for a moment as she continued to walk. "Is it too much to be askin'? She just wants to be goin' home and see her babies. Is that so wrong?" She grasped her chest to help assuage the huge ache she felt welling up. "Was it wrong for her to help me? Did I do something bad?" Honor's eyes brimmed with even more tears as she screamed skyward. "Why must she die"? People began to stare at her and point.

After several minutes, she stopped walking. *"Why don't Ye love her? And why don't Ye love me anymore"?* Honor's loneliness threatened to engulf her, but after a few moments she considered her outburst. She stopped, fell to her knees, and prayed silently, *Please, I'm sorry I got mad at Ye. What I said was very bad, and I'm truly sorry. All we want is to go home. Please find someone to help us make our way home.*

Obadiah, walked up. Immediately, Honor threw her arms around his neck. "I fear that God is punishin' me, and I nae know why."

Startled by the sudden hug, Obadiah didn't know what to do. Without thinking, he put his arms around Honor's waist and pulled her into a tight embrace. "I don't know much about God, and I don't understand why He'd be punishing either of you. And you ain't done any wrong that I know of."

They stopped walking and she put her cheek against his. "God's makin' me be here when He should be keepin' me in Ireland. And Comfort loves me, but He's lettin' her die. I know I've said I hated people and not been nice to thee. I'm sorry for that. Maybe that's why He's punishin' me so much."

"If you'd stop hating me, I could like you some."

She pulled herself out of his arms and turned to continue their walk. He copied her measured steps, walking at her side. They passed the sailor who had watched as Comfort cleaned her up. Honor moved closer to Obadiah, and after they'd passed the sailor, she said, "I shouldn't have gotten sick. Then he wouldn't a'seen me with no clothes."

"I saw my sister once. When she took a bath, I walked in. Do you think that was wrong?"

"Did ye try to see her?"

"No."

"Well, ye are her brother, and it was an accident. That should be different. I don't know. A king named David saw a girl in her bath, and Father Hannigan said that was a big sin."

"Do you really think you did a sin?" he asked.

"Comfort is very sick, and I don't know why! We need each other, and I love her dearly. I need to know if it's my fault. I wish Father Hannigan were here, 'cause he'd know."

●●●

Four weeks later, in early October, Comfort had recovered and the Blissful Lady sailed into Chesapeake Bay. Comfort recovered, in part because Honor talked to her a lot and brought her food and clean water.

"Thank you, Honor," said Comfort. "I needed the help of my little nun and you worked very hard."

Honor beamed with pride. Yes, I did, didn't I?

The horrible journey would soon be over. Twenty-one of the seventy-five people in the hold had been buried at sea. The captain's new task would be easy — to sell the remaining fifty-four indentured servants and tobacco brides.

Once in port, the surviving passengers were taken, one by one, to the junior officer's quarters where they were given two buckets of clean Maryland well water and small pieces of soap with which to bathe. A large tub had been placed in the quarters so the passengers could wash themselves and their clothes with some privacy. Honor and Comfort asked to bathe together and enjoyed the forty long minutes and four buckets of freshwater to cleanse the grime from each other and from their dresses.

Even so, four buckets of well-water were not enough to completely wash away ten weeks of filth. Both women were much worse for the wear. Honor had lost a significant amount of weight; the ripples of her food-starved ribs and gaunt face suggesting the harshness of the voyage. Her once radiant hair had grown dull and now hung in oily snarls. Her glowing skin had been replaced with the pallid whitewash of weeks with little sunshine. She had little left of her childhood beauty. The dimpled smile that had been her Da's delight just a few months earlier was gone, for she could now only muster what might generously be called a grin on the rare occasion that warranted it. Honor anticipated a time of rest and recuperation in a Catholic Church, the sanctuary that would care for her and safely get her home.

Comfort appeared weak and thin, as well. Her skin and her dress were the same pale gray color of neglect. She, too, had lost a lot of weight and looked years older than her age. Unlike her young companion, Comfort's older body ached with a weariness that stooped her shoulders and drew down her countenance. But she, too, had survived and would soon meet a better future.

When they had dressed in their wet but cleaner clothes, a wonderful sense of relief enveloped their spirits. "Oh, Comfort, I'm feelin' like a princess again, and ye are my queen. Perhaps we should call our footmen to bring up the carriage and take us to Church. I didn't tell thee, but I'm fifteen now. My birthday came midway through our wretched journey across the ocean." Honor held up her arm and let her hand droop in feigned superiority. "Soon I'll be goin' home."

Comfort pulled the young girl into her arms and hugged her. "Good cheer. I am happy for you, little one."

Once the two had finished bathing, they were allowed on deck for a hot meal of thick meat stew with hardtack, cheese, and lots of fresh water. They were even given pewter spoons and cups and allowed to sit in the sun. The two women ate the Christmas-like feast with gusto. Comfort and Honor surveyed the port and the city beyond. "We'll have to run like the wind," said Honor. "I'm sure they'll not be tyin' us up when the men come to buy us, and we can make our escape then. We'll look for a church with a cross on top, and we can run there."

The captain and first mate had each passenger brought to them, one at a time. The name of each person and a transportation contract were matched. Each person was handed a quill pen with which they marked an "X" at a place near the bottom of the contract. The first mate then wrote in their names, as best he could spell them.

Honor read the contract, which stated that the undersigned volunteered to be property of the ship's captain or his designee, and that the undersigned would be bound to their contract's purchaser for the purpose of marriage or for a period of indenture of four to seven years. For the indentured servants, it also listed the land and/or property the purchaser and Maryland agreed to give them after their service. The owner had the right to punish the servant or sell their contract, as he deemed appropriate. Finally, it decreed that the penalty for running away could include amputation of their toes by the owner of their contract.

Honor, spoke out, "I was kidnapped and am not here by choice. I will not sign this and I demand ye return me to Dingle."

The first mate slapped Honor so hard that she lost her footing and fell. "If you don't sign the paper, we will keep you on board until we are again at sea and then throw you overboard. We will waste no more food and water on you."

Seeing no realistic alternative, Honor signed the paper and became a colonist in the New World. The issue it created was tricky. How would she persuade some kind gentleman to buy her contract without wedding with her? And how would she recognize him?

Chapter Seven

In early July of 1701, William prepared for a trip to Annapolis, where he would look for a second indentured lad and, at long last, a good woman to wed. He rode over to the Rausch farm to set a date with Walter, who also desired to venture to Annapolis to see about a wife. He found his neighbor building a smokehouse.

"Good morning, Walter."

"*Guten morgen*," replied Walter. "Please come into my cabin for some tea."

Once the tea and small talk were finished, William got down to business. "I've come to tell you that I'm ready to go to Annapolis to look for a servant and a wife. Are you also ready?"

"*Ja*, this *ist gut*. I write a letter to *meinen bruder*, Günther, und he will loan me money to purchase a *frau*.

"That is wonderful news. Your children need a mother."

"*Ja*, this is so. *Und* Günther's *Frau*, Hilda, wants to come with us to find this woman."

"I would like to leave in a week. Can you send a letter to ask your brother and his wife to be ready that soon?"

"This is no problem. Günther *und* Hilda live very close to Annapolis town. They wait for us to come. Then we all go to town."

"Good. Would you be ready to leave next Monday?"

"*Ja*. Do you think a ship will be there *mit* women to choose from?"

"I hope so. If not, they hold a fair with the women who were not sold from earlier ships."

"I don't know about this new world. A fair to buy a wife is unbelievable."

"It does seem different, but in this new world, when we have a problem, we invent a way to solve it. Sometimes our new ideas are easier than the way things were done in the old country. I like that about living in America."

"*Ja*, in Deutschland, we go to a matchmaker who knows all the *fräulein und* widows ready to wed. Then we go to the father or *bruder* and talk. The father speaks to the *fräulein*, und if she is happy with idea, the father tells us to visit for dinner. Sometimes the boy *und* girl will bundle before they wed, and sometimes they will not. It is all complicated."

William sat back and stared at the ceiling. "I think I want a woman who is at least twenty-five years old and a widow. I hope she can read so that she can teach my children. I want a large family, so it would be good if she already had some children. If she has lived on a farm, that would also be good. If she is a bit handsome, I would like that as well." He rubbed his hands together and smiled like an excited child at Christmas. "Walter, what will you look for in a wife?"

Walter smiled and said, "A Christian *frau und gut mutter*."

● ● ●

The ragged old *Blissful Lady* had been tied to a pier in the port of Annapolis the day before William and Walter arrived. Honor was excited, as the first mate and several crewmen visited the passenger deck and distributed a clean, white bonnet to each of the women.

"You will be given hot tea and buttered bread this morning," said the mate. "Once you've eaten, you will be allowed to leave the ship, but you must stay on the dock. There will be sailors on shore to catch anyone who tries to run, and I remind you that you signed a paper giving us permission to cut off your toes if you attempt to escape. Other crew members will be posted near each of you to ensure that your comments to buyers are appropriate. If you attempt to speak inappropriately about the ship or the voyage, you will be brought back inside the ship and chained to your bunk."

Honor thought, Mother of God, help me escape to find a priest! Perhaps a good gentleman will buy me and we can persuade him to buy Comfort as well. Oh, God, please don't be sendin' an ugly old man. If he's young and good, I can tell him that we need to see a priest to hear our confessions. It's but a wee lie. Then when I'm in the confessional, I can tell the priest that we were both kidnapped and he will give us both sanctuary.

The mate went on, "On the dock, you are to stand straight and have a pleasant look. Speak not, save when you are spoken to, and then answer briefly."

Honor's mind continued to scheme. If we're bought at different times, the first could run away and find the priest and speak of the other. The priest can be comin' to the docks and buy the other. The Holy Mother will tell him what to do.

"You have all signed contracts giving the captain the right to sell you as a servant or a bride. Do not dispute this with any buyers. They will come to inspect you. If they wish to look at your teeth or feel your limbs, allow this. Other than that, you will be treated with Christian propriety."

Christian propriety, thought Honor. These heathen be knowin' none of it! They're all thieves and kidnappers. They throw dead people overboard without givin' the last rites. God will never forgive them, and neither will I. There be nary a Christian gentleman among them.

"Should a buyer purchase your contract, he will speak with the first mate, pay for your transportation, and sign the papers. After that, you are no longer under the Captain's protection. The purchaser will own you and treat you as he sees fit. If no one purchases your papers, you will be returned to the ship to wait for the morrow. If you remain unwanted, you will be sold to a slave seller who will dispose of you in some other way."

●●●

A few minutes later, the nervous passengers were led down the plank to the dock. There were many more men than women, ranging in age from early teens to almost forty. Honor and the other women were the first to disembark and stood on the end of the dock closest to shore. Then the men came and stood nearer the ship. It would be a hot day, but the fresh air and steadiness of the dock were welcomed by those who had come from the ship. All were happy and relieved that the long voyage had finally ended.

Honor continued to plot her escape. Once she was purchased and off the dock, she would run to a church with a cross on top. Two such steeples could be seen from the docks. "I'm almost there", she whispered to herself.

The Annapolis waterfront included a long row of warehouses, all painted in bright colors. The dock itself looked like a finger of large rocks covered over with a layer of sand and made smooth with thick wood boards. Along with two other docks, it jutted out into the Chesapeake about a hundred feet, with room for two ships. Near the shore, boxes and barrels of inbound goods were stacked: brightly dyed cloth, household items of glass, along with farm tools and equipment. More barrels on the boardwalk behind the dock held hogsheads of tobacco, smoked fish, and corn whisky, all bound for England. A breeze wafted in from the south, scented with salt and carrying the caws of seagulls in search of food. Horses and carts waited on shore with wheelbarrows, ready to transfer goods one way or the other. The dock area appeared to be a gateway to prosperity and happiness. Comfort smiled as she took it all in.

Honor wore the same dress she had worn when kidnapped, though it now hung about her like an old coat on a peg. She knew she couldn't look very appealing, but neither did any of the other women. Nonetheless, she hoped a kind man would take notice and decide to purchase her contract.

Honor prayed, "Sweet Mother of God, send someone slow of foot who will buy me, and make him handsome and not fat."

She pulled at a few tresses of red hair to frame her pale, freckled face, trying to envision the majestic statue of the Madonna that stood in her Church back home. Then she straightened her back, bowed her head to the left, put her feet together, and clasped her hands as in prayer, staring down in angelic innocence. Should an appropriate candidate walk by, she decided, she would lift her head and smile. Honor may have been thin with a far-too-big dress, but as she stood among the other women from the *Blissful Lady*, she appeared to be an adorable child in need.

Early in the day, three older men and a woman approached the row of candidate servants and brides. They stopped in front of Comfort, and one of the men took off his hat and bowed. "*Guten tag*," he said.

A second man, wearing a yellow blouse and grey knee pants with black stockings, turned to look at Honor. *He's a big man*, Honor thought, *but not fat*. His brown hat sat square on his head, its wide brim almost hiding the small ponytail at the back of his head. Honor smiled and stared into his eyes until he turned his head and scanned all the way down the line. Then he brought his eyes back to rest on Comfort. He entwined his large fingers, turned again toward Honor, and smiled. Forgetting her plan, Honor straightened up and smoothed the front of her tattered dress. She curtsied and returned his smile with the shine of her green Irish eyes. "Good day to you, kind sir," she said to him. "This is my best friend, Comfort Smyth, and my name is Honor O'Flynn."

Honor continued to smile as the yellow-shirted man looked at her for several seconds.

"I was kidnapped, but God wants me to return to Ireland to become a nun," she whispered. He excused himself with a silent bow and walked down toward the line of available young men. *He was about the same age as Da*, Honor noticed, watching him for several seconds longer. *He might be perfect*, she thought. *What should I do now?*

Honor returned her attention to Comfort as she heard the other man ask, "*Sprechen sie Deutsch? I am Walter Rausch und das ist mein bruder und his frau.*" Walter bowed and doffed his hat again. Hilda frowned and stood stiffly, like a sergeant inspecting his troop.

Honor watched as Comfort held out her hand to the woman. "Good afternoon. My name is Ann Smyth. I'm English."

"*Ja*, I am Hilda und this *ist mein mann*, Günther," she said, turning to her left and putting her hand on the shoulder of the third gentleman, who stood off to the side, smoking his pipe officiously. "Günther*s bruder ist* for a *frau* looking." She put her hand on Walter's shoulder who, with old German formality, doffed his hat yet again.

"I am pleased to meet you," Comfort said as she turned toward Honor. "This is my dear friend, Honor. She's from Ireland and wants very much to return to her family. I want to wed and live here in Maryland." Hilda smiled at Honor as Comfort spoke again. "She is but fifteen and does not wish to be wed. The English sailors brought Honor here against her will, and the dear girl is searching for someone to help her get back home."

Honor curtsied. "Top of the mornin' to ye."

Hilda's frown deepened. "But she *ist* old enough to wed, *ja*?"

Comfort smiled at Walter. "She says her father in Ireland will pay her contract and her return fare, as well as a reward to anyone who helps her."

Günthe*r* took over the conversation. "*Und* how old are you, *Frau* Comfort?"

"I am thirty-one. I am a widow with four children back in England."

Hilda looked surprised, "*Und* why did you leave your children?"

"My husband died, and I could not care for them. I left them with my sister and came here for a new start. I miss them very much." Comfort's eyes grew sad. "I hope to bring them over as soon as I can."

Hilda raised her eyebrows.

Comfort turned her eyes back to Walter. "Honor is like my new daughter. Would you be interested in buying both our contracts?"

Hilda spoke for him. "Walter *ist* a widower *mit* four kinder, two boys *und* two girls. He has not much money *und* he has no tobacco to trade."

"That's what I have," Comfort nodded, "two boys and two girls. Perhaps one day I can send for them." Honor took Comfort's arm as the older woman looked down at the ground. "Honor and I would like to stay together. Can anything be done?"

"It must be hard for you, *ja*," said Hilda. "But we have no money for two."

Comfort lifted her arm away from Honor's grip and put it around her friend's shoulder. She hugged Honor and looked at Hilda. "Please forgive my speaking so boldly." She paused and looked down. "I am a very good cook and housekeeper and I am a very good mother. I would never have left my children if I'd had any other choice."

"*Ja, und* what do you wish to be called?"

Comfort dropped her hold on Honor and took a small step sideways. "Comfort," Honor blurted out. "That is what she is, a comfort to everyone. But she would like to go home to her children."

Comfort reached out and pulled Honor close to hug her a second time. "No, little one. You can go home, but I will make my life here."

Walter heard Comfort's gentle admonition. "Günther lends me money, but not for two. You are good woman. If you love *meine kinder* like this, I would ask you to come *und* wed with me. Perhaps another man will come *und* pay for the *fräulein*."

Comfort reached out her hand, as tears of relief welled in her eyes. Walter completed the arrangement with a firm handshake.

Honor could not hide the disappointment that swept over her face. Comfort hugged her again, then pushed her kindly but firmly out of the protective nest that had kept the young girl safe through many weeks of horror. She bowed toward Walter. "I will love your children. And, if you treat me well, I will come to love you."

Walter bowed like the good German he was. "Then it is done." He excused himself and walked with Hilda and Günther to the first mate's table.

Comfort turned back to Honor. "I can't go back to Ireland with you Honor, but I will pray every day that you find a way to get there." The tears finally spilled from Comfort's eyes as she pulled Honor into her arms again. "I have grown to love you as my very own and I will miss you."

"Please, Comfort. What if they cut off my toes?" Honor's eyes closed as the thought of the pain overwhelmed her.

"Don't try to run away. You must put your future in God's hands. I shall pray that your contract will be purchased by a good man who will write your father and send you home soon."

By then, Honor had lost control and begun to cry as well. "Please ask the man in the yellow shirt to buy me." She pointed toward the man. "I don't want to be apart from thee. And, I think he likes me."

"I can't promise, but I will try. I will do my very best. But for now I must go, and you must remain. I will always love you, child."

Comfort released her, turned, and walked away. Honor watched Comfort step to the table where the first mate negotiated the final price for the servants and brides. She saw Hilda reach out to shake Comfort's hand, and Walter walk over to offer Comfort a kerchief. Walter's boys stood by with anxious looks as they prepared to meet the woman who would soon become their mother. At that end of the dock were signs of hope and happiness, while Honor's end remained sad and lonely.

After a minute or so, Comfort looked back at Honor, wiping her tears away with Walter's kerchief. Honor could have used a kerchief as well, but no one came to her aid. Nonetheless, she knew she needed to interest a buyer. She looked at the other man in the group who had smiled at her, watching as he headed over to what looked to her to be the youngest boy of the lot. *Good*, she thought, *he likes younger people, and I'm almost as young as Obadiah. Please, Holy Mother, make him want a housekeeper or a nursemaid for his children.* Honor wiped her tears away, pinched her cheeks, and stood up as straight as she could.

A few minutes later, Honor saw the yellow-shirted man put his pipe in his mouth and shake Obadiah's hand. Both were smiling. *Bless me, we could all be together*, she thought.

The man left the boy and walked back past her to the first mate's table. She strained to hear his conversation with the first mate. "That one's not yet thirteen and comes from a town near Chelmsford. Let me see his contract," said the man. The first mate found the contract and handed it to the man. After reading the paper, the man said, "This contract makes him to be fifteen, yet the lad says he is but twelve. If he speaks truly, you must have a signature from his parent to transport him. Is this the parent's mark?"

"I am not responsible for who signs these contracts," the first mate responded gruffly. "If the paper says he's fifteen, I believe it to be proper. If it be not so, you will have to take it up with the broker in England."

Honor watched as the man frowned and looked again at the piece of paper. "Perhaps I should take it up with the magistrate. Your captain has broken the law, sir."

The first mate stood and looked toward the ship. Honor saw him put his hands on the table and lean forward to face the yellow-shirted man, eye to eye. "Sometimes the brokers bring us wayward youths. If you are interested, such lads can be bought for less than the normal two hundred fifty pounds of tobacco."

"I would never pay such a fee for a lad so young. But, he appears to be a good lad, and no scoundrel. Will you not accept one hundred fifty pounds?"

"Sir," said the first mate, with a smirk, "you must jest. That is too little. I could not accept less than two hundred pounds of prime tobacco leaves."

"I should find another underage passenger and pay you but one and fifty for each of them," the man replied.

With those words, Honor's heart began to beat faster. Should I shout out? she wondered. But the idea of ten lashes frightened her too much to speak. How can I get the gentleman to look at me again?

"You may have this one for one hundred and fifty, but none other," said the first mate. Then he added, "But I must insist that your tobacco be of the highest quality."

"I've come to acquire two, a lad and a bride. I will return on the morrow for the bride." Honor watched as the man leaned over and signed Obadiah's contract. Thank you, Holy Mother, please make him kind of heart and slow of foot.

With that, the man walked back to the young Obadiah, who beamed as he stepped from the line of unsold men. "I will serve you well, but when my time is over, I want to return to become very rich."

"If that is your desire and you remain with me for six years, I will help you in any way I can," the man said earnestly. Obadiah reached out his hand, and the two secured their agreement. As they walked toward the end of the dock, Honor decided to act. Although she had been unfriendly to Obadiah, she took a risk and shouted out, "Obadiah, thank you my good Christian brother, for your help on our voyage. You are lucky to have found such a good master. I will miss you."

Obadiah looked back at her, and she regretted that she hadn't been nicer to him on the ship. She removed her bonnet, unfurled her red hair, smiled, and spoke again. "God go with you. And don't forget me in your prayers."

William looked at her and smiled as well. He spoke to Obadiah, "Lad, is that lass your friend?"

"No, master, she's just a girl from the boat."

William looked again at Honor's red hair and broad smile. He removed his hat and bowed toward her.

Honor shouted, "May I know your name, sir?" She glanced around and saw an ensign looking her way. She ignored him, knowing she had to take this chance. "Might ye be interested in a housekeeper?"

William turned and walked toward her. "I am William Logsdon, at your service. I need not a housekeeper. I am in search of a bride, who will be older than you."

"Kind sir," said Honor inappropriately, "I wish to be bought as a servant, not as a bride."

"Good luck to you then," answered William with a tip of his hat. He and Obadiah turned and walked over to the two-wheeled cart to meet up with Comfort and her new family. Comfort took Obadiah in her arms and hugged him.

Walter, Günther, William, and all three boys began to unload several hogsheads of tobacco, carrying them to a scale behind the table where the first mate sat, waiting to be paid. When Obadiah and William came close enough, Honor made one last attempt, "Good day to you, master. May God go with thee." This time, William didn't smile back.

Honor watched as Walter and his crew climbed onto Günther's wagon and drove off in one direction, while William and Obadiah got into the two-wheeled cart and rode off in another.

The rest of the day, buyers walked right past Honor. One who did stop reeked of alcohol as he lifted her arm and dropped it. Another, smelling almost as bad as the ship's hold, scratched himself in indecent places as he scanned her, head to foot, before continuing down the dwindling row of would-be servants and brides.

Chapter Eight

William and Obadiah brought the horse cart to a halt in front of a boarding house, as its proprietress, Winifred Skidmore, descended the steps. "Brother Logsdon, I thought you wanted a wench as well as a field hand. Were there no suitable wenches at the docks?" William handed the reins to Obadiah and jumped down from the cart.

William wasn't ready to answer the lady's prying questions. He redirected, saying instead, "Sister Skidmore, this is Obadiah Green. He is an ambitious lad and has agreed to serve on my plantation for six years. Obadiah, this is Mistress Skidmore." Obadiah jumped down from the cart, bowed, and smiled at the promise of a warm bed and hot, tasty meals.

William's neighbor, Walter Rausch, had arrived earlier. He now came out of the house, accompanied by William's servant, Isaac, Comfort, Günther, and Hilda.

William spoke again to Winifred. "May Isaac put the horse in the corral?"

Winifred nodded her approval, "Of course, and because you still have bushels of apples and sheaves of tobacco yet to sell, have him put the cart in the barn."

Isaac walked the horse forward as the adults walked toward the house.

Winifred continued, "Brother Logsdon, your bundle is still in the left bedroom upstairs. Your German neighbor will sleep with you. The other Germans will have the center bedroom upstairs. The two servant boys and the German's new wench will be in the two downstairs bedrooms. I put extra blankets on the beds for them. I have venison stew and cornbread for supper."

Winifred's boarding house was a two-story log structure with seven rooms. The front of the house had a large door, as well as two glazed and shuttered windows. The first floor consisted of a large room with an impressive stone fireplace which heated and lit the house. Wrought-iron hooks set into the walls held kettles over the flames, and today's guests were greeted with the aroma of venison, along with fresh bread and boiling vegetables.

Cracks separated the rough-cut floor and ceiling boards, which had long since warped and become uneven. The lack of rugs made for homey creaking sounds whenever people walked about. The walls had been plastered and whitewashed, but were otherwise bare. Whale oil lamps hung in each room, giving off black smoke and mingling fishy smells with that of the damp mold. The sturdy wooden furniture, though uncomfortable in appearance, was a welcome change for Comfort and Obadiah. Eight straight-back chairs stood on either side of the long dining table. In front of the fireplace sat four heavier chairs, arranged in a semicircle, where guests could sit, smoke, and discuss the day's events.

Steep stairs behind a wall led to a root cellar and three bedrooms upstairs. Each upstairs room held a bed, small table, oil lamp, and one glazed window. Thick straw mattresses and warm blankets lay atop each bed for Winifred and her paying guests. Two more tiny rooms with dirt floors and rough wood walls were hidden behind the fireplace on the first floor. They had been additions to the original house, each with a lock on the outside of its door. These first-floor cells had no windows or access to the heat of the fireplace, and no furniture.

Once inside, Winifred again asked William what had come of his anticipated new bride. "I ask you, sir, were you not able to find a wench?"

"I had planned to find a wife," William answered. "But I confess that it be easier to purchase a boy's contract than to inquire of a woman. A boy is a servant for a few years, but a woman would be a wife for the rest of my life. I felt ill at ease when I walked past the women; they just seemed to stare at me.

I could persuade myself to speak to only one of them, but she was too young for me to wed with."

"A man such as you requires a strong and virtuous woman. A wife of noble character is worth far more than rubies." Shapely as a lass, Winifred had grown to be a woman of large girth who spoke her no-nonsense mind without reservation. Her large breasts drew her shoulders forward, which caused her to walk with the waddle of a mother duck.

"I have birthed three children; all are alive to this day. So take my good advice and choose a wife with a strong back, wide hips, and large breasts." She cupped her hands and lifted her two heavy appendages. "Then work her hard and sire her often." William flushed and said nothing.

Later, as Winifred and her guests ate their supper, Hilda inquired into Winifred's family, "*Frau* Skidmore, is your husband away?"

"No. He's been dead for many years."

"I'm sorry," said Günther. "But at least he left you with a good warm house."

Winifred snorted. "Humph. He was long dead when I bought this house, after years of very hard work. I believe a wise woman builds her own house, but a foolish one tears hers down." She stiffened her back and lifted her heavily burdened shoulders. "When he died, I had to become strong and resourceful. I took in laundry and made soap and candles to sell."

"Then you have done well for yourself," said Hilda. "Your Kinder, do they live here in Annapolis?"

"No, Lord bless them, my children are not near to me. The two eldest are in Virginia. The youngest disappeared two years ago, and I know not what has become of him. A disobedient scalawag," she added. "He prefers loose women and strong whisky over his own mother, the ungrateful prodigal." Realizing her revelation, she quickly covered her comment with a cliché: "I love all my children dearly."

William broke in, "I'm sure you did your best. It must be difficult to be a widow. At least you are able to take in boarders and provide well for yourself."

"Yes, and I also take in lads and wenches from the docks who are too sick or too stubborn to be purchased. I fatten them up and teach them what they need to know to survive in this country. When they're ready, I sell them to men who desire obedient servants and well-trained wives. In fact, after today's stock at the docks is picked over, I will look at the dregs. Do you plan to look again for a wench on the morrow?"

"Yes," said William. "I don't look forward to the search, but I do hope to find a suitable woman. There should yet be several to choose from."

"Be it your desire that I should come with you and share my observations? Understand, sir, that I am a good judge of female virtue."

"I do seek a virtuous wife, and any advice you might have would be most welcome, Mistress Skidmore," William admitted gratefully.

"Wise sir, a wife of noble character is her husband's crown."

After sitting quietly through the earlier part of the exchange, Hilda now spoke out. "Master Logsdon, if it pleases you, Günther *und* I will go wit you on the morrow. *Und* perhaps, Walter and Mistress Comfort would go, too. We shall give you whatever advice you will need, und Comfort knows well of the woman you talked to on the dock."

"That would indeed be helpful," answered William. "That will allow us to leave Mistress Skidmore to her more pressing chores."

"Humph," grunted Winifred.

●●●

After supper, the adult guests went outside to enjoy the warm summer evening. Taking a deep breath, Comfort made a bold move as she endeavored to speak with William. "Master

Logsdon, it is not my place, but may we speak in confidence?" Politely, the three Germans walked a bit ahead.

"Of course, speak as you wish." The two walked down the center of the dirt road that ran past the Skidmore house. "Should I call you Mistress Smyth?"

"Sir, please call me Comfort."

"I should prefer Mistress Comfort until I come to know your better."

"Yes, sir. Mistress Hilda says that we will be neighbors, and that you are a good Anglican."

"Mistress Hilda's words do me good report. Yes, we will be neighbors. Walter's plantation is but a short ride from my own. He is a good and kind person, a man of virtue. I'm sure you will be happy here in Maryland."

"I shall do my best to be happy, Master Logsdon, but I fear I shall be ever saddened, as well. I shall miss my sweet Honor. She is such a wonderful child." Comfort searched William's eyes for a sign of compassion, but saw none.

"I met the lass and doubt you need worry. A child blessed with her spirit and charm is indeed destined to a good life. I don't know when I have seen such a delightful child. If she were my daughter, I should be indeed smitten with her smile."

"Did you know, sir, the English sailors kidnapped Honor and brought her here against her will? She has a dream to be a nun in Ireland. I pray that someone kind will purchase her as a servant girl and send a letter to her father for the funds to free her and send her home." Comfort clasped her hands to her chest, looking down at her feet. "It will be hard for me to be happy until she has found such a Christian gentleman."

William bowed his head toward her. "Mistress Comfort, she told me of her plight and desire. I shall join my prayer with yours."

Comfort looked up with her humblest, yet most beguiling smile. "Kind Master Logsdon, my prayer is that you might be that gentleman."

At first, William said nothing. Then, as the group turned and walked back toward the house, he replied, "Mistress Comfort, the lass is indeed charming, but I seek someone older. I cannot afford to buy the contracts of both a wife and a servant-girl."

"Master William, it would make me very happy if you chose to save her from a fearful fate. Would you be displeased if I were to pray that none suitable for you to wed would remain when we visit the ship on the morrow and that Honor be yet available?"

He looked at Comfort with a pensive smile, having just moments before considered Honor none of his concern.

Chapter Nine

The next morning, Winifred asked William whether or not he wanted her to lock Isaac and Obadiah in their room to keep them from escaping.

William responded, "That will not be necessary, Mistress Skidmore. They will not run away. We have an agreement, and they are honorable lads."

"Brother Logsdon, it is my experience that few indentured servants are honorable. They must all be beaten and kept locked up until they are too afraid to run."

"Madam, I came to Maryland as a contract servant myself, and I was never held prisoner. Nor did I ever run. My master and I had an agreement, and I have made such a pact with these two lads. They shall explore your city while I look for a bride."

Winifred turned and glared at Obadiah. "Lad, if you try to run away, the authorities will catch you. It is against the law for anyone to help a runaway from the ships. If you attempt to flee, you will be caught, and the authorities will place you in my care. I will not treat you with foolish trust."

●●●

Later that morning, as William and the Germans approached the docks, seagulls soared overhead screeching their coastal greetings. From her place in the row of unsold servants and brides, Honor watched young men with wheelbarrows busily loading cargo onto the *Blissful Lady*, while others unloaded the goods the ship had brought from England.

Far fewer men and women remained unsold today, and Honor feared her last chance to escape could be at hand. If I don't find a kind, slow-footed, older gentleman to buy me, I dread what else may happen. They won't take me back to

Ireland. They'll probably sell me as a slave or throw me into the ocean, she thought to herself.

Then Honor noticed William approaching the dock. "Please, God", she whispered. She glanced at the competition, counting at least two other women who she believed might be appropriate to William's needs. Perhaps he desires none of them and has decided he wants a servant girl rather than a wife. Or might the German woman with him consider a servant girl? Surely one of them will buy me. She stood tall, smoothed her dress, and put on the dimpled smile that had attracted William's eye the day before.

As the entourage walked past the first mate's table, the young officer called out to William, "Sir, once you have signed the papers, the lad is for you to deal with."

"I am well pleased with the lad and have no desire to return him," said William. "Today I have come for a bride."

The mate exhaled with relief. "Beg pardon sir, I misunderstood. I still have a few good wenches for you to choose from."

Walter and Günther hung back while William, Comfort, and Hilda walked past the first mate out onto the dock. William scanned the unsold women. His eyes stopped at Honor, and both smiled.

Hilda said, "She is age of Walter's daughter, Petra. Perhaps she is not yet ready to wed." Hilda knew about Honor from Comfort's comments the day before. The three walked directly toward Honor. Nonetheless, when the group reached Honor, Hilda reached out and shook the young girl's hand. "Take off this cap and show me your hair," she commanded firmly, but not unkindly.

Honor obliged with a smile of expectation. Honor looked at William as she brought her hair to the front of her dress, combing it with her fingers.

Hilda went on with the interview. "How old are you, *fräulein?*"

"I be fifteen, mum, and I could be a good housekeeper or governess. Comfort is me very best friend." She looked back at William to find his eyes still focused on her. "Perhaps you've changed yer mind about a wife and be interested in a house servant?"

"*Nein*," answered Hilda. "Master Logsdon does not look for servant girl. He needs wife." Hilda turned and pulled William forward.

"Yes, mum," Honor responded. "Master Logsdon told me this yesterday when he bought Obadiah's contract." Honor thought for a moment. "And the man over there bought Comfort's contract." She pointed at Walter but stared directly at William. "If he can't find a suitable wife, then he might be interested in buyin' me and sendin' a letter to me da in Ireland. Then, at a later time, he could find a better wife than any on this dock. Again, Honor gave William a bright smile.

She returned her attention to Hilda. "I could be a very good house servant for you, as well, or for Mistress Comfort." She looked at Comfort. "Comfort be like me own ma, and I'm bein' like her daughter." Shifting her attention back to William, Honor put her weight on one foot, smiling like a flirty child seeking a favor. "Comfort and I would like to be together."

"Walter has no need for servants. He has two sons and two daughters. And now he has a wife." Hilda looked up at William and then back down at Honor. "You are fifteen. It *ist* time for you to wed. Someone will come, *und* you will have to go with him. Herr Logsdon is a good man and in need of a wife, not a servant. This *ist gut* for you, *ja*?"

Honor raised her eyebrows in false shock. "Oh, no, I would not be a good wife. God needs me to remain pure, like the Virgin Mary."

Hilda bowed and said, "This *ist* not for you to say. Life *ist* never easy for a woman. You will wed with any man who buys you." She turned, took William's arm, and pulled him away. Loud enough for Honor to hear, she said, "This one *ist* too young for you. There are other women to choose from."

Honor took Hilda's words as the rebuke they were intended to be, and her countenance turned immediately to disappointment.

William walked down the line toward the shore. "This is not easy," Honor heard him say.

They took two more steps, when Hilda tugged on his arm. "I see one who would suit you," she said, pointing toward the next woman in line. "*Ist* that lady there."

William looked at a woman in a red dress, standing very near the ensign's table and the shore line. He stopped suddenly and took a deep breath, causing Hilda to lose her grip. "That one by the officer," he said.

The German woman reached out, took hold of his arm again, and tugged at it. "*Gut.* We will both meet her."

Honor looked on, her face clouded with discouragement. *What did I do wrong?* she wondered to herself.

William and Hilda approached the woman in red. "Good morning, my lady," Honor heard William say to the woman. "May I learn your name?"

The woman tipped her head to the right, smiled, and did a slight curtsy. "And a good day to you, sir," she said. "My name is Elizabeth." Standing at average height, she weighed a bit too much to be perfectly appealing. The open neckline of her brightly colored dress had a string pulled tight, just below her well-cleaved breasts. With dark brown hair and a rather plain face, her nose was a bit large and bent to the left. "I'm please to meet you, sir."

"What age are you, Elizabeth?" inquired Hilda.

The woman responded, never taking her eyes off William. "I am younger than most of the other wenches here."

"*Ja, und* where from you come?" asked Hilda.

"I'm from Ipswitch, near London." She smiled at William. "And I'm just twenty-four."

Hilda continued her interrogation. "Were you wedded in this Ipstitch?"

The woman turned to Hilda, trying to hide her annoyance with a stare. "My husband got his self killed in the mills about five years ago. I was a very young widow."

William stepped forward, saying, "I'm sorry about your loss. Did you have any children?" Honor stared in envy while Comfort prayed quietly to herself.

"My husband could not have children, though we tried." The woman looked back at William. "Do you have children?"

"No," said William. "I have never been wed."

Hilda reinserted herself. "Of course, it *ist* wife's duty to have children."

Elizabeth's face showed anxiety at the apparent questioning of her fertility. She looked at William. "My husband was not a complete man, but he provided well for me. I am no longer young, and want to have a big family while I am still able. She looked directly at William. "Sir, I'm sure I can produce sons for you."

"How you do know this?" asked Hilda pointedly.

"I just know," replied Elizabeth.

Hilda spoke up again. "For five years, you have no husband. How have you lived?"

"It ain't been easy, mum. My family would not take me in, so I had to find work as a seamstress."

"Could you make support as seamstress?" Hilda queried. "In Germany, it *ist* very hard for woman without man."

Elizabeth looked at Hilda, her eyes defiant in an attempt to put an end to these questions. "I did what I had to do."

"At least you had no babies to support," Hilda acknowledged. "Did you volunteer to be transported here, or were you ordered?'

The woman responded with a sigh. "I volunteered to come, because I want to find a new life."

"And I wish to find a new wife," William said, smiling at the woman. She returned his smile openly. Honor just turned her head away, biting her lip as punishment for her earlier mistake.

Comfort took a step toward Honor and whispered to the girl, "I met her before, in the magistrate's office. She was convicted of prostitution and sent to the Colonies."

William smiled again at Elizabeth and shook her hand. "I seek an Anglican wife. Do you attend the Church of England?"

"I am so glad to hear that." She turned her eyes from him and looked down at the dock. "I am a true believer, but my first husband would not let me attend church."

"Let me speak to the officer," William said, stepping away from the woman. The discussion made him quite uncomfortable, and he wanted no more of it. He bowed, and turned to walk away.

●●●

Comfort walked over to join the Germans. She was uncomfortable with the situation and felt she needed to say something.

"Mistress Hilda," Comfort exclaimed. "This is wrong. I know of this woman, and she is not who she claims to be. She is not a match for a good man like Master Logsdon."

"*Ja*, I think this *ist* true," said Hilda. "You should speak with him."

"I could not be so bold." She looked at Walter. "Perhaps you can relay my concerns. She is a woman of the streets." Walter looked at Comfort for a moment, then stepped over to William, who stood in line waiting his turn to negotiate with the first mate. He pulled William to the side.

"*Mein guter* neighbor," Comfort heard Walter say. "Comfort knows of this woman. She *ist* not a lady and she *ist* not *Frau* for you."

William looked at Comfort, wondering if she might be manipulating him on Honor's behalf.

Walter went on, "You have been *guter* neighbor for me. I speak *gut* for you. You must not wed with this woman."

Frustrated, William stepped out of line and walked over to Günther, Hilda, and Comfort. "Buying a wife is most difficult," he said in frustration. He stared at Comfort and spoke in a concerned fashion. "Do you know something about this woman that I should know, as well? Please, be very truthful."

Comfort feared she might have stepped over a line and was now in serious trouble. She looked him in the eye, concern on her face. "Sir, it is not for me to meddle in your affairs, particularly as I have already spoken of my desire for Honor."

William's face grew more confident, and he smiled. "What do you know of the woman?" he asked, insistently.

"Sir, my master in London accused me of thievery and had me taken before the magistrate. I did not steal from him, but the magistrate offered only prison or transportation."

William's countenance took on a look of serious annoyance. "What does that have to do with the lady?"

"Sir, she came before the same magistrate on the same day. The prosecutor accused her of unspeakable behavior. The judge gave her the same offer he gave me. Sir, I am sorry, but you are a good man and deserve better." William looked at Comfort. His eyes appeared dejected and further frustrated at the new information.

"You are correct; it is not for you to meddle." William walked away, not toward the first mate's desk but toward his cart, parked near the port's warehouse.

Comfort looked to Walter and said, "On the ship, she often used coarse language."

He answered, "It *ist* not a woman's place to speak of another. You must learn to control your tongue."

"Walter," Hilda put a hand on her brother-in-law's arm and said gently, "If someone sees a neighbor in danger, *ist* it not good to warn him?"

"This *ist* man's job," scolded Walter.

"Then, you must speak again to Wilhelm," said Hilda. They all followed William to the cart.

Walter spoke first, "It *ist* your need to find a good *Frau*. Perhaps one of the others *ist* better suited to you."

"I am uncomfortable with all of this. Walter did well indeed, but I could find none who seemed like the woman I seek. How can a man know anything about a woman after a small handful of words? Perhaps it would be wiser if I were to ask Sister Skidmore to find a good match for me."

"The young girl that came with *Frau* Comfort, she *ist* young and still a virgin," said Günther. "Perhaps you should buy her, even if she does not wish to wed. The law says you can demand she gives you children."

"Günther," said William. "I'm thirty-seven, old enough to be her father. I'm looking for a woman near twice her age. And I have no need for a house servant."

"I pray, sir," said Comfort, "that you will forgive me for speaking boldly again, and I hope that the Lord will give you a good wife as soon as possible. But, sir, perhaps it is not time for you to wed. If no one suits you as a wife, perhaps you could buy Honor's contract and help her return to her home. I would be very grateful."

William turned away and put his hands over his face, exhausted by the whole affair. "Perhaps you are correct. I will talk again with the lass. But you must leave me and return to Mistress Skidmore's. I have had enough help."

●●●

Honor watched as William helped the others onto Günther's wagon. As they rode off, he walked back toward Honor. She wiped her reddened eyes and removed the bonnet she had been given, revealing for the second time the wispy glory of her golden-red curls. Though a bit disheveled, her hair had been washed, and the sun turned it into a frizzy halo of ginger color. In fact, she looked to William like the angelic child that every man hopes for as he dreams about his own daughters.

"Good day, Obadiah's master," she said. "I am so ashamed of my rude behavior earlier."

"My name is William Logsdon. Please do not call me Obadiah's master."

"Then may I be callin' ye Master Logsdon?" she asked, inhaling her sniffles.

"You may. I know that Mistress Comfort loves you very much."

"And I her... without Comfort, I would have had nary a soul to help me and might surely have died on the voyage. God gave me to her and her to me."

He watched as she wiped her eyes with the sleeve of her tattered dress. "Why do you cry?"

Honor avoided the question, "I pray she will be happy, and always be walkin' in sunshine."

"I'm sure that Walter will be very happy with Comfort. I could have been happy with her as well. I, however, have not yet found another suitable Anglican wife."

"Sir, I be Catholic. I was stolen from the beach in Dingle in County Kerry, Ireland. I should nae be here. All I want is to go home to fulfill my pledge to God. I'm to become a nun."

"I'm looking for an older woman and I want her to be Anglican."

"I know that the German man be an answer to Comfort's prayers," Honor said as she nervously touched William's hand. "I am sorry that God has not given you a good Anglican wife. Were I nae Catholic and too young, I would be interested in your need. I can see that you are a kind and generous man. I'm sure God will be findin' a good wife for you." She pulled her hand away.

A strange look washed across William's face as he stared into Honor's eyes. "Yes, then," he said with a quiver in his voice. "I am surprised to see you yet here. I would wager that some young man will soon find your smile delightful and purchase your contract before the day is out."

She smiled shyly. "Two younger men spoke with me at length yesterday, but I could nae speak well to either of them. Thanks to Our Lady, they both walked away. I can nae wed anyone. That is why I seek an older man who needs a housekeeper." She then made her plea. "Sir," she whispered, clasping her hands as in prayer. "Would you help me get back home? If you would, sir, please take me away and lead me to a priest. He will write to my father, who is rich and will send money. Da will also reward you handsomely for your favor."

"I've been told of your desire. But I cannot help you find a priest, for there are no Catholic churches in all of Maryland. For some years, Catholics have had to convert to the Church of England or go without a priest. Besides, as I have told you, I am in need of a wife, not a housekeeper."

"The Holy Church is banned here, as in England?" Honor gasped, wide eyed. "God forgive your country," she said, crossing herself. "Master William, the children in my village need a teacher. Perhaps you could buy me as a daughter. Be as my father and help me, but don't take me to be your wife. God will bless you."

"Yes, child, but your father may not be able to send the money. Even if he did, it would take six months to get here and I have not enough tobacco to buy a wife and a servant girl, too."

Honor knew more than she could let on. "Please sir. The Captain told us that if we were not bought soon, he would sell us as common slaves or throw us into the sea to drown. Sir, I am a young girl and not yet a woman," she lied. A new plan for escape had come to her mind, but she would have to continue to hide the truth. "Perhaps you could purchase my contract, and if Da does not send the money in six months, perhaps I would by then become a woman. A few months are not that long to wait, and God will bless you for your inconvenience." She smiled at him, showing off her most alluring dimples.

William chuckled, touching her cheek, and tried to hide the proud father look in his eyes. He gave a small shake of his head, but it said enough. Honor shut her eyes and silently thought, *Holy Mother, now is the time that I most need your help.*

William lifted Honor's chin, looking at her red hair and the tears of fear that were more than moistening her eyes. She reached out, put both arms around his waist and hugged him. "Please, sir. I could decide to wed with you, but not if Da sends the money."

She looked up and saw him gulp back the lump in his throat. "Honor, he said, "I know what you desire of me, but a righteous girl should not hide the truth. You want to give your father time to send the money. And you are already a woman. I confess, you are delightful and I want to take you home and treat you as a house servant for six months. But, if your father's letter does not arrive in that time, I will take you to Mistress Skidmore's and she will find a husband for you. If no letter arrives, you will have to make your life elsewhere in Maryland." With that, he put the pipe back into his mouth.

She leapt up and hugged his head, as she had often hugged her father. "Thank you, Master Logsdon. I will not hide the truth from you again."

William put his arms around her and held her tight as he set her feet back on the ground. Then he kissed the top of her head. She had never been so close to a man as when his hand dropped to her waist and pulled her to himself. Not even her father.

Chapter Ten

As Honor and William arrived at the Skidmore boarding house, Honor felt relieved that she had turned the corner in her plan to return home. Winifred came outside as William helped Honor down from the cart, looking concerned as she approached the man and the girl.

Large and imposing, Winifred walked over to the slight girl and lifted her chin. "I see you selected a very young wench." Winifred smiled with condescension at Honor, "You're pretty enough, but too skinny. Nevertheless, I'm sure I can fatten you up." Honor recoiled from the woman's touch. The boardinghouse mistress turned to William. "You've chosen a feisty one. I'm sure she ate little on the ship, but she will fill out and learn to behave soon enough."

"I'll not be staying long enough for that," Honor challenged the older woman.

Winifred looked at the girl with gentle admonition in her eyes. "Speak when you are spoken to, child," she said, turning back to William. "It's not my business the kind of wench you take to your bed this night. Should I be putting bundling boards in your bed? That way, you can reach your hands over and enjoy her."

Honor jerked her head up, "Sir," she said. "I'm to be a Catholic nun."

"No, Mistress Skidmore," said William, "Master Rausch and I will share a room, while Mistress Comfort and Mistress Honor sleep in a downstairs bedroom."

"I see," Winifred said. "Then you don't desire skinny Catholic girls. I am glad to hear that. I wouldn't want a Papist in my house either." Winifred turned on her heel and walked away.

●●●

At breakfast the next morning, Winifred took charge. As Honor looked on, the boarding house operator spoke to both William and Walter. "I'm sure both wenches are of good stock and will make good wives. However, before you leave for home, you must take them to the Anglican Church and wed with them. That is the law now."

William corrected the misunderstanding, "Thank you sister, but the girl I brought back will not be my wife. She is much too young. I will keep her as a house servant until she is able to return to her home in Ireland."

"So that's why you bought her contract? She'll be an indentured servant. It makes good sense to keep her close but not wed her. Do you have a chaperone in your home?"

"No, I have no other women in my home, and she's not indentured. She is as free as you and I," said William. "It seemed proper to simply help her return home. I intend to write a letter to her father and get from him the funds she will need. Until then, she will act as my house servant."

"But sir, she can't be your house servant if you don't have a chaperone. Both wenches must go to church and be wedded today. I cannot allow you to take her home unless you're wed or have an appropriate chaperone. Such a thing is against the law, and I cannot permit it."

"I know not of this law," said William.

Winifred explained, "You know well, sir, for every woman in the colony, there are near ten men. So the law says that an unwed man cannot have an unwed woman, not even his own daughter, in his house without a chaperone, lest that man abuse the woman. If you are caught, you will be fined and placed in the stocks for ridicule."

Honor spoke up, "Is there no exception for house servants?"

"I'm sorry, my dear," said Winifred, her tone now softened from its earlier abrupt tenor. "There are no exceptions. If you wish to live with him, you must wed first. Otherwise, I would have to speak to the authorities."

"No!" cried Honor.

William walked over to Honor and put his hands on her shoulders. He spoke, "Child, what shall I do with you? I'm Anglican, and you're Catholic. Neither of us wishes to be wed, and I may now have to take you back to the ship."

Honor said nothing, but her mind began to race. I can't be wed to him. Yet if I have to go back to the ship, an evil man may buy me and force himself on me. I need to find a way to escape.

She went to her cell, closed the door, and dropped to her knees. "Holy Mother, help me escape and keep my promise," she prayed in a whisper. "I know that being wed is not what you want. Please tell me what to do." She finished by crossing herself and then, to emphasize her sincerity, said an Our Father.

After the prayer, her escape ideas began to foment again. She considered her options. If I run away, Obadiah or Isaac will be runnin' to catch me. If I refuse to say the vows, the Master will be takin' me back to the ship. If I take the vows, I'll be an Englishman's wife and will never get home to Ireland. Saints above, I am needin' a plan and I'll be needin' it quick!

Honor returned to William and heard him ask Isaac to harness his horse to the cart. Obadiah also went to hitch Günther's horse to his wagon. Honor jumped to her feet. "I'll go help the boys," she said. Once away from the house, she asked Obadiah if he would help her. "I know I was not very nice to you on the ship, and truly I am sorry. But I need a wee bit of help from ye today. I cannot be wedded, for I must remain pure. I am going to run away, and when I do, ye must not run to catch me. Ye must also slow Isaac down if he gives chase after me. Please, will ye be me friend and help? God will bless you for it."

"Honor, we are not friends, and Master Logsdon has employed me to serve him. If he asks me to catch you, I will. If not me, you know he will send Isaac."

"Perhaps he won't be sendin' anyone after me. I must find a Catholic family and seek refuge. They will help me. If I run, ye must let me go. And if he sends ye, please run slowly."

"No," Obadiah insisted. "If you run away, I'll not wait for him to ask. I will chase you and I can run very fast, so don't try to escape."

Honor's eyes grew wide with fear at the thought of what would happen if William chose to make her his wife — or didn't. After a few moments, the rest of the entourage emerged from the boarding house and Honor stared at her new master, anxious and afraid. She got onto the cart, sitting cross-legged, and leaned forward as far as she could.

●●●

The wagons stopped first at a broker who bought the remainder of William's tobacco. Then they went to the milliner's shop to buy the clothes Honor and Comfort would need: everyday dresses, underclothing, coats, and bonnets. Honor needed shoes, as well, since she'd abandoned hers near the Dingle docks. Comfort would also require fabric, buttons, needles, and thread to make and repair clothes for her new family.

As they entered the shop, William tapped his pipe on his palm, emptied it of the tobacco, and deposited it into the pocket of his vest. Comfort stood, in awe of her good fortune, whereas Honor remained somber and anxious. She stared at the floor as the milliner approached the group.

"Why do you look down, child?" asked William. "I don't understand. Aren't you happy to be free and on your way back to Ireland?"

She said nothing, but stood silent, the thoughts persisting: *I don't want to go back to the ship.*

"Are you afraid? Surely you need new clothes that fit." He reached out to hug the girl, but she stepped away from him. She looked up and tried to force a smile. Then she stepped over to Comfort and took the older woman's hand. "Don't let him send me back to that ship." William continued to hold out his arms in invitation to Honor.

"No!" she insisted.

"Master Logsdon," Comfort spoke. "May I take the girl outside and talk with her?"

William nodded, and the two went outside, walking far enough away to be out of hearing range. Comfort was upset with the girl. "Miss Honor, what are you trying to do? Master Logsdon has been nothing but good to you, yet you reject his kindness."

"He can't be takin' me to his house, so he plans to send me back to the ship. Comfort, I can't," she wailed.

"What is wrong with you, Honor? He won't send you to the ship. He has said he will help you get back to Ireland. He's a good man and he will keep his word." Honor looked up, her eyes full of fear. Comfort went on. "He is buying the things you will need to stay here and asks for very little in return, only that you show some appreciation. Why didn't you let him hug you?"

"He hugged me and kissed the top of my head at the boarding house. I didn't like it — he held me too close."

"Is that so bad? Did not your father hug and kiss you? Young lady, you have such a childish notion of right and wrong. It's time for you to grow up."

"I'm not his daughter." Honor drew closer and put her arms around Comfort, but the older woman did not return the embrace.

"You have the charm of an angel when you have a need and the appreciation of a spoiled child when help is offered. We will go back inside, and you will hug Master William and treat him like the father he's trying to be."

Honor remained anxious. "It would be a sin to be kissin' him."

"He has gone out of his way to help you," Comfort said, backing away from Honor's embrace with a mother's frown set on her face. "All the while, your foolish ideas about propriety make you very unworthy of his help. It is time for you to accept your new situation and be grateful to those who try to help you."

Chastened, Honor looked down. "Tell me what to do."

"Apologize and hug him … very close."

Tears welled up in Honor's eyes. As the women returned to the shop, the milliner was showing yard goods to Walter and Hilda. Comfort left Honor at William's side and took her place next to Walter, grasping his hand and standing close. He said, "I can afford only one dress, but I can buy the material for others. Can you sew?"

Honor watched Comfort through tear-washed eyes. She took William's hand and touched her head against his shoulder.

In addition to the yard goods, Comfort acquired a warm coat and other items in preparation for the coming winter. With her shopping complete, Comfort hugged Walter and thanked him for his kindness. "I will love your children as my own," she promised.

Honor stepped in front of William, hugging him with both arms. "I'm sorry. You're a good man and I be lovin' you for helpin' me."

Honor's turn had come. The milliner stepped toward her and commented on her red hair. "I have the perfect dress for your beautiful hair, but it's for Sunday wearing. She looked at William, saying, "The girl will be very pleased." She went to a hook on the wall and pulled off a beautiful dark green dress with a white bodice that laced up in the back. It had short, white sleeves that ruffled around red ribbons and red bows down the front. Below the waist, the green skirt had a white apron bordered in green. The dress seemed a bit large for Honor, but it could be taken in to fit.

Honor's eyes opened wide. She forced a smile, and Comfort said. "Well, my dear, you said your Da called you as Irish as the shamrock and as Catholic as the rose. This dress suits you well, but it may be too expensive. Perhaps a simpler frock would be better."

Honor turned to William with a more sincere smile. "Master William, this dress is quite beautiful, but I need something simpler."

"Know that I will ask your father to repay the cost of the dress," William answered.

"Yes, sir. And he will pay you, but a simpler dress will do."

"Then you shall have a simpler dress."

Honor reached up and, with one arm, hugged him. "I'm sorry for being childish before. Thank you for helping me."

Waiting until she backed away, William looked up at her. "Thank you for the nice hug."

"Please don't send me back to the boat. They'll throw me into the ocean, and I'll drown."

"I wouldn't do that. Besides, they told me they won't take anyone back. I'll have to find somewhere for you to stay until the letter comes. Perhaps Sister Skidmore will take you in."

Honor nodded and turned her attention to the milliner. After a bit, she decided on an everyday dress and other appropriate clothing. The dress had long sleeves, a light brown bodice, and yellow laces down the front. The burnt orange skirt, completing the warm colors of fall, required petticoats to billow it out. All Honor needed now was underclothing and simple brown shoes.

The men paid for the purchases, and the group bade farewell to the milliner, who was now quite a bit wealthier. After visiting the cobbler to purchase shoes, the entourage drove to St. Ann's, where Comfort and Walter were to be married.

●●●

St. Anne's Anglican Church was located on Duke of Gloucester Street, a mile north of the Skidmore boarding house. The five-year-old Church stood an impressive two stories high, with a tall bell tower and a beautiful winding staircase. From the tower, one could see the entire village of Annapolis.

The group found Parson Blyth in his Tudor cottage, next to the Church. The entrance to the two story house sat at the end of a path bordered with green shrubs and red flowers. Large brown timbers framed the exterior, with smaller timbers branching off at odd angles. The resulting spaces held plaster panels that were painted white. The second story was a bit wider and deeper than the first, causing it to hang over like the top of a mushroom. The shakes in the roof were uneven, the peak sagging in the middle, and white painted chimneys protruding upward like three soldiers standing guard.

Comfort stared at the familiar style and said, "God bless England. It's like being home."

Parson Blyth opened the door, welcoming them. "Good day to you all." He then reached behind to bring forth a lady who carried an infant on her hip. She, too, came out to greet the visitors. "This is my wife, Clara."

"Good day to you, Ma'am," said William.

Clara wore a tan colored dress with a bright yellow scarf. She shifted the baby from her right side to the left. Tall for a colonial woman, and robust with dark brown hair tied tight behind her head, she had given birth only once, at age twenty-six. Clara looked at the two women and said, "How beautiful you both are."

Comfort squeezed Honor's hand. "Such a beautiful child, how old is he?"

The proud papa answered, "Henry will be a year next month. Would you believe me if I said he already knows the twenty-third Psalm?" He smiled and pushed his tongue into his cheek. "Won't you come inside? How may I help you?"

"My name, sir, is William Logsdon, and this gentleman is Walter Rausch." William paused as the entourage entered the cottage. "We live on neighboring plantations near Reisterstown. We have acquired these two ladies from the ship in the harbor. Their names are Comfort and Honor."

Comfort curtsied, and William continued. "The lads here are my servants. They are Isaac and Obadiah." Both boys bowed.

"May God bless you all, please come and have a seat in the parlor." The parson motioned to the room to the right of the doorway.

William studied the beauty of the cozy room, enjoying the color and scent of the fresh flowers that filled a vase sitting atop a graceful pedestal table. He listened to the gentle creaking of the floorboards as the others walked through an archway into the sitting room. He scanned the bookshelves that lined one wall as a backdrop for two padded lounge chairs, each with its own footstool. A bowl on one of the tables held a quantity of ripe, summer apples, while an expensive-looking book lay open on the other. He glanced at a three-person wood bench and two matching rocking chairs that formed a grouping on the opposite wall, and studied the glowing fire beneath the mantle on a third wall. Finally, he breathed in, as though he could smell the beams of bright morning sunlight that came through two glass-paned windows.

Clara said, "Would you boys like an apple?'

"Yes, mum," said Isaac, stepping toward the bowl.

With the baby on one hip, she used her free hand to pick through the selection to find the two biggest apples, and handed them to the boys. "Why don't you sit on the floor by the door while you eat them?"

The parson spoke up. "Can I assume you've come seeking a double wedding ceremony?"

"Walter and Comfort wish to wed," answered William, "But I wish to help the young girl return to her native Ireland."

"Well, then, please sit down." Parson Blyth took a place at one of the bookshelf chairs, and Clara took the other. With the grace of a queen, Clara arranged the skirt of her dress, fanning it out around her. William and Walter sat in the rocking chairs opposite them, their backs straight, and proper. Comfort and Honor sat on the bench.

Parson Blyth looked at the two women. "And which of you is Comfort?"

Comfort spoke up, "Yes, sir, I am Ann Comfort Smyth, and this is my dear friend ..."

Honor blurted out, "Father, my name is Honor O'Flynn. I'm fifteen and was kidnapped by English sailors. I cannot wed because I'm Catholic and want to be a nun."

The parson smiled, looking at his wife. He returned his gaze to Comfort. "And do you wish to be wed with this man?" he asked, indicating Walter.

Comfort nodded, "Yes, Parson. I'm from London and wish to start a new life here."

As part of a well-established practice, Clara stood. "Well, it is early for lunch, but I would like to invite you all to share some refreshment. Come with me, boys," she said as she headed toward the kitchen area at the rear of the house. Isaac and Obadiah stood and followed her, not yet finished with the first course of what they hoped might be a feast.

Blyth turned his attention back to William. "Help me understand, sir. You purchased this child's contract but don't want to wed with her. Instead, you want to send her back to Ireland. Is that correct?"

"Yes, sir. I came to Annapolis with the tobacco needed to acquire a second field hand and a wife, but none of the women on the ship suited me. Honor is a friend of Comfort's, who asked that I consider helping the girl. I agreed to buy her contract and help her get home. I plan to write a letter to her father to ask for the funds to repay me and secure a return fare. I had planned to bring her home as a house servant, but I have learned that this may be against the law. I need your help to find a place for her until the letter from her father arrives."

Honor spoke again, "Surely there is a good Catholic family who needs a house servant?"

"I am sure that something can be worked out." Blyth turned to Walter. "Do you two wish to be wedded this day?

"Ja, this ist so."

"German," said the parson gleefully. "We have many Germans in Maryland. Some have come from Europe and some form Pennsylvania, to the north. From where have you come?"

95

"I come from *München*. I have two boys, *und* two girls, but no wife. She *ist mit Gott*."

"I see you've chosen a fine English lady as a second mother for your children." He smiled at Comfort, then returned his eyes to Walter. "You have chosen well but, you should have brought your children to meet their new mother."

"They meet *mit* Comfort yesterday. This morning they go with *meinem Bruder und* his *Frau*. We will see them later today, on the way home."

Clara and the boys returned with a tray of cheddar cheese and a pitcher of apple cider. She sent them back to the kitchen for a tray with wooden noggins as she began to pass apples and the cheese to her other guests.

Honor had never before tasted cider, and only knew cheddar cheese to be a Christmas day delicacy. "Take two noggins and sit by the door, boys," said Clara. "If you want more apples, help yourself. I must serve cider to the adults first. Then I will give you some."

The parson spoke again, "I shall say the blessing." All bowed their heads, and Honor crossed herself. "Gracious Father, we thank you for the food which Thou hast provided, and we thank Thee for the safe journey which brought these new people to our shores. Most importantly, we ask for Thy blessing on all who share this meal. May Thy will for each of them come to pass. I ask this is in the name of our Lord and Savior, Jesus Christ. Amen."

The others mumbled their own versions of "Amen."

Clara passed thick slices of cheese, first to the two ladies and then to the men. Finally, she served Isaac and Obadiah, whose eyes had grown big. Clara saw that Honor ate the delicious treat slowly.

"Honor, you have such beautiful hair," said Clara. "With a name like O'Flynn, you would be expected to have red hair. There are many young girls from Ireland here in Maryland."

Honor took a sip from her noggin, then answered, "The English kidnapped me, but I don't want to live here."

Comfort addressed her sternly, as a mother would, "Honor, behave yourself." Walter reached over and put his hand on Comfort's arm. She looked up. He smiled, and she stopped talking.

Parson Blyth spoke, "Many of our Irish boys and girls came as victims of unscrupulous sea captains. It is a wicked practice. Many of those girls have taken husbands and attend our Church, though they remain Catholic." Obadiah and Isaac had gobbled their cheese and Clara reached for the tray to offer each another piece.

"Yes, Father, but I can nae wed," said Honor. "God wants me to be a nun."

At that, William spoke up, "Parson, she is a very determined girl. I would have taken her home as a maid servant, but Sister Skidmore reminds me that this is not possible. Can you help us?" William looked at Honor and smiled.

Parson Blyth turned back to Honor, "Did you know that the Anglican Church is Catholic, just not Roman Catholic? And did you know that priests in the Anglican Church are called Parson and not Father?" Blyth smiled. "My child, what if it is not God's will that you go home? Perhaps …"

He couldn't finish his sentence before Honor interrupted, "Please, Father, it is God's will. I know it is. He wants me to teach the children. They need me, so you must find a Roman Catholic family where I can live until I go home."

"Honor, I am not a Catholic priest. You need not call me Father. Parson will do."

"Please, Parson," she answered, "I could work to repay my keep. I know Da will send money for my return. Could you please write a letter to my Da?"

"Child, is that not what Master Logsdon wishes to do?" he smiled at the girl. "Understand that it could take many months for such correspondence to be complete."

Clara got up and poured more cider into the boys' noggins. "I have some fresh bread. Would you boys like some?"

The boys nodded vigorously as William spoke up again. "Since I live in the back country, I would like to ask her father to send his response to your church. I would leave the letter with Mistress Skidmore to be taken via an eastbound ship, perhaps ..."

Honor interrupted again. "I could be a maid servant until Da's letter gets here. Do you need a maid servant, Parson?"

Comfort could sit silent no longer. "Honor, you are not to speak again unless you are spoken to. For such a sweet girl, I cannot understand why you are so rude."

"Comfort, I am afraid."

"We all know that, but being afraid is no reason for misbehaving."

Blyth smiled at William. "Do you have a woman relative who could live in your house as a chaperone?"

"No, sir, I have no family here except the two boys, and my cabin is very small."

Blyth looked back at Honor. "What you ask may not be possible, as I know of no Roman Catholic families who have need for a servant girl."

"Could I just live here with you and your wife? She could be a chaperone." Honor looked at Comfort, not wanting to upset her further.

Blyth smiled broadly. "No, child, our house is small, too. We have no room that would be appropriate for a maiden."

Honor thought for a few seconds and adjusted her plan. "Is there a home for maidens without families in the village?"

Blyth shook his head. "There are so many men without wives that unwed maidens your age are not to be found. We have a few boarding houses. You must either wed Brother Logsdon or live with Sister Skidmore, and that is assuming Sister Skidmore will allow you to live with her, and Brother Logsdon is willing to pay for your keep."

Honor looked fearful again. "Mistress Skidmore has said she will not allow a Catholic in her house. There must be some other houses where a Catholic maiden can live. My Da will pay twice whatever me keep might be, I promise."

Blyth responded, "Brother Logsdon, Sister Skidmore often takes in unwed women whom she buys from the boats. She might consider purchasing Honor's contract, if the price were acceptable. Would you consider selling the girl?"

William thought for a minute. His heart still wanted to take Honor home to *Brotherly Love*. "No, Parson, but I will speak with Mistress Skidmore about Honor becoming a boarder, and when I write the letter to Ireland, I will include that expense in my request."

After the refreshments were eaten and decisions made, the visitors thanked Clara and the parson and walked outside. They went together into the church, where Parson Blyth married Walter and Comfort. Honor had never attended an Anglican ceremony, and marveled at how similar it was to the Catholic weddings in her hometown of Dingle.

●●●

With the wedding complete, the guests prepared to leave. Clara hugged Honor tenderly. "You're a darling girl, Honor, but you have not learned to hold your tongue. A woman can make few demands in this world, and children may make even fewer. Wherever you come to stay, keep your thoughts and fears to yourself. And if you stay with Mistress Skidmore, you'll be happy there."

"I would like to stay with Mistress Skidmore. I know I will be happy waiting there."

Comfort hugged and kissed Honor several times, and both felt tears at parting again. Comfort said, "If you come to Master Logsdon's plantation, I will visit you; we will be but a short wagon ride away."

"Oh, Comfort, that is such a good idea. I love you so. God bless you."

William, the boys, and Honor walked to his cart, while the others loaded themselves onto Günther's wagon. They started off in different directions.

"Sir, I am very sorry that I spoke rudely to you but I must take care of myself until I get home."

"That is all right, child. If I were you, I might be just as afraid as you are." He stepped back. "What if your father does not send the money? You must decide what you will do in such circumstances."

"Da will answer, I am sure of that. But you must ask him to act quickly. If he can't send the money, I will find another way." After a few seconds, she went on. "Sir, might it be possible for me to stay with Comfort at her cottage?"

"No. Their cottage is even smaller than mine, and they have six people living there."

Before they arrived at Mistress Skidmore's house, Honor found herself speaking up once again. "I will pray for you, always, sir."

Chapter Eleven

The next morning, both Rausch families left for home, and William took his horse-drawn cart to town to buy some paper, ink, and a quill, as Mrs. Skidmore had no need to keep such things on hand. Upon William's return to the boarding house, Honor listened as he spoke to Winifred. "Sister Skidmore, I too will be leaving this morning, and would like to leave Honor in your charge for five to six months. How much would you ask for her keep?"

"She is a most darling girl, and I will be pleased to teach her. I would ask one pound per month, and another pound when the letter from her father arrives. I will also need the authority to act in your best interest, as I seek to guide the child."

"I have not enough to pay the whole fee now but offer three shillings for my stay, and three pounds to pay for Honor's board. I will give you the rest when I return this fall to sell more tobacco. The final payment will have to wait for the letter from Ireland. Is that acceptable?"

"Of course," said Winifred, ever the smart businesswoman.

"Does the fee include the use of a sleeping room upstairs?"

"Certainly, and it covers her food, as well. Am I to believe that you wish me to teach her the ways of a proper wife?"

"Such would be useful," said William. "But my plan is to have her return home. However, should her father not be able to send the money, she will have to make her life here. Anything you can teach her that will make her life easier would be, of course, appreciated."

"Brother Logsdon, I warrant that she is a dear girl, but she is Catholic, and more than a bit willful. I will be happy to have her if I also have the right to discipline any misbehavior. You must sign a contract promising to pay for her keep, and you must give me your permission to teach her obedience. Would you write out such an agreement and sign it?"

"Of course I would." Winifred dictated the contents of the contract:

For the keep of Honor O'Flynn, William Logsdon agrees to pay Winifred Skidmore one pound sterling per month for the keep of Honor O'Flynn in her boarding house. Winifred agrees to educate Honor O'Flynn and discipline her, if needed. Honor O'Flynn agrees to obey Winifred Skidmore for as long as she remains in residence with Winifred Skidmore.

William wrote out the document and signed it. He then asked Honor to sign it. She smiled at him as she carefully signed Honor O'Flynn to the bottom of the page. Putting his hand on Honor's shoulder, William said, "Child, let's write a letter to your Father. Shall I tell him that you could have a good life here in Maryland? It would save your Da much money if he did not have to send for you, and you could become a nun here in America." William ignored a deliberate cough from Winifred, who was listening to every word as she prepared a vegetable stew for supper.

Honor ignored his question, his words causing the girl to pause. "Sir, ask Da to send the needed money soon. Da is the mayor of Dingle. If he cannae manage the full funds, I am sure the townspeople will assist him."

"Will you allow me to include a few encouraging words of my own?" William persisted. "Instead of paying to send you home to Ireland, I could suggest that your family immigrate to Maryland. Such a trip would cost little more and could be of great profit for all."

"If me Da were to choose for our family to travel to Maryland, I would be true to his desire and become a nun here." A harrumph came from across the room, as Winifred carefully considered William's suggestion and Honor's reply.

"You are a determined girl." said William. "I shall include my encouragement in the letter."

Sitting at the Skidmore table, William drafted a letter to Cillian O'Flynn, Dingle, Ireland. Honor read over his shoulder as he wrote:

"Sir, I am your humble servant William Logsdon of Brotherly Love, Maryland, and I have had the privilege to purchase the contract of your most charming daughter, Honor. She has said that an English seaman kidnapped and brought her here against her will and asks you to send the money needed for her to return to you. She sends her salutations of love, hoping they find you and your family in good health, as is she, having been so since her arrival in Maryland... praise God for his blessings. It would cost thirty pounds for Honor's expenses and return trip to Ireland. If you are able to forward these funds, I recommend you send the money in care of Parson Blyth at St. Anne's Church in Annapolis, Maryland. However, I believe such monies could better be used to bring yourself and the rest of your family to America. Having met and being much in admiration of your daughter, I would rather see her stay in Maryland. She has agreed that I might attempt to encourage you rather to join her here than to send her home.

There is not one immigrant in my neighborhood who is not thrilled to be in this country and would leave their native land again to come here, should the opportunity present itself. Maryland is the best colony for working folk and tradesmen from anyplace in the world. It is a healthy, beautiful country. Land costs are very low, from ten to a hundred pounds per hundred acres, depending on the quality of the land or its location. Also, land grows in value each year because of the vast quantities of people who migrate here annually. Therefore, I would encourage you and your family – or anyone else – to hurry and make passage, the sooner the better.

An Amish neighbor of mine has traveled most of this region surveying the land and has found many fine tracts. Because he is curious and somewhat difficult to please, he waited to buy land until the second day of October last, when he bought a tract consisting of fifty acres, for which he paid 45 pounds. It is excellent land but uncleared, with the exception of about 10 acres for which he has a small log cabin and orchard planned. He might have bought less costly land, but it would not have been to his satisfaction.

Another friend visited near my plantation for three months and then rented a farm five miles from there with a good brick house and two hundred acres of land for four pounds a year. Together with my acres, we sowed about two hundred acres of wheat and seven acres of rye. We plowed our summer crop in May and June with a yoke of oxen and two horses, expending no more effort than one would with double the animals back in Ireland. We sowed our wheat with two horses, as the land is almost free of rocks. A boy of 12 or 14 years can hold a plow, and a man can drive the plow by himself, working an acre in a day. The stronger men can plow two acres in a day.

Provisions are plentiful at the Annapolis market, where growers gather to present their commodities for sale. These markets are held on the fourth and seventh days of each week. The region also abounds in so much fruit that it is difficult to find a homestead without an apple, peach, or cherry orchard. As for chestnuts, walnuts, hazelnuts, strawberries, blueberries, and mulberries — they grow wild in the woods and fields in vast quantities. These fruits and nuts are good safeguards against poor harvest, whether roasted, boiled, used in cakes and tarts, and even in rum. People harvest these wild crops so that they can eat and drink their plenty.

A reaper is paid two shillings, three pence a day, while a mower is paid two shillings, sixpence, and a pint of rum, in addition to meat and drink. No workman agrees to labor without food and drink included as part of the bargain. A laboring man is paid eighteen or twenty pence a day, even in winter.

The winters have not been as cold as expected, nor the summers as hot as we anticipated; both are more moderate than we were told. In summertime, people wear but a shirt and linen drawers/trousers, which are breeches and stockings all in one. They are fine, cool wear for the summer.

Anyone, except indentured servants, may leave the region at will, and servants when they have served their time may leave, if they please, though it is rare that any leave the region, except when a man's business requires such travel.

When you come, bring wool and linen cloth, shoes, stockings, and hats. Such things are sold here, and a man can earn more for a suit of clothes here than in Ireland, because a workman's labor is paid so well. I would have you bring two or three good felling axes and three iron wedges, for they are of good service here. Plow irons are valuable, too, so you should bring as many as your monies will allow. You might also bring plow chains as they are in demand, as well.

Honor fears my encouragement will be of little effect because you are so happy with your lives in Dingle, but you may be assured that if I did not respect your daughter and your family so much, I would not have written such a long letter."

Yours in God's blessing,

William Logsdon.

Once he finished his letter, William said to Honor, "Please write something so your father will know the letter also comes from you." William handed the letter to her, and she read it over again. The fact that she could both read and write amazed the colonists, including the illiterate Winifred Skidmore. Honor sat, thought for a moment, and then wrote: I am as Irish as the shamrock and as Catholic as the rose. Honor.

Honor's new petticoat swished as she walked around the table to hand the letter back to William. He read her words out loud and then stared at her. She had cleaned up, groomed her hair, and wore one of her new dresses. Everything about her had turned desirable and William once again felt a sense of pride in his effort to help the girl. "You are an amazing young woman, Honor," he said

Honor reached up and gave him a reluctant girl's hug.

William rose from the table, saying, "I come to Annapolis every three months to buy what items I need, and will come again in October. We will see each other then, and again in January. By then your father's response should have arrived." He turned to Winifred, "If word from Ireland comes sooner,

Parson Blyth will send someone to fetch me." He handed his letter to Winifred, asking her to give it to the captain of the *Blissful Lady* before the ship sailed for England. Winifred folded the document and placed it in her apron pocket with a small pat.

William, Isaac, and Obadiah walked outside and climbed aboard the horse cart. It had started to sprinkle, and the wind blew a bit harder than before. Honor and Winifred followed them out. "Here are some Johnnycakes for you and the lads to eat on their trip," the old woman said, handing him a small satchel. "I believe I know how to persuade the wench to stay. She is a sweet girl, and would be a good wife to one of your boys. I shall try to change her mind."

Honor looked at William. "No. I be wantin' to go home."

"Sister Skidmore, I think Honor is well fixed in her desires. Perhaps events could change her mind, but neither you nor I will likely have any influence."

William smiled and thanked Winifred. "Take good care of her. She is like a daughter to me."

Honor smiled.

"You're a wonderful young lady, Honor, and I'm sure your family anxiously awaits your return. But if that is not possible, I will do what I can to make you happy here in Maryland."

He put his hand behind her head and drew it to himself. She reached uneasily around him with a squeeze normally reserved for her father. "Thank you for helpin' me, and God bless ye. I'll be prayin for ye always," Remembering Comfort's admonition, Honor reached up and rubbed her lips against his cheek.

With his business complete, William smiled and began his ride west toward the Patapsco River, which served as the cart path back to *Brotherly Love*.

After waving goodbye, Honor looked at her new mistress. Winifred looked back, commanding, "Come inside, wench. It is about to storm." Honor felt the strong grip on her elbow as she entered her new home.

●●●

It would take about ten hours for William and the boys to cover the forty miles along the river from Annapolis to *Brotherly Love*. Long before they reached the plantation, a storm began, and William knew the water in the river would soon begin to rise. He decided that pushing through for the last few miles would be unwise, so they found a clearing to wait out the rest of the day. Obadiah tethered the horse in a small grassy clearing, as Isaac positioned the cart to offer some shelter. William gathered some dry tinder and started a small fire under one end of the cart, while the boys collected what dry wood they could find around the campsite. The cold wind pierced the insufficient layers of clothing the three men wore, making them shiver with the damp. The three travelers huddled between the cart wheels as near to the fire as possible. William passed around the deer-jerky he and Isaac had brought along and gave the boys the remaining Johnnycakes and the last of the apples.

"Tell me about your plantation, Master Logsdon," said Obadiah. "How far is it from here?"

"We are but three or four hours from my land. Most bountiful, it sits between two creeks that join to become the river we are upon. I have three hundred acres of good land, about forty of them cleared for crops. There is a cabin, an orchard, a small barn for horses, and a cellar for storing meat, fruits, and vegetables. I also have a smokehouse for preserving the meat we harvest from the forest. Isaac lives in the cabin, as will you. He is fifteen, with two years more on his contract. You two will be good company for each other." Isaac smiled at Obadiah, happy to know he would have someone new to talk to and hunt with.

"What type of work will you have for me?"

"Well, there are more crops to harvest, and the winter crop needs planting. During the winter months, we will clear more land. I hope to use the trees we fell to build a small tobacco barn, and I want to start a new cabin for my family. You will help with that. Have you ever cleared trees or built a log cabin?"

"I have cut small trees but know naught of the building."

"When the new cabin is built, you and Isaac will move into the old cabin. We shall also take time to hunt for deer and turkey. Isaac loves to hunt, and I am sure you will, too. Have you ever fired a gun?"

"Oh no, sir, the master of my village does not allow citizens to have firearms. You can be jailed for killing one of his deer. However, I wish very much to learn to hunt."

"In this country, every man must practice the use of a gun. Not just to hunt game, but also to fight if the Indians come to raid. A band of Susquehannocks live about six hours north of my land. Mostly, we live in peace. But other times they raid plantations to steal food, tools, horses — and sometimes women and children. Raiding is their ancient practice, and missionaries have not yet brought them to the Christian way. I will teach you how to avoid these raiders and how to fight them if they ever attack you."

"Being a soldier will be such great fun. I shall enjoy living in Maryland!" Obadiah declared to Isaac and William.

"Know, son, that life here is harsh and sometimes very dangerous. You must never consider these realities as fun. Know also that it is not God's will for us to fight with Indians, except to protect ourselves and our loved ones."

Isaac changed the subject. "Do you desire to wed the red-haired wench, Master William? Will she be coming to live with us?"

"No. She is but a child in need of help, and I am much too old for her. You are much closer to her age, Isaac. Perhaps you have noticed that Honor has many pleasing gifts. Do you favor her as well? If she could see *Brotherly Love*, I know she would be happy there. And if I can find a wife soon, Honor could come to live with us as our maidservant."

●●●

Once William and the boys had gone, Honor and Winifred went inside to get acquainted with each other. Honor stood near the table, offering herself as a friend. "Da always said that however long the road shall be, there always comes a turnin'.

I'm happy that my troubles are over and I can live here with you until my money comes. I shall help in any way I can and be of no trouble at all. Thank you for havin' me."

"I am quite sure you will be no trouble," Winifred smiled, her voice friendly. "I have taught many a wench the ways of Maryland and have cared for each one dearly. I will treat you well and teach you like the others. That is, of course, if you're strictly obedient."

Honor turned away to look around the room. "This is such a nice house. I shall enjoy my stay here. I am good at gardenin' and washin' tableware, and I will be most obedient."

"Remember what the proverbs tell us: 'The sluggard wants and gets naught, but the diligent are satisfied.' So be diligent and work hard and you will do just fine."

Honor changed the subject. "Might I ask which room will be mine? It will be nice to sleep in a bed again."

"You may use the upstairs room on the left," said Winifred, as she started toward the stairs. "We will begin your education in the morning. If the rainy weather breaks, we will make some candles." Winifred made her way up the stairs. "You must excuse me for a moment."

Waiting until Winifred appeared again, Honor continued the conversation with a shout. "I would like very much to begin in the mornin'. Back home, Da is the mayor. Our family is rich, and I am like a princess." Honor grinned at her own humor. "Ma buys our candles, but I would very much like to learn how to make them myself."

Winifred answered in a loud voice from above. "We have no princesses in Maryland. We will begin in the morning. Today, however, I must post Master Logsdon's letter with the ship's captain. I want you to stay inside until I return." With that, Winifred came downstairs, donned the warm cloak she had brought from her room, and left the boarding house without another word. It occurred to Honor that the large woman walked with the strut of an English bulldog.

*This letter was adapted, with changes to correct the language and to fit this story, from a letter written in October 1725 by Charles A. Hanna of Chester, Pennsylvania (60 miles north of Annapolis). I use that letter to illustrate how people like William spoke and felt about life in Mid-America at the time. The letter can be found in Alden T. Vaughan's America Before the Revolution, 1725-1775, Prentice Hall, Inc., Englewood Cliffs, New Jersey, 1967, pages 25-27.

Chapter Twelve

A few days later, Winifred approached Honor and said, "I will need to go shopping for about two hours. Get your cloak so we can be on our way." Honor had other thoughts, telling her mistress she would rather not go on the errand trip. "Can I trust you to stay inside the house?" Honor lied easily, agreeing to stay home. "Then sweep the house and wash the floors," Winifred said gruffly. The opportunity of two hours of freedom excited Honor's imagination, so she agreed to the chore.

Soon after Winifred left, Honor wrapped her arms around herself and spun around joyously until she fell against the table. "Oh, thank you, Holy Mother," she prayed. She quickly swept the floor and then skipped to the door. She jaunted out, heading down the street without a shawl. The air felt warm and moist with promise. Honor walked around the block of stone and cut wood houses that made up Winifred's neighborhood. The buildings, yellow, red, and other colors, gave the neighborhood the look of a bouquet of flowers, noticeably different from the drab, brown houses of Dingle. While Honor's home village had four footpaths and a few houses, Annapolis had numerous crossed streets and a great many houses. At one corner, she turned right and saw a row of shops. Her jaw dropped as she saw, for the first time, the center of abundance in America.

In just minutes, she found the shop with a dress and woman's hat painted on the sign over the front door. Honor stood before the millinery shop where William had taken her the day they visited St. Anne's. She went in and greeted the shop owner who had waited on them that day. "Good day to you, child," said the milliner. "I see you're wearing your new dress this afternoon. Let me look at you." The proprietress took Honor's hands and held them out to the side. "You look as pretty as the fairest young ladies in all of Annapolis. What brings you here this warm August day?"

In colonial days, millinery shops were almost always owned by women. They carried not only dresses, but also provided fabric from which to make aprons, kerchiefs, cloaks, hats, and underclothing, as well as finished versions of these items. Almost all millinery customers were town folk or the wives of wealthy plantation owners. The poorer women of the community had to spin their own flax and cotton fibers into thread and weave them into material themselves. Poor women's dresses were drab natural tones or tinted with the juices of local berries, but the brightly colored fine silks and linens sold in town were imported from England.

The milliners' apprentices were young girls who desire to develop their sewing skills or widows in need of employment. The tasks of cutting, fitting, and sewing fell to those apprentices, whereas the shop owners handled the sales. Honor figured this might be a place for her to earn a few shillings.

"I be lovin' my dress, ma'am. It is very pretty." Honor spun around, letting the skirt flair and swish. "Master Logsdon has gone to his plantation and I am out for a short time to meet the neighbors and seek a way to support myself."

"Yes," said the milliner, "I heard from another customer that he left without you. Why didn't he take you with him? You're such a sweet girl." The milliner guided Honor deeper into the shop, hoping for a morsel of juicy gossip. "Where are you staying, child?"

"With Mistress Skidmore."

"I see," the shop owner said, lifting her eyes in intense interest. "And does she beat you?"

"Oh, no mum. She treats me very well."

"Why did your master leave you there?" the milliner inquired a bit forcefully.

"Because I cannae be weddin' with him, and there is no chaperone so I cannae act as a house servant. Instead, I agreed to stay in the boarding house until I can return to my home in Dingle."

The milliner smiled and invited Honor to sit and tell her all about it. "So, he chose you to be his wife and you refused him? As a rule, tobacco brides have not much choice in such matters. Why did you not tell him before he purchased your contract? Did you not speak of wedding before he bought you such nice dresses? Or did something happen after I met you yesterday?"

"We spoke of it. I be Catholic, you see, and he be English. And, I'm quite young while he's very old. But he's a good man and I am most happy for him. He treats me as a daughter and has provided for me to stay with Mistress Skidmore. There I will be for a few months."

"Oh my, you're Catholic! That could be a problem. Did he not take you to his bed?"

"Of course not! Mistress Skidmore did suggest we could sleep together, but I couldn't. I must remain chaste."

"But how will you repay him for his expenses? There must be some arrangement."

"Yes. Me Da will send the money. He wants me back. The children are needin' me, and I want to be needed."

"And until the money arrives, you are staying with Mistress Skidmore? That is not good, child. Master Logsdon has done you no service in leaving you with that woman."

"I sense that Mistress Skidmore is sometimes a bit harsh, but there should be no problem."

"Harsh, indeed. Does she force you to sleep in one of those dreadful small rooms?"

"Nae. Master William told her that I am her boarder, so I sleep in one of the soft beds upstairs."

"Listen to me, child." The milliner put her arm around Honor and whispered in her ear, as if someone might be listening, even though not another soul was in the shop. "Be careful, dear girl. Mistress Skidmore has had several young women in her house over the years, and all were locked in the small rooms at night. I heard from a friend that one was even forced to sleep without blankets in the winter. She also has been known to sell girls to unsavory men who offer her considerable sums. Watch yourself. Maryland has many unsavory men and few available women."

Honor smiled at the milliner, believing she had the situation with Mistress Skidmore under control. The girl came to the point of her visit. "Mistress, would you be needin' a lassie to work in your shop?"

Eager for access to periodic updates about Winifred Skidmore, the milliner offered the girl employment. "Well, I could use a girl every Saturday to sweep the floors and tidy up the shop." A smile pulled at the corners of Honor's mouth. "I could pay you a shilling a week, but you would have to work quite hard."

Honor's eyes lit up with elation. "That would be wonderful. I am so grateful and shall speak with Mistress Skidmore this very afternoon," she said, shaking the milliner's hand. "Oh, Mother of God, I must get back at once," Honor added, realizing it had been more than two hours since Winifred had left.

Excited about the opportunity to work, Honor returned to the boarding house ready to share her good news. She'd not expected to return to an angry Mistress Skidmore. "Where have you been?" demanded Winifred. "I told you to stay in the house. You neither kept your word nor did the chores I asked of you. What's more, you have no shawl and could catch your death in this weather."

"Oh, Mistress Skidmore, I just had to explore your beautiful city. I met the dressmaker, and we talked a wee bit longer than we should have. But, saints be praised, she has offered me an apprenticeship. Isn't that wonderful?"

"I see. Nevertheless, I must punish you for disobeying me." Winifred folded her arms and clenched her jaw.

"Mum, I am a border, not a servant."

"You have been a disobedient girl. You must understand that you cannot just walk off whenever you wish. I told you not to leave the house. For that, you will not sleep in the upstairs bedroom for three weeks, but in one of the downstairs rooms. There will be no bed, so you can sleep on the dirt floor. Winter is coming, but you will have no blanket. And, until you show me that I can trust you, you will remain on the property at all times.

"I am sorry, mum. But I need a wee bit of work. I must earn money to pay for the clothes and supplies I'll be needin.'"

"And work you will, I assure you. There is always need for an obedient wench. I will find ways to rent you out, and what you earn will go toward your keep."

Knowing nothing of a slave's life, Honor didn't grasp the meaning of Mistress Skidmore's comment. She made another plea, "Could you at least help me find a priest to hear my confession? Master Logsdon would want you to do that. He knows I be needin' to see a priest."

"No, child. That I cannot do. You need no priest to be forgiven, and finding one is nigh impossible in Annapolis."

The severity of Honor's situation began to dawn on her, as her prerogatives appeared to be vanishing quickly. This woman was nothing like Comfort and could never be considered a friend. But with some care, Honor and Winifred could, at least, get along for the months until Da's letter would arrive. Nonetheless, she made one last plea. "Perhaps I can visit St. Anne's, and the priest there will hear my confession. He seemed like such a nice man.

"Parson Smyth hears no confessions. I will take you to church when I go, but you shall not visit there on your own."

"Glory be, Mistress Skidmore. I just want to give my confession and stay pure until I return home."

"You signed a contract saying you would be obedient. I know very well what to do if you try to run away, and you will be caught and punished severely."

Remembering the threat of losing her toes, Honor said, "Mistress Skidmore, I promise I will not run away. I am your boarder for the next few months, and you should do as Master Logsdon instructed."

"Understand, wench, as far as I am concerned, Master Logsdon does not want you and has given you into my care. You are little more than a slave girl, and you must obey me completely."

●●●

The next morning, Winifred let Honor out of her cell very early and had her bring in several armloads of firewood before they sat down to eat. The weather had turned quite chilly.

"That's enough wood," Winifred instructed. "Now build up the fire and heat some water for tea." The widow sat comfortably at the table, wrapped in a shawl.

"Mum, may I be havin' another shawl to keep me warm?"

"No, you may not. You will be warm enough once the fire heats the house."

Teary eyed, Honor placed tinder on the embers, blowing on them to get the fire going. During breakfast, Winifred said, "It is hard for me to be as strict as I must, but I know that life is very hard for women in this country, and you must learn to survive." She cut an apple in two and offered half of it to Honor.

"But need you punish me so harshly? Can't you just tell me what I'm to do?"

"Yesterday I told you to stay home. What did you do then?"

"I said I was sorry. I thought it was unimportant, that finding employment was more urgent," came Honor's plaintive response. The tea had warmed her, but the room remained cold. "Certainly you must have another shawl?"

"Women like us have no rights and no freedom. We are often uncomfortable. If I don't teach you your place, you will be bitter for the rest of your life. It is better that you learn now, while you are young."

"That's why I'm wantin' to return to Ireland where I am loved and looked after."

"That, dear," Winifred said with a hint of sneer, "was before you signed the contract, giving all your rights to the ship's captain, and then to Master Logsdon, and then to me. Today you must obey or be punished."

"I nae wanted to sign it, but they would have thrown me into the sea."

"You are correct. Sign it or be thrown into the sea. You have no rights."

"But Mistress Skidmore, Master William is not like that."

"Have you any idea how men treat slave girls? Since your master purchased your contract, he owns you. If he calls you to his bed, you must go. If he chooses to beat you or keep you in the barn with his animals, you go without speaking. He can even kill you and tell the sheriff that you grew ill and died from a fever, and no one will do a thing. You stupid child, when will you realize that you have no rights?"

"God would not let him do those things to me!" Honor protested.

"It was your God who let the English seaman capture you so that the captain could bring you here. God set you under Master Logsdon, and Master Logsdon has put you in my charge while he is away. I will train you to obey fully and without complaint. You must learn to obey if you are to survive."

When they had finished eating, Winifred spoke again, "We will begin your training this morning. Have you ever canned vegetables?"

"I'm sorry for bein' disobedient Mum. I promise to be doin' better."

The old woman looked at Honor, anger brimming in her eyes. "I asked if you know how to can vegetables."

● ● ●

Nearly every home in colonial Maryland had its own vegetable garden and root cellar. In the Skidmore house, the large cellar below the kitchen contained several shelves of ceramic jars filled with cooked fruits or vegetables, sealed airtight with beeswax. Winifred grew much of her own food in the garden behind her house. She canned in the summer and fall and brought the food out for the housekeeper and her guests in the winter and spring.

Surrounded by a stick-and-wattle fence, Winifred's quarter-acre garden produced an abundance of food. She had built the fence by cutting stiff, strong sticks and hammering one end of each down into the soil every three or four feet. Long, supple sticks were then woven between the vertical posts. A two-foot fence would keep out all small animals, while a scarecrow fended off the birds.

By the time Honor went with Winifred to work in the garden, all the corn had been harvested. The ears had been air dried and stored in barrels. The corn stalks were tied together into shocks, which resembled teepees, and stored in the root cellar, as well. They would be used later to stuff mattresses for the upstairs bedrooms. The remaining carrots, along with the zucchini, butternut, acorn, yellow, and crookneck squashes needed to be harvested, washed, pickled, canned, and stored away in half-gallon ceramic jars.

As they picked, Winifred continued Honor's education. "It's not just slave girls who have no rights. Few women have any rights. We must learn to make our way by being clever."

"At home, Da lets me play and have fun, even while doin' my garden chores."

"Aye, and he's the father with a spoiled wench for a daughter."

On her knees picking beans, Honor said nothing, for a change.

Winifred stooped to reach the squash. "How often did you smile at your father like a silly child so he would give you what you wanted?"

Still, Honor said nothing.

"And when he told you to do something, did you bat your eyes at him so he'd be thinking he's in charge and you were obedient?"

"Of course Da likes me to smile."

"Do you flirt with Master Logsdon the same way?"

"Sometimes," Honor said slowly, "when he's nice to me."

"Do you flirt with me?"

"Of course not!"

Winifred stepped over to Honor and used her foot to push over the basket of beans the girl had collected, spilling them across the ground. "Henceforth, you will smile at me whenever we're together. Now pick up those beans and say you're sorry."

Bewildered, Honor looked up at Winifred's angry face. After a long minute, she smiled broadly. "Yes, mum. I'm sorry and won't be forgettin' again."

Winifred returned to her basket of yellow squash. "That's better."

●●●

It would take several hours to pick the ripened vegetables, and two days to do the preserving, all under Winifred's demanding and unforgiving eye. Together, the woman and the girl carried the bounty into the kitchen and scrubbed off any remaining dirt. Winifred inspected each item before setting it in a pile on the table. They worked together to cut the squash into small pieces, shoveling the chunks into a large metal pot. Winifred fired commands at Honor, one after the other. "Scrub this one again. Go fetch more clean water. Watch the sizes of the pieces. I told you to cut off all the stems. Don't you listen? How will you ever learn if you don't listen?"

With a timid smile, Honor looked at Winifred. "Thank you for being patient with me."

Soon the pot was full. "Fill the pot with hot water, toss in a small handful of salt, and put the pot on the wrought-iron hook in the hearth." Honor did as told under Winifred's patient tutelage. The widow went on, "That's too much water. Don't waste so much salt. It's expensive. How many times must I tell you? Don't put the pot directly over the flames."

The heated water would not be used to cook the squash, only to kill any bacteria remaining on the skins. The salt would preserve the food. While the squash simmered, the women carried several one-gallon jars up from the cellar. Winifred wiped the dust from them with a clean rag.

"Check the pot. We don't want the squash to turn mushy. As soon as the water boils, remove the pot from the fire."

Again Honor learned how to flirt with her mistress. "Oh, mum, this is such fun. Can we eat some squash for supper?"

Winifred ignored her. "These small jars hold enough for several people for several days."

With a rag to protect her hands, Honor took the pot from the spider, and together they spooned the squash pieces into the jars. "Now watch what I do and learn everything. First, I sprinkle a small handful of cornmeal with some mustard and turmeric on the still hot slices."

"Why do you do that?"

"It gives the squash a good flavor. Now cover the pieces with clean water and add a little cider vinegar and some salt for more flavoring. The vinegar will pickle the vegetables and kill anything that might rot them."

"How long does it take them to pickle?"

"A week or two. Soon a yellow scum will float to the top of the jar, and we must remove it. When that process stops, the pickling is finished and we can use wax and a wood plug to seal the jars and keep the air from contaminating the vegetables."

"I love your squash. It's delicious. Thank you for teaching me how to do the cannin'." Honor had learned the technique well enough to satisfy Winifred's controlling nature.

Winifred looked pleased. "Bring the next pot over here, and fetch me the other jug of vinegar. Hurry up, wench. We don't have all day."

It took well into the evening to finish that day's canning. The steps would be repeated several times during the next few days. When they finished, Honor dropped with exhaustion.

"You did well, wench. I will make supper while you rest awhile. Tonight we shall both eat an extra share."

●●●

At *Brotherly Love*, William continued to think about Honor's future. He considered the facts that Obadiah knew her well and that Isaac was her age and would soon be freed. As the men harvested William's vegetable garden, he wondered what would become of the girl. *What if Cillian doesn't send for her? Perhaps Isaac or Obadiah will come to see her charming ways, the bright red hair, and her beautiful smile.* He picked the remaining acorn squash and set them in a basket. *She can be a real charmer when she wants to. Any man would love a daughter with her gifts.* Isaac pulled up the now brown, harvested corn stalks, chopped off the roots, and stood them up in shocks.

William's thoughts wandered on. *I wish she were ten years older – then things might be different.* He dug up the remaining carrots and onions. *I should have wedded years ago. I'd have my own children by now.* He rose, rested his chin on the shovel handle, and looked at the Indian summer sky, savoring the sensation of possibility. Men older than I often wed younger girls after losing their first wives. He shook his head, coming back to reality. *If Isaac or Obadiah were interested in her, I could help them acquire land nearby. That would be proper.* William spent some time with the question of whom the red-haired Irish lass might wed if the money failed to arrive. *That way,* he thought, *she could stay nearby, and I could enjoy my charming, newfound daughter for a long time.*

"Obadiah," he said that evening, as they ate supper, "I saw Honor walk with you before we left the city. What do you think of her?"

"I think she thinks only about herself and is in a hurry to get back to Ireland. She doesn't care about anything else."

"Pray that she might change her mind. If she had a reason to like Maryland, she might want to stay," William mused as they ate trout that Isaac and Obadiah had caught that afternoon.

"Her desires are fixed, Master Logsdon. No one can change her mind."

Turning to Isaac, William said, "On the morning we went to the church, she went with you to harness the mare. I think she likes you."

"No, she just wanted me to help her escape," Isaac responded. "She was planning to run away and tried to talk me out of chasing her. I told her I would chase her and catch her and bring her back to you." Isaac pulled two carrots from the wooden bowl in the center of the table.

"Of course she wanted to run away," said William. "She felt alone and needed a friend. Isaac, why did she choose you to ask for help? Perhaps she's fond of you. She didn't ask Obadiah to help her."

"I think she's pretty," said Isaac who, at eighteen, was approaching the end of his indentured time. "I have never seen such bright red hair. It's like the leaves on a maple tree."

William smiled broadly, "Isaac, it's time for you to consider your future. You'll need a woman, and she is a charming girl." Reaching over and touching Isaac's shoulder, he encouraged, "If she isn't able to go home, I'll give her to you and even help you acquire some good land next to mine."

Obadiah looked at Isaac and laughed. "No, he'd probably run away with her. He could become a pirate and she could be his maid. They'd sail the world over, raiding Spanish ships and stealing everyone's gold."

William laughed, as well. As he pulled the meat from the bones of another trout, he remarked to Isaac, "I thought you wanted to be a rich planter. Be wise and know that tobacco is almost as valuable as a pirate's gold, but much easier to acquire."

"Yes, sir, but it's Obadiah there who wants to go back to England and become a duke or something. It's he who'll be needing a lady to serve tea to the king. Besides, I know he likes her. He talks about her often enough."

"Not me. It's you who goes on about the wench. Perhaps, you want to hold her hand and court her," Obadiah laughed rather nastily.

"Boys, I'm serious," said William. "What is to become of her if her father doesn't send money to pay for her trip home? She is both smart and beautiful, and her smile can light up a room. I want to help her, and I would like her to come here to *Brotherly Love*. If she sees this place, I am certain she will want to live here. But she needs to be wed first, and I am too old. Either of you would be the right age for her." William pointed his fish-covered finger at the eldest of his servants. "Perhaps, Isaac, you should court her. In a year, you will be free of your indenture. You could not do better than to wed that girl and clear the land just north of here."

"Sir," said Isaac. "With all respect, shouldn't Mistress Honor be your wife?

Chapter Thirteen

After two weeks of sleeping on the dirt floor without as much as a piece of hay for comfort, Honor was shocked to hear Winifred say, "You may move your things back upstairs today. Then I want to show you how to make johnnycakes. Henceforth, you will arise early, bring in wood for the fireplace, and prepare cakes for my breakfast."

Honor's old dress offered little protection against the cold. To garner at least a bit of warmth, Honor built up the fire with the first load. She took her time rearranging the remaining armloads of firewood so she could warm up; the heat felt good.

Soon after, Winifred brought a basketful of dried corn ears and two knives to the table. "Have you ever taken the kernels off the corn ears?"

"No, mum, but I want to learn." The girl sat watching Winifred for a few minutes. With the bowl on the table next to her, she grabbed an ear of corn. Holding one end, she used a knife to pry off the kernels, letting them fall into the bowl.

The old woman watched Honor as she worked. "That's too slow. When the kernels are dry, twist them off with your hand."

Honor did as Winifred instructed. The old woman stood behind Honor, watching the girl work. Some of the kernels spilled over the side of the bowl, onto the floor.

"Take care, wench! Do not waste the food," yelled Winifred. Honor picked up the spilled kernels and put them in the bowl. She set her jaw in defiance, prepared for whatever might come next. Winifred did nothing, but said, "You smell awful. After we make the johnnycakes, you must take a bath."

In time, all the corn ears were twisted clean, and the bowl was half-full of dried Kernels.

"Now get the quern and bring it to me," Winifred said, pointing to two stone corn grinding tools near where the fireplace. The bigger, rougher stone was saucer-shaped with a shallow depression on its top. The smaller stone was hard, smooth, and round. Honor set the small stone in the depression and heaved both pieces to the table.

"In the city, women buy cornmeal from the miller, but in the country they must mill it themselves. Let me show you how to do that," said the old woman, putting a small handful of kernels into the depression. Crushing the kernels with the smaller stone, Winifred continued, "You must pound and grind the corn until it's as fine as bread flour." When she finished her demonstration, the old woman handed the smaller grinding stone to Honor. "I'll bring you another bowl for the meal. And don't spill any more — we can't afford to waste food. I must get some water. Do not leave the house." Winifred wrapped her shawl around her shoulders, grabbing a bucket as she left the house. When she returned, she poured some water into a pot and hung it over the fire to boil.

After an hour of hard work, Honor's arms ached. "May I rest a wee bit, Mistress? My arms hurt."

"Yes. Sit there until I return." Winifred went down to the basement larder and returned with a pitcher of milk. "My last daughter was younger and smaller than you when I last saw her. But she was strong and well trained. I brought her up to be a good wife."

"Dear Lord, how long has it been since you lost her? You must feel terrible."

"I stopped feeling years and years ago. My job was finished." Winifred mixed two handfuls of cornmeal with boiling water, cold milk, and a pinch of salt. She stirred the mixture into a gritty, damp lump, which she placed on the table. "There, now you do the same while I put the spider in the hearth and get the skillet to fry the cakes." The old woman left for a moment, returning with a slab of bacon. "You have to fry some bacon to grease the pan before you put the dough in."

"Where is your daughter now?" asked Honor.

Winifred didn't answer, gazing at the sizzling fatback preparing the skillet to fry the johnnycakes. By then, Honor had produced several more lumps of cornbread dough with the remaining meal.

"Tell me about your children? How many did you have?"

"Stop talking," Winifred admonished. "My business is not yours to know." She spread the dough across the sizzling skillet.

Honor could not see the old woman's face as the johnnycakes fried. Soon, they were sitting at the table eating the hot cornbread cakes and slabs of bacon.

"That breakfast tasted wonderful," Honor, said "This is really good. I love the blackberry jam and bacon. Could I have some more tea?"

When they had finished, Winifred's mood turned somber, and she wiped a few tears from her eyes. "Come here."

Honor walked to Winifred, who hugged her, saying, "You did well this morning."

After that hug, Winifred's disposition grew almost sunny. She gave Honor four shillings and handed the girl a well-worn wrap, telling her to walk to the miller's shop and purchase ten pounds of wheat flour. "We will make bread this afternoon. But you must come straight home. While you are out, I will visit the neighbor to the east to see if she wants to buy some vegetables and fresh bread."

"Oh yes, Mum." Honor was delighted at the opportunity to wander about again, this time with permission.

Winifred went on, "You may look into the other shop windows, but be back in one hour."

"Oh, thank you, Mum." Honor curtsied and smiled up at the older woman. She wrapped Winifred's old cloak about herself and left the house quickly. She ran to the street where the shops were located. The first shop that caught her eye had a picture of a wooden barrel painted on a sign above the door.

●●●

Honor looked inside the shop and saw a man in a grey apron that covered all but his strong arms. Watching him hammer an iron ring around the wood stays of a new barrel, she said, "Good day to you, kind sir." She put on her most charming dimpled smile. "My name is Honor."

The cooper looked up and smiled at his visitor. "And a good day to you, lass. I'm John the cooper," he said with the lilt of Erin. "What can I be doin' for you this fine, brisk mornin'?"

"I'm new here and be wantin' to meet the neighbors." Honor was immediately reassured by the cooper's Irish accent.

"And your voice speaks of the Green Isle of Saint Paddy himself." The cooper crossed himself. "I've nea seen ye before. Might I ask how long you have been in Annapolis?"

"Several weeks now. How long have ye been here?" Honor watched as the cooper doffed his tricorner hat at someone looking in the door behind her. The girl turned to look just as the visitor moved away, and then returned her charming smile to the cooper.

"I've been here a bit longer than two weeks," he said with a smile. "Ten years have passed since I first came to this place, and near twelve since I last saw Ireland."

"And what do you do in your shop?"

"I make shipping barrels. Would you be wantin' to see how they are made?"

Honor nodded and walked over to the cooper's workbench. He picked up a round disc which had been made from four boards, joined with glue, and strengthened with dowel pins. It had a groove cut just inside its round parameter. "The first thing I do is make a top and bottom for the barrel. Then I use a pattern to cut out the staves." He set the round piece down and handed Honor another piece of wood that appeared wider in the middle than on the ends. "I arrange the staves around an end piece and glue them together. Then I hammer iron rings around the staves to hold them tight. And with that, I have a new barrel." He turned the palms of his hands upward. "It's quite easy." The cooper put one foot forward and took a swashbuckler's deep bow.

Honor smiled with delight. "And why, Cooper John, did you come to Maryland?"

"I came to worship as God leads me, not as the King of England demands. What brings you here child?"

"Saints be praised. You must be Catholic. I'm Catholic, too, and I'm wantin' very much to find a priest."

The cooper smiled. "Then God has blessed us both."

"Might I ask where you celebrate the Mass? I am told there are no Catholic Churches in Annapolis."

He smiled again, nodding at her, "Might I share a cup of tea with you, lassie? It's time for me to rest some and the pot is already boilin'." Honor nodded. The cooper walked over to a raised brick smithy's hearth with two more iron rings resting on bright red coals. Next to the rings, a steaming tin pot of tea sat whistling. He poured two cups and, with his back to the girl, asked, "Do you take a wee bit of milk, lass? Or may I call you Miss Honor?"

"Yes, please. I had tea for breakfast, but haven't had it with milk for such a long time. Ma gave me brothers and me tea with milk and honey every morning. I miss all of them very much."

"Then I shall have to start keeping honey in the shop. That way, ye might visit often and tell me of the green land of our fathers."

"That I would do, and you can tell me of this new land." Honor clasped her hands with joy at finding new kinship.

They both smiled. He asked, "And where are ye livin'?"

"I be livin' with Mistress Skidmore and I be callin' my benefactor Master Logsdon, out of respect. They both be helpin' me get home. I would like to call you Master John, as I hope you can help me as well. You still haven't told me where you go to see the priest.

"No child, you must call me Cooper John." He handed Honor a cup and sat down on a bench, crossing himself again.

"Let me bless the time we'll be havin' together." Honor sat next to him and nodded her approval. "May the God of hosts bring peace to those who love Him. May the peace of His word bring joy to those who serve. And may the joy of hot tea bring happiness to both our tummies." He flashed his own Irish smile.

Honor laughed, for the first time in a long while, she noticed. Then she grasped the cup with both hands and blew across its steamy hot nectar.

After a few moments, the cooper said, "Maryland started as a place where English Catholics could come to worship freely. I suppose the King wanted Catholics from all his land to leave and bother him no further. For years, we were the greater part of Maryland, and the Church grew. But ten years ago, a Puritan force defeated our Catholic army in a wee bit of a war. Assuming the power to elect their own, the Puritans banned the Catholic Church from the entire colony. A shame it is that such a wicked thing could be done. Since then, we Catholics worship in homes and meet in secret. In fact, I cannot tell you where we meet, as I am sworn to secrecy."

"I have met the parson at St. Anne's," she answered. "He seems like a nice man."

"Aye, Parson Blyth is all that, lass, and more. I am sure he knows where we Catholics meet, but he would not speak of it, either. Sometimes, when I see him on the street, he doffs his hat and shakes my hand. 'Good day, my friend,' he says to me, as though I were his equal. Can you imagine that? Me bein' his equal?"

The two sat and talked about Annapolis and Dingle for almost an hour. The cooper wove stories with the blarney of his heritage. Honor told him about the ordeal from which she had only recently escaped. "Did you know God wants me to be nun and teach the children?"

The bell at a nearby church tolled twelve times for noon. Honor rose from her chair, smiling at her new Irish friend. "It is way past my time to get back to the boarding house. I must leave you now."

"God bless you, Honor. I shall say an Our Father for you and look forward to your visitin' with me again. We have much to talk about. And remember, good women keep their tongues in their pockets until they wed. Or, in your case, keep it there until you return to Ireland."

"Thank you, kind sir," she said with a curtsy. "Please give my best to your dear wife."

"Top of the mornin' to ye, child. And by the way, I've never been married." said the cooper.

●●●

The miller from whom Honor would buy the flour was only three doors down from the cooper's workshop. The small front room of the miller's shop had creaky wood floors, a small counter, and shelves stacked with bundles of wheat, rye, and corn flour. A scale rested on a workbench, ready to be used for measuring and bundling the fresh, fragrant products. A layer of soft white powder covered the whole shop, finding special hiding places in the cracks between the floorboards. *Oh Lord,* thought Honor. *How these smells remind me of home* — a smell that offered the promise of hot bread and delicious cakes to all who entered.

"Good day to you, sir," Honor said, as she walked toward the miller. "Mistress Skidmore has sent me to purchase some wheat flour." She smiled at the miller, like any youngster taking pride in newfound responsibility. However, concern about being late again and the knowledge that Winifred would not be pleased soon wiped away her smile. She needed to complete the transaction as quickly as possible.

"Good day to you, sister. You have come to the right shop," the miller responded. He walked behind the counter and pulled a package from the shelf. "You shall have ten pounds of my best flour." The package had been wrapped in paper and tied with a string. "You must be the new girl at Sister Skidmore's."

"That be true, sir, but how would ye know that?" she answered with surprise.

"Earlier this day, she came to visit and said you'd be coming this forenoon. I suspect you got a later start."

The miller stood only a few inches taller than Honor, his girth suggesting that he frequently sampled the breads and cakes produced with flour from his shop. A jolly man, he wore a white apron that covered his chest to his knee britches. His loose green shirt had large wooden sticks for buttons that made bumps in his apron, and he wore black shoes with brass buckles and white stockings. The brown kerchief wrapped around his oversized bald pate and the stubby hands resting on his equally oversized belly gave him the look of a storybook gnome, fresh from beneath a stone bridge. All in all, Honor thought him a very pleasant fellow.

"What wonderful people live here in Annapolis," she said.

"Well, if that includes me, I thank you, but one can't eat compliments. I still must charge you three shillings for the flour."

"I fear that I'm terribly late and in a most fearful hurry," said Honor as they exchanged the money and flour. She waved a pleasant good-by, running out the front door and down the walk toward the boarding house.

●●●

As she drew closer to the house, Honor saw Winifred waiting on the landing, her furious scowl visible from a shocking distance. The girl walked quickly into the house and laid the package on the kitchen work-plank. Winifred stormed into the house behind her, shouting, "What did I tell you? You're a stupid girl."

Honor said nothing. With her arms clasped tightly to her chest, she listened closely, anticipating that the older woman would come charging at her. *I'm not that late*, she thought to herself.

"Answer me! What did I tell you to do? I just can't trust you to obey me."

Still, Honor stood silent. She hoped her remorseful look would offer some degree of protection. She sat down on the bench at the table, wrapping her arms around herself. The cold in the room chilled her less than the anticipation of the coming verbal attack.

"Did I tell you to stop at the barrel shop? Come over here now!"

How did she know that, thought the girl? Then Honor remembered the cooper doffing his hat as someone walked by. "*She followed me. How wicked*!"

"Why do you continue to disobey me?" Winifred bellowed, like a bull elephant announcing its presence to a broad savannah neighborhood. Honor watched Winifred climb the stairs without waiting for an answer. *She spied on me. That's not right. I'm a free person and I have a right to visit whomever I please. I can't trust her either. I must learn to be more careful.*

About ten minutes later, Winifred came back down, speaking this time with calm in her voice. She carried Honor's old tattered dress in her wrinkled hand. "Put it on," she said, handing the garment to the girl. "We need to make bread this afternoon, and I don't want you to get your new dress dirty."

Honor stepped forward, taking the tattered dress from the old woman. She removed her good dress and its petticoats, exchanging it for the shabby one she had worn on the ship. Her eyes followed Winifred as she rose from the bench by the table and walked over to the hearth.

Calmly, the older woman said, "I don't know what to do with you, but somehow I must teach you again to obey completely. I know you think you were a princess or someone important back in Ireland, but this is Maryland, and in my house, you're just a slave girl. As a woman, you have no rights at all. I must make you understand that, or your life will be very harsh."

"Mistress Skidmore, Master Logsdon didn't leave me here as a slave. He is my protector." She took a few steps toward the older woman, thinking she might not be punished. "You must treat me as a guest in your house." Winifred turned around. The venom in her eyes cast a chill over the girl and she trembled visibly. Honor decided she must establish her status once and for all with this woman. "Da will be sendin' money as soon as he receives Master Logsdon's letter. Then I shall return home and be no more bother to you."

"You are a foolish child. Your father will never send money for you. What you are now, you shall be from here on out." Winifred stood a few inches from the girl, and Honor took two steps back, in a quick move of self-preservation. Winifred stepped toward her, grabbed Honor's left arm, and slapped the girl hard, forcing her back on her heels. "I thought my father loved me, but he sold me to a stranger when I was twelve years old and not yet a woman. The man who bought me took me in his house that very morning. I had never been told about such things. I have never known such pain. Not once did he woo me. He just threw me down and used me for his pleasure. Understand, I don't dislike you for being such a useless little worm. I am upset because you won't learn your place."

Winifred lifted her skirt to reveal legs that were striped with scars. "He also beat me every day for weeks. Do you want me to do this to you? I have whipped useless worms before, and I can do it to you, too."

My God, thought Honor, she is truly evil. I didn't know such evil existed, except maybe among the English. What am I to do? "I am truly sorry for misbehaving as I did," Honor said, her voice a plea for leniency.

Winifred continued her tirade as if she hadn't heard a word from Honor. "My husband used to call me 'Whinny.' He'd force me to my hands and knees and make me bray like a mule while he beat me like an animal." Winifred sat down again. "Once, I burnt his food, and he made me eat it off the floor. I could do nothing to stop him. As my husband, he knew he could do anything he wanted to me, and that I was powerless to fight back."

Honor had never envisioned such treatment by men. "Your husband must have been truly evil. I'm so sorry."

Winifred walked toward Honor and slapped her across the face again. "You're a stupid, stupid girl. All men are evil! Wait until your nice Master Logsdon mounts you. Wait until he beats you with a stick," she sneered. "Then you'll understand why I must be harsh with you. You must learn that the punishment for doing as you please is very harsh."

"Master Logsdon is not like that. He cares about me and treats me like a father."

"Does he drink beer and wine?"

"Mum, I don't know what he drinks."

"When he is drunk with wine, he will beat you. Mark my words — I know about men."

"Maybe he's not like Da. Perhaps he is evil and wants me in his bed. I do not know. But Da will send the money, and I will soon go home. I must just stay here until the letter comes. Mum, could you not have run away and got help from your Da?"

"Of course I tried that, but my father just sent me back." Winifred raised her hand to strike again. "He didn't want me either."

Honor bent over, covering her face with both hands and crying out, "Please, don't beat me!"

Winifred hovered over Honor. "Once, my husband kicked me so hard that I lost my baby. My father did nothing to help me." She grabbed a handful of Honor's hair and pulled the girl erect. "You see, my father signed a contract and sold me away, just like your contract."

"I know that some men are evil," Honor sympathized with the bitter old woman. She was beginning to understand. "But you said that your husband left you. All those evil things are in the past. You can be happy again."

"After I turned twenty, he lost interest. He ran off to Virginia with a sixteen-year-old girl. 'You're too old and too fat.' That's what he told me, leaving me with nothing but a scar-covered body, three children, and a rundown one-room cabin."

"I'm sorry about what happened to you. That is why I want to go home. Then Master Logsdon cannae hurt me."

"I was forced to sell two of my babies. I had to become hard just to survive. I had to do disgusting things, things I can't even mention aloud." Pain appeared on Winifred's face, and for a brief moment, Honor saw tears in the hard woman's troubled eyes.

"I am so sorry for the hard life you had, Mistress Skidmore, but God will not let such things happen to me," said Honor. "He won't allow Master Logsdon to abuse me that way."

"I tell you, if you do not learn to yield to me now, in a few short years, you will be alone on the streets, selling yourself to any man with a few shillings."

Winifred sat on the bench next to Honor, who immediately grew fearful, her eyes filling with tears. The girl sat on her hands, and stared into infinity. Neither Comfort, William, Parson Blyth, the milliner, the cooper — nor even the miller — had spoken to her this way. *There must be another, better reality,* she thought. Honor put her hands together, raising her fingers to her chin. She silently prayed an Our Father, rounding out the last phrase in a mere whisper, "…and deliver us from evil. Amen."

Honor looked up at Winifred. "I'm sorry for my transgression. How will you punish me?"

"I must move you back into the downstairs room, and I will lock the door whenever I leave the house. You can bathe once a week, and you must wear the old dress until Master Logsdon returns. That way, you can't run away again because everyone will know that you are a slave. Perhaps in the next few months, you will grow hard and obedient."

That night in her cell, Honor had an imaginary conversation with William. Sir, you know how much I miss you. Please know now how much I'm needin' you. This is not a good place to be, and I pray to the saints that you hurry back and save me. Sir, please come and take care of me. At the end, she quickly added, And please don't do to me what her husband did.

●●●

On the same day Honor visited the cooper, Comfort and Walter went to call on William and the boys. They delivered some supplies they had purchased for him in the hamlet of Owings Mills. "*Guten tag*," Walter said, climbing down from his horse. He dropped the reins and helped Comfort down.

William responded, "And good day to you. Thank you for the flour and salt." He held the bulky paper-bound packages in one hand and shook Walter's hand with the other. "Might I offer some refreshment? We have hot tea, corn bread, carrots, and venison for supper. Can you stay?"

"*Ja*, we will stay." The three friends walked toward the cabin. William whistled for the boys to come in from the field where they were hoeing the weeds from around the tobacco plants. Walter waited for William to set the packages on the table, and then handed him some change from his purchase.

After supper, while Comfort and the boys cleaned the dishes, the two men remained at the table and lit their pipes. William pulled a jug of home-brewed applejack from a shelf and poured it into the three noggins he'd kept on the table following the meal. "Have you heard from the *fräulein* in Annapolis?" asked Walter. "*Meine frau* speaks often of her. I tell you, they are *gut* friends."

From the kitchen board, Comfort corrected her husband. "Speak English, Walter. It is 'my wife,' not '*meine frau*.'"

"We all are learning the English much *besser*," This is *sehr gut*, I think."

"Very good," repeated Comfort. "Very good. Not '*sehr gut*.'" She came over to sit on the bench next to her husband, leaving Isaac and Obadiah to finish the dishes. Comfort patted Walter's hand. To William, it appeared to be some kind of signal, rather than a sign of budding love.

"No, I have not heard from Honor," William replied. "I was hoping you might have heard something," William said, nodding at Comfort. "You are her good friend, but I am just helping her get home." Then to Walter he said, "I admit, I do think of her often. That girl has more spirit than a young colt that has just learned to jump." He passed two noggins of the fruity drink to his guests. "Did you know that she can read and write?"

"Yes, I do and thank you," said Comfort, accepting the mug. "Honor has many gifts and she has no trouble telling everyone what she wants." She looked at William and smiled. "If anyone can find a way to get back home, it will be that lass. On the ship, she spoke of her many ideas for escaping, and on the dock, she found you, Master Logsdon. God will bless you for what you've done."

"Yet I worry about what's best for her. Life must be hard for Catholics in Ireland. I wrote her father that there's good land here, and if he can afford the cost, he should bring the rest of his family over here, rather than taking her back to Ireland. There's land available across the creek from you. The girl is a joy, to be sure."

"*Und* why would bringing her father here be the best?" asked Walter. "He, too, is Catholic, and it is no *bosser* for his family here than in his own country."

"Because we are building something new here, and we need good families in Maryland."

"*Ja*, it would be *sehr gut* for Maryland." He corrected himself, "Very good. But what truly is best for Honor *und* her family?"

At that Comfort spoke up. "Walter, you know that Maryland is what's best for Honor. God has much to do here, and there are too few people. With Honor's spirit and dedication, life here would be full of opportunity. If she wants to serve her church, Maryland is a place that needs her. If she decides to wed, where better to raise a family?"

William responded with the question that had been bothering him. "I have wondered what I should do if her father fails to send the needed funds. Who could I find to wed with her?"

"*Ist* okay you sell her to someone in Annapolis, perhaps a *gut* Irish shopkeeper?" asked Walter.

"It is very possible," answered William. "But would she be happy?"

Comfort patted Walter's hand again. "Master Logsdon, what are your own thoughts? Beyond her spirit, what do you like most about Honor?"

He smiled broadly, and continued "There is much to like about that little girl. Her Irish way of speaking delights me, as does her beautiful smile. And I can see, even now, those green eyes and her red hair. Maybe what I like the most is the way she teases when she wants something. She just puts on a disappointed look to tease you into letting her have her way. I was indentured when I was her age, so I had no time to learn the ways of young ladies. It is hard to resist her charm."

"That, sir, is her great strength. It is a charm that comes from being naive and innocent," said Comfort. "I, too, admire that most about her. She is like the first flower of spring, filled with hope and promise." Then she spoke indirectly. "Youthful charm would make her a good wife for a wise man."

Returning from his thoughts, William said, "I would think him indeed blessed."

"Why is that, Master Logsdon? Would she be a good helpmate and keep a good house?

"Of course she would. She has lived a farm maid's life, and she is strong willed."

"And would she be a good mother to a man's children?"

"That too. She is educated and she knows of God. She would be a good teacher to a man's children." William's countenance turned quiet and he again stared into the distance.

Comfort gave him a few seconds further to be lost in his thoughts. "She would be a good wife for some man, don't you think?"

Finally seeing through Comfort's last comment, William responded abruptly, "No. I am too old, and she too young."

"Then you have thought of keeping her for yourself, if her money doesn't arrive, of course," Comfort prodded.

"I have thought about Obadiah or Isaac wedding with her, but they reject the idea."

"If she were ten years older, would you take her as your own?"

"I believe I would, as she is most charming."

But William wasn't ready to end the conversation. "That's true. But she has spoken several times of her wish not to wed with me or anyone else. She is forever Catholic, and I am Anglican. So I want to help her get home to Ireland... that is all."

"Master Logsdon, I fear you deny the gift that has been placed before you. I fear you will rob yourself of the very joy that is within your grasp. And I fear that you will rob my precious Honor of her happiness, as well."

"Enough!" said Walter with command to his voice.

Chapter Fourteen

A week later, after a breakfast of hot tea and johnnycakes, Winifred descended the stairs to the root cellar and returned with two wooden buckets. She handed one to Honor, saying, "It is time to begin your next lesson. I will show you how to make candles and soap. But first, we will go to the butcher and buy some tallow."

Winifred nodded toward Honor as she put on her shawl, and they left for the half-mile walk. Honor soon ached from the cold. She had on naught but her thin old dress and a tattered shawl. She soon began to shiver in the chilled air. "Walk faster," commanded Winifred. "The exercise will warm you."

The narrow butcher shop occupied a small space in an alley behind two other shops, the sign in front depicting a large ham. As they entered the shop, Honor saw a heavy wooden table and a row of meat hooks that held the carcasses of deer and pigs. Rows of sausages hung from more hooks lining one wall, and cages of live chickens rested against another wall. Bloody sawdust covered the floor, and the spicy smell of animal flesh reminded Honor of a similar shop in Dingle.

When the middle-aged butcher saw the red-haired girl behind the older woman, he set down his cleaver and walked around to the front of the shop, wiping his red-stained hands on his bloody apron.

"I've heard of this one," he said, smiling at the girl. "Ain't she a pretty little thing?" Honor smiled back, and the stocky man put a huge hand on Honor's arm, pulling the girl away from Winifred. "A neighbor told me all about you. She said you're new to our city and haven't yet found a husband." He squeezed her arm and worked his eyes down to her wrist, as though inspecting a carcass. She jumped when he grabbed her other arm and opened her shawl, like it was a curtain in a tawdry peep-show.

Without letting go, the butcher looked at Winifred and went on, "Good day to you, Mistress Skidmore. Everyone is talking about this lass — the pretty Irish girl, that's what they call her." Honor stepped back and pulled her arms out of the huge man's bloody grip.

Winifred became angry. "Who told you that I have a new guest?" She glared at Honor before turning her stare back to the overweight sausage and ham purveyor.

"As you know," he said smugly, "since my old woman died, I've been in the market for a new wife. I need a woman to look after those eight children. When folks hear of an available woman, they often share the news with me." Fully grasping the man's meaning, Honor looked with fright to her overseer, while the butcher continued to stare at her hair.

"Master Logsdon has spoken for me," said Honor pertly. "I am not available."

Winifred followed, "She's from the docks, is useless, and has much to learn." Winifred turned to Honor, her hands on her hips, and glared. "She thinks her father is going to send her money for her return fare to Ireland. Not likely. And Master Logsdon of *Brotherly Love* has no interest in her, save getting his money back for her contract. I believe she will be available, come spring."

The butcher continued to stare, while Winifred went on talking. "If the funds do not arrive, I believe Master Logsdon will be interested in selling her contract. If so, a sale could be arranged, but she'll be very expensive. I doubt you have that kind of money."

"I like skinny girls," said the sneering butcher with a slimy voice.

"We shall see. For now, all we want is twelve pounds of tallow."

"I have that much and more, a good stock of fat today." He laughed at his own joke, slapping his obese belly. Taking hold of the two buckets Winifred and Honor had set on the floor, he turned and walked away. On his way out the back door, he passed an odorous gas that caused Winifred to wince.

"Sir, you needn't be rude. We are ladies," Winifred admonished him, putting a handkerchief to her nose. After the butcher had stepped through the door to the rear of his shop, she looked at Honor. "Let that be a lesson to you. I've yet to meet a man who is not, from time to time, crude and smells like a barnyard. Even your Master Logsdon, I would suspect, is crude when he fancies it."

When the butcher returned, he set the two buckets down, each full of pinkish-white animal fat. "That will be six shillings," he said. "Three shillings a bucket." Winifred paid and they left.

The two women walked toward home. Winifred gave her bucket to Honor. "Here, you carry my bucket, too. My shoulder hurts. Now, hurry along."

When they reached the boarding house, Honor spoke out, "Mum, you cannot sell me to that man!"

Winifred just humphed and farted. "Can't be helped," she said, shrugging her shoulders. As they entered the house, Winifred commanded, "Set the buckets on the table." Then she went to retrieve two smaller buckets from the root cellar. On returning, she exclaimed, "Now, we must pick bayberries."

They left the house again, turning toward the nearby forest where plentiful myrtle bushes could be found. The temperature started to warm.

"Mistress Skidmore, Da will send the money. He has to."

Winifred said only, "Hurry up. We haven't all day."

●●●

Winifred explained to Honor that bayberries are the red and black fruit of the myrtle bushes, which are abundant in Maryland because they like the moist weather. The marble-sized fruit look a bit like raspberries and contain a high percentage of wax. In fact, it takes fifteen pounds of berries to make one pound of candle wax. Candles made from animal fat have a putrid smell when burned, so mixing in the bayberry wax makes for a much more pleasant odor.

The two women walked to a spot in the forest where the trees had not yet dropped their fall colors and still shone in a glorious array. Squirrels scampered about, burying acorns. A fearless young fox scampered across the women's path, looking for something interesting to play with. The orange-red animal stopped to inspect the two women. Robins swooped from branch to branch, searching for food in preparation for their flight south. Twenty minutes after leaving the boarding house, Winifred and Honor came upon a patch of myrtle bushes and began to pick. Honor made a contest of the picking, working rapidly with two hands to make sure she would collect the most berries. By four that afternoon, each woman had two heavy bucketsful of the waxy fruit.

"That should be enough. It will be dark soon, and it's time to head home," said Winifred.

On the way back, Honor said, "It was good fun in the forest today. I worked hard to gather the most."

"That's as it should be. You are younger and should work faster."

"Thank you for taking me berry picking," Mistress Skidmore.

"Remember, if you wed a backcountry gentleman, you will have to pick many more buckets of bayberries to keep on hand. Then, every time your master kills a pig or a spring bear, you can use the new fat to make candles with the berry wax you've stored away." Winifred put her hand on Honor's shoulder. "In the city, you can buy candles if you have money. But if you're poor, you'll have to make them. Believe me, it's easier to be the woman of a rich city merchant than for a poor country farmer."

Honor said nothing, though she thought, my plans do not include making candles for anyone!

"You should be pleased if the butcher or some other city merchant wants you. It would be such a blessing to buy candles and the other things that make life easier."

Honor caught the reference to the butcher and responded appropriately, "Come spring, I'll be expectin' Da's letter, and I'll be returnin' to Ireland on the next boat. So I have no thoughts of butchers or any other men, city or country."

"Stupid girl, when will you accept that returning home is not going to happen? You will have to satisfy Master Logsdon's desires, or someone else's — perhaps the butcher, who has already expressed an interest."

"I think not, Mum. My master be a good Christian man and he will nae allow me to be sold into the bed of a butcher."

"With that bright red hair and your little-girl look, many a man would pay a handsome sum to put you in his bed. They're like that, you know. The younger the wench, the better the old men like them. Every last one of them." Mocking Honor's youthful beauty, Winifred paraded in front of the girl, swaggering her wide hips. She turned to face Honor. "I used to be young and pretty, too, you know."

●●●

That evening after supper, Winifred said, "I'm tired. You pick the stems and leaves and put the berries in a kettle. When you're done, cover the berries with water and boil them for a short while. After a few minutes, remove the kettle from the fire and set it aside."

By the time the culling and boiling task was finished, the old woman was asleep upstairs, and Honor had the opportunity to lie down in front of the warm fireplace. She had a cozy sleep there that night.

Before the sun rose the next morning, Honor found Winifred in the kitchen, spooning the wax off the top of the berry brew. "Good morning, child," she said as Honor walked into the room.

The young girl quickly went about replacing the wood and the fire building. Winifred said and did nothing unpleasant as

Honor ran to the wood pile. *I hope things will be easier today.* The sun peeked over the eastern horizon, the clear sky offering the promise of a warm, beautiful day.

When finished with her wood chore, Honor stood next to Winifred to learn the next steps of candle making. The old woman reported brusquely, "The berry wax had stems and pieces of leaves in it. Why didn't you do as I told you?"

Honor spoke with false humility, "I'm sorry for the stems and leaves. It was late, and I was very tired last evening. I should have been more careful. But I'm awake now and I will do a better job."

"You most certainly will. Take the berry mash out to the pigs, and bring the kettle back. Then cut the tallow into small pieces and put them in the kettle." Honor picked up the kettle and walked toward the door. As she left the house, Winifred said, "Make sure to cover the fat with clean water once the kettle is full." It took ninety minutes for the girl to finish the dicing chore.

"Good," Winifred said approvingly. "Now get some more wood and start a big fire in the pit out back. Make it quick this time, for we haven't all day." Honor obediently carried two armfuls of chopped wood to the backyard fire pit. Then she went to the kitchen, picked up the little shovel next to the hearth, and collected some glowing coals from the fire. In little more than ten minutes, the outdoor fire blazed brightly.

The old woman came out of the house, carrying one kettle of fat and water. "You did well. As a reward, you can eat a hearty breakfast with me." Winifred hung the kettle on the iron spit over the flames. While the water came to a boil, they ate a breakfast of biscuits, apple butter, and fried bacon. To the girl, it was a meal well worth the work.

"Soon, we'll make soap, and I'll bring the tub up from the cellar so that you can take a bath with hot water. Would you like that?"

"Oh, yes, Mum. It's been ages since I had a bath with soap and hot water."

"I've been thinking of allowing you to sleep upstairs in a bed again. You see, I can be quite nice when you do as I say. In fact, if you were my daughter, you might even come to like me."

Honor had been mulling over the woman's comments about William on their way back to the boarding house with the bayberries. "Mistress Skidmore, why do you think Master Logsdon wants to take me as his wife?"

"Why? Well, who are you to him? Why would he spend his valuable tobacco to buy a young girl just to send her home to her family?"

"Because he's a good Christian, and an angel has spoken to him."

"Ah yes, an angel has spoken."

"Don't you believe in angels?"

"I most certainly do believe in them," Winifred said with a smirk. "They speak to me all the time. Humph!"

"Then why don't you believe they encouraged him to do only good on my behalf?"

"As I told you before, I've seen him looking at you when your back is turned. I have seen men with that look before. Remember, I was once young and pretty like you." Winifred helped herself to another thick slice of bacon and bit off a chunk. "Why would he hug you if he doesn't want to hold you closer than is appropriate?"

Honor stared into the distance, like a deer sensing an unseen hunter's presence. *Holy Mother*, she thought to herself. *Does he mean to have me?*

● ● ●

After the meal, Winifred divided the tallow in two equal parts, using half to mix with the berry wax for candle making. "We'll use the other half for the soap," she explained. She had Honor build the fire up in the backyard pit and put the mix of tallow and berry wax back on the spit. "In an hour or two, the candle mix will be ready for dipping."

They walked back to the house to retrieve some string. Honor asked innocently, "When you said 'if you were my daughter,' what did you mean?"

"I spoke foolishness," said Winifred. "I was thinking of my own girls. Just forget what I said."

"I understand, Mum." Honor remembered Comfort saying something similar. "Are you missin' your babies?"

"Yes," Winifred said, her voice barely above a whisper. "I might regret selling them."

"Ye must have been in terrible trouble to have come to such a situation."

"My garden was poor that fall, and I had few goods to sell. Had the girls stayed with me, we would have starved."

"I'm sure ye loved them very much. How old were they?"

"Tilda was old enough for a man to wed, and Elizabeth would have reached that age in a year or two."

"So they must both be wedded now." The two women left the house and walked back to the fire pit. "Perhaps you have grandchildren now. How long have Tilda and Elizabeth been gone?"

"Eight years. Elizabeth's birthday would have been this month. She was ten when I last kissed her."

"My God," said Honor, taken aback by the young age of the girls when they were sold. "Do you remember Mistress Comfort? She had to give away her children, as well. She gave them to her sister. On the ship, she told me I was like her new daughter, and that I eased her loneliness a wee bit."

They sat down on the bench beside the pot of tallow and bayberry wax. Honor reached up and touched the side of Winifred's white bonnet. "Perhaps I could make your loneness more bearable, too. "

Winifred, whose heart was badly scarred, said only, "Humph. I have no need of another brat."

"Oh, please, Mistress Skidmore. You may think your sin was great, but I could pray to the saints for your forgiveness. They hear me prayers."

Winifred turned on the bench and faced Honor for a few long seconds. Then she slapped the girl so hard that Honor fell off the bench.

Honor sat on the ground, stunned, not understanding what she had said to warrant such an intense reaction. Meanwhile, Winifred began to cut lengths of string, tying one end of each to a small weight. The strings were arranged on a stick and hung down straight and stiff. She made two sticks, with six strings each.

"Sit up and watch me dip the strings," demanded Winifred. She lowered the weighted strings very slowly into the hot wax, and pulled them out again nearly as slowly. As though she had never punished the girl, Winifred smiled. "You dip the strings in right to the top and slowly pull them out. Then you set the stick of candles aside to dry. I'll cut string for six more candles."

Honor repeated the first dipping exactly as she had seen Winifred do it. Her eyes looked bewildered and her hands shook. "I'm sorry, ma'am."

"That's good. It seems the warning I just gave you has worked, and you are finally learning. Make no assumptions about winning anyone's affection."

"Now re-dip the candles again." Honor did so, and the first six candles grew a bit fatter.

"Very good. Now wait until the wax is dry, and do it again, continuing until the candles are as big around as your thumb. When both sticks are finished, you can do it all again to make another dozen. Then we will put the remaining wax in the shed until we need to make more." Winifred got up and walked back to the house. "If the candles are well made, I will let you bathe and sleep upstairs tonight."

●●●

Sometime later, after she had bathed with hot water and soap, Honor heard Winifred come down the stairs. "Are you hungry?" she asked sternly. "Do you want to have supper?"

"Yes, mum."

"Then go out to the shed and fetch more wood for the house. Bring three armfuls."

Winifred smiled as Honor returned with the last load of wood. "You can sit here and eat supper." Winifred, who had almost finished her own meal, pointed to the bench where she sat. "Sit next to me."

Honor nodded, but began to walk toward the hearth. Winifred stopped her. "You're to say 'Yes, mum, but may I warm myself first?' And don't walk away from me."

"Yes, Mum," said Honor as she bowed and looked at the floor. "May I stand by the fire for a few minutes?"

"Of course," Winifred responded, waving away the small rejection. "If you're hungry, there is some stew in the kettle and cornbread on the counter." After a time, Honor walked to the plank on the kitchen wall, found a bowl, and ladled out some stew from the pot hanging inside the fireplace. She returned and sat, saying, "Thank you, mum."

"You will find me generous, once you learn to regret your mistakes," Winifred explained. "Until you do, I must be harsh. Know that I do this for your own good." The wind continued to blow outside, the single candle on the table providing little light through the darkened Skidmore house.

Tis not I who needs to repent,"thought Honor. But aloud she said, "Yes, mum, I will pray daily, wishing not to be punished any further."

"I receive no joy in it," said Winifred dubiously. "Master Logsdon has engaged me to train you to be a good wife. We shall see if your Da truly wants you back. If not, I will sell you as a bride." Winifred arose from the bench and climbed the stairs to her room.

Some minutes later, Winifred returned to the table. As though the conversation hadn't missed a beat, she said, "By the time I reached fifteen, I had wedded and birthed my first baby. My husband Daniel was a big man. He taught me that a disobedient woman is the devil's tool, and swift beatings are the Lord's best cure.

"Master Logsdon is not like that. He be a lovin' man."

"Daniel was a good man, too, but I have many scars from the lessons he had to teach me. You must do difficult things in Maryland to survive." She was silent a moment before adding, "My second baby lived only eighteen months. He was too weak. I birthed him without any help and I dug his grave alone."

Several days went by with nary a ripple before Winifred came home after visiting with a friend. Her angry look spoke volumes. Removing her shawl, she said to Honor. "A neighbor told me that you visited the dress shop?"

"Yes, mum. I told you about my offer of an apprentice position."

"Did you tell her that Master Logsdon bought you, and that you are staying with me?"

"Yes, that is the truth."

"And you told her that I said he might bed you before you were wed?"

Honor simply looked at the angry woman with a blank face. The hard slap came quickly, spinning her around on her heel.

"That is for speaking to the milliner. Remove your dress and shoes and put them on the table," the old woman's voice was dark and ominous. "I must punish you for spreading rumors about me."

"No, mum. I cannae undress in front of you."

Winifred went to the kitchen and returned with a hickory switch. She flicked the switch like a striking snake, resulting in a painful sting on Honor's forearm. "Keep your mouth shut!"

"I'm sorry," cried Honor. Winifred swiped the switch again. This time, it found Honor's cheek and cut a wound that began to bleed immediately. Honor screamed, grabbing her cheek and turning her back on the old woman. The wooden snake struck her, yet again, on her backside.

"You will never speak ill of me again. And you will do what I tell you with haste, or I will rip that dress from your limbs."

Honor bent and pulled the dress over her head, leaving only the thin chemise to cover her. Holding her bleeding cheek, she cowered in fear. Winifred struck a hard blow to her rump, cutting through the cotton and leaving yet another bleeding wound.

Honor lost her breath and started to cry. She dropped her dress on the table and placed her hands over the new wound. Between wails of fear, she begged, "I'm sorry. Please don't beat me. I won't do it again."

Winifred grabbed her by the hair, pushing her head toward the table. "Put your hands on the bench." Honor obeyed, immediately receiving three more sharp blows. Honor's backside stung more with each blow, and the chemise began to stick to her body. Then Winifred threw the dress at Honor, telling the terrified girl, "Dress yourself. I can't stand the look of you."

Honor clutched the dress in her arms and stood erect, crying with pain and fear. Winifred grabbed Honor's hair again and marched her to the six foot by six foot, dirt-floored cubicle. She flung Honor inside and down to the ground. The old woman spoke again. "You will stay in that room until you starve to death. I'll bring you water only after you beg me. And if you don't apologize this day, I will whip you again tomorrow."

The door slammed shut, and Honor heard Winifred pull the wood bolt into the iron latch, locking the cell door. The light of day turned to utter black, and the hope of returning to Ireland evaporated as the rock-hard thought of starvation became a reality. *My God*, thought Honor. Still shaking, she sat up and grabbed her knees, but the bleeding wounds on her bottom stung with such pain that she had to roll over onto her side. She huddled into a corner, where the two walls gave her what little security they could.

After a long time, her thoughts turned to the experiences Comfort had spoken of, the times she described had to put her nose against the wall. She remembered Comfort's admonition, "Hide with God inside your head, and never, ever talk back." In her head, Honor repeated Comfort's prayer, her mind focusing on the last line: "You will never leave us or forsake us; that neither death nor life, nor things present nor things to come, can separate us from the love of Christ Jesus our Lord. Amen."

Honor clasped her hands and silently prayed, "Holy Mother, why are you allowing these things? Why did you allow Master William to help me and then send him away? Please bring him back quickly". Then she said something that came from an unknown place inside her. Out loud she said, "Please ,Master William, I will wed you for it."

Many hours passed before Honor fell asleep.

●●●

After a long day preparing the fields for new tobacco planting, William needed refreshing sleep. He and the boys ate a hearty meal of venison, boiled vegetables, and hard tack. Then they climbed up to the attic and went right to bed, William in his big straw bed, and the boys across the room on the floor. The fire in the hearth below burned bright, its rising heat bringing a measure of relief to their aching muscles.

William was very tired, but following his habit, he closed his eyes and set about erasing the problems of the day with pleasant thoughts. His mind soon turned to Honor, wondering whether she was well, and imagining her beside him as they talked together. He recalled the last moment of their parting and the warm feeling that filled him as he lifted her off her feet and kissed her cheek. With that, his lips turned to neutral, his eyelids turned down, and he fell quickly into a world of dreams.

His dream, however, returned him to the workday he had just left behind. He saw himself standing behind his plow horse in a field of endless tobacco plant stumps. As the horse came to the end of a row, he looked back to gauge the straightness of his furrow. The turned earth had disappeared, as though no plow had ever passed over it. Discouraged, he wiped his brow and turned the horse around. He looked up toward the cabin and saw not cleared land, but stumps of harvested tobacco, which seemed unwilling to make room for his plow. His own inadequacy overwhelmed him. His dreamy fears became audible as he yelled out, "Damn you, go away!" Across the room, the two boys awoke and looked at each other.

Then the dream shifted to a happier sound. William heard the voice of a girl. "Papa," she called out, "I've brought your supper." He turned and looked back, wondering how the girl had come to be there. Her essence seemed to be walking through a wispy fog in spring. She appeared to be about ten years old, with the red hair of a younger Honor. Her soft white dress covered her from head to toe, with bows and flowers sewn here and there and a high waist tied with a kelly-green belt. He saw the white ribbon in her hair as it vanished into the auburn where her tresses fell to cover her shoulders. She stood next to him and smiled. "Are you hungry, Papa?" He reached out twice to touch her face, but both times his hands passed though her like vapor. On the third, try she grew substantial and he drew her in to kiss her dimpled cheeks. She whispered, "I love you, Papa."

A breeze from behind the girl lifted the strands of her hair and blew them around his fingers. She tilted her head down, as though embarrassed, but lifted her eyes to him in adulation. Every bit of frustration vanished from his soul. It was a brand new dream.

William took the platter of buttered bread and the cold water she had offered. She hugged him, pressing her head into his chest. In a dreamy instant, the two were sitting on a fallen log next to a babbling creak in the forest. She sat close beside him, with her head bent toward his shoulder. The wind gently waved the tree branches, and the birds sang a tune that might have been written by a master composer.

"Papa, look," the girl said, pointing as a young doe leapt across the creek and bounded further into the forest. A large gray buck followed in graceful leaps, and the girl giggled.

William smiled. "Child, where's your bread? You need to eat so that you can grow big and strong."

"That's silly. I'm not a little girl anymore."

He turned to look at her. She lifted her neck, pulling her shoulders back and rubbing her hands down the front of the pleated white bodice of her dress. She was no longer a little girl, but a fifteen-year-old charmer. Suddenly, her chest was bare. "Honor," he exclaimed with a bit of embarrassment, "behave yourself. You shouldn't be undressed in front of me."

"Don't be silly, Master William," she said with her Irish accent. "I'm your wife now." She reached out to take his hand and pulled it toward herself. William continued to avert his eyes. She said, "I've come a long way to be here, and I'm not goin' to leave you.

"Please, eat something," he said, nervously pulling off a large piece of bread which he offered to her without looking her way. When she didn't take it, he turned and saw that she had walked away from him and into the creek.

The barefoot woman was clothed in white linen, which glowed brightly in the sunlight. She appeared taller now, and clearly much older than Honor. Through the white material, he could imagine a mature woman, wholly capable of making his heart race, and the image did just that.

He marveled at her auburn tresses, parted straight down the back of her head, flowing over the soft white shoulders of her dress, and disappearing out of sight. She moved her outstretched arms up and down for balance, as she waded from stone to stone through the ankle-deep water. Mesmerized, William set his food down and stared, his jaw beginning to quiver.

Then, in the blink of an eye, she faced him and knelt down in the water. Naked, she sat on the heel of one foot with a small child sitting on her other leg. She reached into the creek for a handful of water and used it to bathe the baby. Like a tiny stream, the water ran down the baby's belly, over its leg and back into the creek. The baby boy looked up at William and reached out to him. As William's hands began to shake, he tucked them under his arms to hide his reaction to these sensuous thoughts.

The woman rose and walked out of the water toward William. He tried to look into her face but couldn't make it out. Her body glowed like Grecian marble — perfectly carved, graceful, slender, and full. He reached out to the vision as she knelt down before him, offering him the baby. She murmured, "Here, William, hold your son." He took the child, and the woman closed his eyes with soft fingers, kissing him on the lips – a soft kiss, a warm, pure kiss.

Suddenly his eyes opened again, and he sat up in his bed. He shook off the dream. "My God!" he said aloud. "She's just fifteen. What am I thinking?"

●●●

William rose before the sun, ready to finish the plowing and take on a new chore: preparing shallow wood flats to start new seedlings. A worrisome frown, left over from his reaction to the dream, rested on his face. He climbed down the ladder and opened the windows to let in the early morning sun, rebuilt the fire in the hearth, and washed his face in the cold water from a bucket near the door. Then he went outside and got to work pulling down the flats and setting them on a work bench in the covered space between the cabin and barn.

Isaac and Obadiah soon came down from the sleeping attic and took up their chores of making coffee and hot cornbread with bacon fat and jam. They also set out some apples from the cellar. A half-hour later, sixteen-year-old Isaac called William in. "Master, breakfast is about ready." After William washed his hands and sat at the table, Isaac spoke again. "Sir, your dream woke us last night. Is everything well with you?"

Thirteen-year-old Obadiah spread jam on a thick piece of cornbread. He took a big bite, looking toward William and wanting to hear his master's answer. "I'm fine," said William. "I just had a bad dream."

Isaac spoke again, "You must have been dreaming of a girl, 'cause you yelled out, 'She's just fifteen.' And you were sitting straight up in your bed."

Obadiah nodded his agreement. With his mouth still full, he said, "You woke me, too. What was happening in your dream?"

"Don't worry about it. It's all fine now. Let us get to work. We have a long day ahead of us. The seedling flats are waiting to be prepared, and you two need to finish the plowing."

"Did you do something wrong?" asked the older boy, who sometimes had his own dreams of girls, featuring events he thought deliciously wrong. Isaac looked at Obadiah and went on. "The girl in your dream, sir, was it Mistress Honor?"

"I don't know. At first I thought I saw Honor. She brought me my supper. She was very nice."

"Uck," said Obadiah. "On the ship, she was never nice. Honor didn't like me because Mistress Comfort did."

"Come now," William replied. "She's just afraid and wants to go home. She could never be mean."

"Never?" asked the younger boy, incredulously. "You don't know Honor like I do, sir. It's more like she could never be nice. I once had to give her my shirt because her dress smelled, and all she said was 'I hate you.' That's the truth."

William said, "Later in my dream, the girl changed. She was much older and very pretty. I don't know what any of it means."

"I admit sir, she is real pretty, but too skinny," said Isaac. "I have dreamt about girls myself, and they are sometimes very pretty." He added, "But I don't dream of them too often."

"Uck," repeated Obadiah. "I could do very well without them, except when they clean and cook and make themselves useful."

"In my dream, the girl was much older," William repeated. "Not skinny at all."

Isaac suggested, "Perhaps you've come to desire Honor as a wife."

"No, she'll soon be going back to Ireland, and I desire someone older."

"Sir," said Isaac, "I've seen how you look at each other."

"I don't want to talk about my dream anymore. Let's get to work."

"I think that is wise," responded Isaac. "I don't talk about those dreams either."

● ● ●

Nonetheless, as William prepared the flats of tobacco seeds, he couldn't get the dream out of his mind. In fact, his thoughts about it seemed more suggestive than the dream itself. *She is fifteen years old – why does she vex me this way?* He arranged the freshly mulched dirt into a flat, smoothing it gently with his hand, perhaps more than necessary. To his hand, the dirt felt like satin softness.

I must not think this way, he thought. Then he set down the flat and took up a shovel to put more dirt into the container on the workbench. With his hands, he mixed new dirt with the old, breaking up clods and picking out small stones. He walked around the barn to see how far the boys had progressed in their plowing chore. He watched as Obadiah guided the plow and Isaac led the horse in a straight path.

Walking back to the seeding bench, his thoughts returned to Honor. I know she's charming and very smart. She would be a joy to me and an excellent teacher for my children. But I want an older, stronger woman, one experienced at hard work in a garden and around a cabin. At the bench, he poked holes in the dirt and placed a tobacco seed in each new hole. The fresh dirt under his fingernails made him close his eyes and swallow.

"For heaven's sake," he said out loud. Yet he finished the thought running amok in his head. She wants to be a nun in a school somewhere. She wants to remain unwed. I promised to help her, and my bond is my word. Someone who wants to wed with me and give birth to my children will come along soon. But

I must confess, Honor will be most desirable in a few years. He took a ladle of water from the bucket and, flicking with his fingers, splashed some on every seed. He closed his eyes and let his mind try to see the water dripping from the baby's foot.

William took two handfuls of water from the bucket and splashed his face. She needs a younger man, he thought, not an old fool like me. Isaac is ready to wed, and Obadiah will be ready in a year or two. I wish I could convince them of her value. They could take the land just north of here and make a good life with her. Not one girl in a hundred can read and write like she can. We could build a school for the children in the country. She could even teach the adults to do sums and write their names.

Returning to his chore, he smoothed moist new dirt over the seeds.

"Everyone will spurn me for taking a bride twenty years my junior." He spread some straw over the flat to help hold in the sun's warmth. "But everyone will be envious of me when all my children can read and write." He carried the flat to the rack on the south wall of the barn, where it would get the full morning sun.

"Wouldn't having her as a wife be wonderful?" he spoke the words out loud. "Perhaps I will speak to her of it when we go to Annapolis. What I want has changed. Perhaps I want more than to just help her get home."

Chapter Fifteen

William spent several days trying to discern what his dream meant and wondering what he should do about it. Had his interest in Honor changed to something more serious, or had his interest in finding a wife just focused inappropriately on Honor? That might depend on what she thought about him, now that she had been in Maryland for more than five months. Perhaps she had grown fond of Maryland while under Winifred's care. She might be ready to change her mind about going back to Ireland. He thought to himself, *If she has decided to stay and is willing to be wedded to me, I will take that as a sign that I should wed with her. Otherwise, I'll look for another bride next summer.* He decided that seeing Honor face to face would help him know what God wanted him to do.

In mid November, two weeks earlier than planned, he hitched the horse to the cart, loaded up the last of his tobacco for sale, and took Isaac and Obadiah with him to Annapolis.

Honor didn't see them approach as William drove the cart up to the boarding house. With her back to them, she walked toward the door with a load of firewood. She looked dirty, gray, and as gaunt as she had been six months earlier. She wore the same rags he had met her in, clothed in nothing but a thin dress and torn shawl. Her feet were bare. How had nothing improved after twenty weeks in Mistress Skidmore's care?

William shouted her name, and Honor turned to see him and the boys. Honor dropped the firewood and ran to them. "Oh, thank you," she yelled. "I've been praying to the saints that you would hurry." She jumped into William's arms and hugged his neck tightly. Her unwashed shawl smelled, as did her hair. "Thank you for coming to get me," she wept as she kissed his cheek. William took his pipe from his mouth and pulled her nearly into a bear hug, with one hand holding her head close to his. He kissed her cheek. Honor whispered, "She hates me."

Honor dropped out of William's strong grip, stepping to Obadiah and hugging him. He pulled his head back to limit the pungent contact. William picked up the fallen shawl and put it back in place around her shoulders. "Why are you wearing these smelly rags when I bought you two nice new dresses?"

Winifred stepped out of the house. "Brother Logsdon," she said. Honor turned at the sound of the door closing. The look on the old woman's face showed both surprise and embarrassment. "It is my good relief to see you so soon. Pray, have you come for this troublesome girl? She is none but disobedient and lies at every opportunity. I can't trust her or let her out of my sight."

"Good day to you, madam." William said, making a small bow toward Winifred. "Why is Honor dressed in rags?"

"I have treated her with a mother's love, yet she has been everything but good in return. All she ever says to me is 'No' and 'I will not.' She refuses to help with the house chores, constantly staying in her room. If I had given her new clothes or a shawl, she would have run away and taken up with some unsavory character. I feel bad about her dresses, but she left me no choice."

"That is not true, sir," responded Honor. "She is an evil woman and has been treatin' me with every cruelty. 'Tis through my Irish luck that I am forced to live here, and it is she who keeps me locked in a dirty room without a bed and nary a blanket. She even tried to interest the disgusting butcher into buyin' me, while I still belong to you."

"There, you see, she cannot even tell the truth to you," Winifred said, trying to wriggle out of the uncomfortable situation. "I tried to serve your wishes, and have never put her up for sale, but she is as strong-willed as a mule. The girl refuses to learn, and speaks badly of me to the neighbors. Twice she has tried to run away. I had no choice but to dress her as a slave, for fear she would run off to go searching for a papist priest."

"No, Master William, she took my new clothes the day after you left. She has beaten me again and again, and makes me sleep on the dirt floor. I get water for bathing once a week, and it is not heated."

William turned to Winifred. "Can this be true?" he demanded. "I paid you well to take care of her. Did you not allow her to sleep in one of your beds?"

"Pray that I could, sir, but after great patience, I could no longer. She is so intent on returning to Ireland that I had to put her in a downstairs room, as the downstairs rooms have the locks. I prayed for her all that night, lest she would escape whilst I slept. Had she escaped, you would have been left with nothing to repay your investment. You cannot trust her."

Honor turned to face William and embraced him with both arms around his chest. "I swear, sir, on the name of the Holy Mother, that I have not been tryin' to run away or make trouble." She stepped back and made the sign of the cross. "I have been waitin' for you and for Da's letter. The children need me back home."

William told Honor that a letter could not be expected for another two or three months. It could be even longer, should a winter passage through the North Atlantic be deemed too dangerous and the ship captains decide to wait for spring. "It could take six to eight months for a ship to take my letter to Ireland and many more for another to return to Maryland with a response."

Winifred spoke again, "If she returns home, good riddance to her. And if you want her, pay me the four pounds fifty for her board, and you can wed her, take her to your home, and do with her as you please. As for a letter, mark my words. She will not hear from her family. I have no doubt that she vexed them as she has me and is unwanted by them, as well. I am quite sure that they sold her to the sea captain to be rid of her. I desire the same."

Honor spoke, tears running down her cheeks. "You know that's not even a wee bit true," she cried. Now fear gripped her face. "You wouldn't take God's will from me. Please take me away, but not to bed me. Master William, you know I am to remain chaste."

William said nothing. He pulled Honor's head into his chest and smiled at Winifred. "The boys and I shall stay two nights and leave for home on Wednesday. It seems unfortunate, but clearly it is best that Honor moves elsewhere. I shall find a place on the morrow, and we can agree on your fee when the letter from her father comes. Would you warm some water and give her some soap so she can bathe? She has an odor most unpleasant. And give her one of the new dresses. You may put Honor and me in the upstairs rooms with beds, and the boys can share one of the downstairs rooms."

●●●

At dawn the next morning, William came downstairs to greet Winifred. "Good day, Mistress Skidmore," he said, stepping outside for a brief look at the beautiful new day. On returning, he smiled at the old woman. "The morning looks sunny and refreshing, a good day for a walk with Honor. I love the late fall. In my mind, it seems to bury all our yesterdays and offers us a fresh new start. I feel so good when the weather starts to cool."

Honor came down the stairs wearing the light brown work dress that William had bought her all those months ago. After breakfast, they took a walk. "I hope that in spite of some unpleasantness with Mistress Skidmore, your stay in Annapolis has persuaded you of the advantages of freedom and the opportunities that accompany life in the New World." And so he began his formal attempt to learn whether she had decided to accept her new life, and whether she would spend it with him. She took his arm, like a proper lady out walking with a suitor. After only a few steps, he attempted to continue his argument. "Tell me about your stay in Maryland."

Honor's answer was not what he wanted to hear. "Mistress Skidmore has not been good to me these past weeks and months. She beat me with her switch and starved me, insistent on teaching me that women in the New World have no rights." While William had no reason to doubt her, the stories she related did not fit into the conversation he had scripted in his mind. He knew she had been poorly dressed when he arrived and had gained no weight since he last saw her. But it was not beyond possibility that Honor had behaved like a spoiled pony, resistant to the ways of an old work horse. Honor might simply have been too playful, and Winifred too serious. Besides, a teenage girl would be more likely to exaggerate than a grown woman.

"Come now. How often did Sister Skidmore take the switch to you?" he asked with the concern of a father.

"Often, master, often. Sometimes my wounds bled." Her response landed like unexpected bad news on an otherwise happy occasion. "I tell ye the truth — she's been whippin' me at least once every week. She beat me yesterday morning, before you arrived."

"Why?"

Honor folded her arms about herself. "Because I made the cornbread wrong, and it tasted too salty."

"Was it too salty?"

"Aye, I may have used too much salt, and the bottom may have been a wee bit burnt, but that is sometimes the case. Lord knows, there's none perfect, here or in Erin."

"Where does she strike you?"

"She struck me on my cheek," Honor said, pointing to slightly scabbed skin, suggesting a recent injury.

"I see the mark. Where else did she strike you?"

Honor paused for a few seconds. "It might be a sin to tell you where she whips me. But I can tell you this," she nodded her head and raised her eyebrows, "it is sometimes very hard to sit down." William watched her cover her mouth and blush in a way that teased him. Then he heard her go on with her sweet modesty, "I shouldn't have even spoken such, as you might think ill of me." She added a smile to her tease, and he smiled back, loving the naiveté that made her remark even more intimate.

The conversation had taken a positive turn, and William grabbed hold of her teasing words like a hungry fish. "Child, it is not wrong to speak of your backside." He turned his head to look at the back of her dress. "A very pretty backside, I might add." They turned a corner and continued their walk along another street.

Honor took hold of William's arm and teased him with a squeeze. "Master Logsdon, what are you thinkin'?" She looked up, pressing her tongue to her upper lip. He flipped his eyebrows up and down, suggesting thoughts of naughty things.

"I am not sure. Perhaps I think of how grown up you are." He tugged her a bit closer. She enjoyed the compliment, smiling, pulling her head up, and walking a bit taller. William looked at her, a smile crossing his face, too. The look gave her a warm flush, and she touched her head to William's arm. With that victory, William changed the conversation to the subject of domesticity. "Honor, how do you make cornbread? Would you like to make some for me?"

"Oh, yes, I make it every day," she bragged. "You ate my cornbread for supper last evening. It tasted good, didn't it? First I grind the corn. Then I mix a measure of flour with the meal. I add a little sugar and a little salt to improve the taste. I use a wee bit more sugar than Mistress Skidmore told me to use, but not so much that she should notice and I should be beaten. I stir in a measure of milk and eggs. I mix and mix it until the dough is nearly smooth." She held an imaginary bowl in one arm and stirred it with an imaginary spoon. "Mistress Skidmore has a special pan for cornbread. I spread the dough in the pan and set it on the stone in the back of the hearth. When it's golden brown and the wood stick comes out dry, it's ready. We let it cool and eat it for supper. I like it best with butter, but she gets to have honey, as well."

"It sounds as though you are at least being well fed. So why are you still so thin?"

"I get little to eat, only two meals a day, and I work very hard. I often am hungry. Sometimes, when I can, I hide food in my pocket. Mistress Skidmore eats much more than she gives to me."

"Two meals each day is not unusual. And now that you've grown into a woman, working hard is to be expected. Besides, Mistress Skidmore is a large woman. Perhaps her treatment of you is not as bad as you suggest?"

Honor stopped walking and looked at him. He continued walking, and heard her speak from behind. With a touch of demand in her voice, she said, "Master Logsdon, I do not wish to stay any longer with Mistress Skidmore. I want to go home with you to be your house servant." She added, with a touch of pleading, "But, please don't ask me to wed with you."

William's thoughts took a negative turn as he moved several steps further ahead of her. He kept walking and didn't respond to the rejection he thought he had heard. Instead, he tried another approach. "I think of you often, Honor. Perhaps I have grown too fond of giving you whatever you request of me." This time he stopped walking and waited for his words to take effect.

When she caught up with him, he put his arm around her shoulder, as though he simply wanted to bring her some warmth on a cool day. But in reality, he did it out of his own need to touch her. He said, "I would like to take you with me. But as we both know, the law prohibits it. We would have to wed first. I know that I would be most happy to have you near me, but properly in the eyes of the law."

She teased him with a move all teenage girls use to exercise their power over boys: Honor snuggled into his hug and said, "Oh, thank you. I love you so." Then she added, "Master Logsdon."

William savored the first part of her words, and ignored the addition of the formality. He waited for Honor to say something that would allow him to push forward with a proposal of his own. When it didn't come, he pressed forward bluntly, "Honor, I have the highest regard for you, but my wishes have changed. I have come to desire to be wed with you."

Honor's first reaction was not at all what he wanted to hear. "I fear a horrible life with a smelly old butcher."

"Butcher?" asked William. "What does the butcher have to do with my wanting to wed with you?"

"Nothing, sir. But what would be improper about me being only your house servant? You know that I will be going home to serve where God needs me. I promised Da, and you wrote a letter to ask him to send funds for my return. Perhaps we could tell people that we are wedded, even if we are not. You could continue to treat me as a daughter. No one else need know."

Like a slap from an evil angel, William's felt a sting as his hopes began to fade. He answered, "No, Honor. You don't understand. I could not trust myself with you so close. Besides, Mistress Skidmore would know we were unwed. And, unless we lied to them, so would Master Rausch and Mistress Comfort." He added, "I cannot bear false witness for your convenience, and neither should you ask it of me."

Honor made it very clear that she did understand what he wanted, and took umbrage at his last remark. "Why do you accuse me of a sin? A nun must remain chaste, and Mistress Skidmore wants to sell me to some old butcher. My need for your help is more important than a little lie. I love God and I've made a promise to me Da. If I told you that I love you, it's a different kind of love than the one you speak of."

William turned his back to her. He closed his eyes, trying to contain his disappointment. *Has God spoken* he wondered to himself.

But turning his back only angered the woman-child. "I know you only want me for your bed." She finished her thought with words that contained meaningful pauses between them. "If we wed ... and you take your privilege with me ... I ... will ... come ... to ... hate ... you."

This is not the girl I met on the docks, he thought to himself. *Why is she accusing me?* With an unwise choice of words, he said. "You make me wonder if you desire only to use me, and care not at all for my feelings and desires? Is that not evil, as well?"

He turned back to her and saw her eyes filling with tears. She said, "William, please understand. I know you love me, but …"

"But what? It is you who doesn't understand. My love for you is no longer that of a father. So, if you decide to hate me, the sin will be on your account, not on mine."

He watched her jaw drop and her eyes grow wide with remorse. "I'm sorry. I shouldn't have said I would hate you. I'm just afraid," she said, stepping forward to be within inches of him. He saw the tears glitter in her eyes as she whispered, "Mistress Skidmore told me of her husband. She said all men in the New World are hungerin' for young girls. I did nae want to believe her, but your words make me fear she is correct. She said you would beat me and make me lay under you, even against my will. It would be your privilege to do whatever you like with me, if we were to wed. Then, when I was older, you would leave me for another, younger girl. I just know I cannae be with any man."

Her whispered tone and the accusation of his being as evil as Winifred's imagination were the fatal stab to his proposal. "Then perhaps my visit here has been of no profit. I should take you back to Mistress Skidmore where you will be safe. You feel nothing more for me than a need to use me until your letter arrives. And then it will be you who leaves me. After all, I'm already too old."

He knew his words would stab her heart in a way he momentarily intended, but very much would have preferred to avoid. He knew he had hit his mark when her tears transformed into audible sobs.

I've killed her good feelings for me, he concluded to himself. Why did I say such a cruel thing?

"Darling, Honor," he said, with a soft, apologetic tone. "I'm sorry. But you must know that I'm not like that man, Master Skidmore."

Honor said nothing for a long time; she just cried. When she was finally composed enough to speak, she tried to explain herself another way. "I am in your debt, Master Logsdon. But if my needin' ye be a sin, at least my reasons are praiseworthy. I truly believe that God sent ye to me. What else could I do but prevail upon your feelings?"

"Such decadent feelings, I must admit. I want to hold you, to kiss you, to have children with you. What about my needing you? What about my reasons? Are they not praiseworthy as well?"

"I understand now. I may be very selfish. But when you bought me, you said you wanted to be like my Da and help me. Master, let me love ye forever. Please let me go home."

"I will do so, but you cannot live at *Brotherly Love* while you wait. I've dreamt of you, Honor. In my dream, you were my wife completely. You gave me a son." He was silent for a moment, before saying, "Let's just go back to the boarding house. Tomorrow we will find another place for you to stay."

●●●

The rest of the day, while William and the two boys sold their produce, William's mind kept returning to Honor's comments about her fear of him and his intentions. *I acted with a Christian man's love for a child in need when I paid for her contract, and I had no desire for anything else at the time. After all, it was only a dream. I felt a father's love when I returned so soon to see her. Could the dream have just been a foolish man's fantasy?* William fretted over those questions throughout the afternoon and into the evening and night. *I do desire to have a wife and family, but that has nothing to do with Honor. Even with red hair and green eyes, the woman in my dream couldn't have been Honor. That woman appeared to be much older and much friendlier. Yet, I could not deny that I dreamt of Honor more than once — pleasurable dreams which often included hugs and kisses. The skip in her walk and the lilt in her voice have somehow worked deep into my dreams. Have they also worked themselves into my flesh? No, no. I wanted to see her again. Yet when I watch her walk and hear her talk, I sometimes have to deny the urge to touch her. Perhaps I should not have kissed her. Should I have refused myself that gesture which pleases fathers? How could one kiss prove more pleasurable than self-control and good behavior would allow. Yes, the loneliness of my bed also drives my want for her to come back with me. What is wrong with that? She is old enough to wed, and, I did buy her contract."*

With that, he realized that his motives for buying Honor's contract and for his return to Annapolis were both good and suspect. He had promised to help her get back home, and he must keep his word. Her remark may have hurt, but it was also true. Before William fell asleep that night, he decided that he knew God's will.

Chapter Sixteen

Early the next morning, while Winifred served up breakfast, William did not even look at Honor, and she knew that her remarks about his intentions had put some distance between them. Yet Honor needed William, and she silently hoped the distance would be short lived. After eating, she heard the decision that would seal her tenuous fate. William looked at her and said, "We will visit Parson Blyth this morning to see about finding another place for you to stay. If that's not possible," William looked at Winifred, "the girl will be staying here for a few more weeks."

Honor shot a pleading look at Obadiah, who denied her obvious request for help. Instead, he queried, "Master Logsdon, might Isaac and I go to town with our money?"

"Yes, but be back soon. I wish to leave for home this midday." Without waiting for a response from anyone, William stood and walked outside.

Honor had not felt this insecure since standing on the Annapolis dock, afraid of being purchased by an old man. She had slept little the night before, and with a repentant cast, went upstairs and knelt beside her bed. She confessed to God, "I'm just a foolish girl. He's been so good to me. I shouldn't be accusin' him like that. Please tell me what to say. I nae want to stay here any longer."

Honor came down the stairs and walked outside to join William, who was busy harnessing the horse to his cart. A northern wind had blown in the night before, leaving a beautiful, brisk morning. "Come with me," he said. Without a word, she helped herself up to the cart's bench. He got up and sat far enough away so as not to touch her. Together they left for Saint Anne's parsonage. She watched while the boys walked toward town where, she was sure, they would enjoy searching for something to spend their money on.

"I am sorry, sir," Honor offered, as they rode off. "It was evil to speak as I did. I'm sore afraid that I've lost the best friend I have in Maryland. Please, forgive my foolish girl's talk." William made no response to her apology.

By the time he brought the cart to a halt in front of the parsonage, he was ready to speak. "I confess to coming to Annapolis because I have missed you and wanted to be with you. My thoughts have been filled with foolish ideas. I have dreamt of you in ways that are inappropriate. I wanted to wed you and take you to *Brotherly Love* as my wife. You've shown me that my wishes were foolish. I will keep my promise to send you home."

"But, I wanted very much to be seein' you as well, and you are in my prayers every day, too."

"Have I ever been in your dreams?"

She clasped her hands and placed them in her lap. "I do remember once, I dreamed we were together after pickin' bayberries in the woods."

"And what else did we do in your dream?"

"I'll not be rememberin' that part," she said innocently. "Maybe we made candles."

"In my dream, you handed me my son," he concluded, climbing down from the cart.

●●●

The Parson's wife, twenty-six-year old Clara Blyth, greeted them at the door with the Parson's son in her arms. "Good day to you sir," Clara said with joyful eyes and a wide smile. To Honor, she added, "Come inside, dear." Clara hugged Honor with her free arm.

Once the door closed, Clara continued, "The parson is riding his circuit today, but perhaps I can be of help." A fire burned brightly in the stone hearth. The room felt warm, and Clara smiled at Honor like a mother seeing her lost daughter return, "It is a joy to see you again. I've heard about your stay with Sister Skidmore and want you to know that I've been praying for you."

William answered with terse sentences, "She is not happy there. She wants another place to board. Can you help her?"

Honor saw Clara stare into William's eyes. After several long seconds, she looked at Honor, who bowed her head to project a somber countenance. Clara said, "I remember the situation from three months ago. He wanted to take you home, but you would not wed and wanted to stay with Sister Skidmore. Has something changed?"

Honor smiled and shook her head no.

"I have just made some tea," Clara said pleasantly. "Please sit down and join me." She pointed to the table and chairs in the room across from the parlor. Honor sat on one side of the table, William on the other. Clara handed ten-month-old Henry to Honor, who accepted the toddler with a slight smile. When Clara returned with three pewter cups and a teapot, she sat at the end of the table, between Honor and William. The baby leaned toward his mother and reached out, but Clara left him in Honor's care. Instead, she poured the tea. "I should like to bless our time together." Reaching toward her guests, she took the hand of each of them. "May the Lord who gives us warm sustenance also give us peace."

After a few seconds of silence, Honor lifted her eyes toward Clara, "I fear that I have accused Master Logsdon of bein' improper with his intentions when he has been none but a gentleman. I am very sorry, and I'm needin' to say a contrition."

Clara sipped her tea and turned to William, "And as I recall, the girl wants not to wed, but to return home and become a nun."

William nodded. Then Clara spoke to Honor. "You have such a beautiful name and a soft heart. Should God grant that I have a daughter, I might just name her Honor after you, and hope that she be as wonderful. I believe God has blessed you."

In Honor's mind, Clara's remark echoed the priest's blessing from many years past. Her frown turned to a smile as she said, "Oh, thank you, mum."

"Remind me of how old you are, dear."

"I be fifteen and am wantin' to do whatever God wants of me."

"And when did you ask Him what He wants?"

"When I was twelve."

"So, you prayed, 'God tell me what you want me to do?"

"Yes, mum. Maybe I said 'Do you want me to be a nun?'"

Clara smiled and then turned to her other guest. "As I recall, Master Logsdon, you bought her from a ship's captain and wanted her to be your wife."

Honor looked at him and saw the disappointment in his eyes. He said, "That's not quite correct. I desired an Anglican wife and just wanted to help Honor get home. I wrote her father to ask that he pay for her return. I confess lately, though, that my feelings for Honor have grown deeper, even though she remains Catholic and continues to insist that she does not wish to wed with any man."

Clara understood the situation completely. "When I drink hot tea on a beautiful fall day, I feel like the Good Lord is blessing all of me, from the inside out," she said. She returned her gaze to Honor, "Tell me child, why do you want to be a nun?"

"I think God wants me to do so, just like He wanted Mary to be Jesus' mother. I hope to serve Him a wee bit like the Holy Mother."

"I see. Mary had a visitation. Has an angel visited you to tell you what God wants of you?"

"Of course not," Honor smiled with a small, fake laugh. "Father Hannigan said the children need a good nun like me. He put it in my heart."

"Who put that idea into your heart? Was it God, or Mary? Was it the priest or your own desires?

"Mistress Clara, I don't know what you mean, wasn't it God?"

"And have you asked God why He has brought you here to Maryland?"

"Oh no, mum. The English brought me to this place. Perhaps I'm like Jonah. Do you know about Jonah? He did not do what God wanted, so a fish swallowed him. I think the ship was my fish. Once Jonah did what God wanted, everything was all right."

"And were you not doing what God wanted?"

"They tied me in the bottom of a ship. It was terrible."

"As I recall, God wanted Jonah to go to Nineveh. Could Maryland be your Nineveh?" Clara didn't wait for an answer. She reached over and touched Honor's cheek. "Honor, dear, there's something I want you to know. You have a child's simple clarity, and I cherish that in you. But in a woman's world, life is not so simple."

Honor smiled and said, "Thank you, but the English king is the one who wants to take the children out of Ireland. God wants me to help them stay."

"And did you accuse Master Logsdon of stopping you from becoming a nun?"

"No, mum," she said, pausing for a moment to decide how to say what she wanted to communicate. "I accused him of wantin' to take me to his bed. But if I did that, I couldn't be a nun, and I couldn't go back to Ireland either. Ma and Da would forget about me, and I would not be buried there." She stopped and looked at William. "I need Master Logsdon's help until the letter from me Da arrives."

Clara poured herself some more tea, but her guests' cups were still nearly full. To give herself more time, she got up and walked to the hearth to pour more hot water into the teapot. She returned to the table.

"Describe Master Logsdon for me," Clara encouraged Honor.

"Well, let me see, now. He's big and very strong. He has a good heart, and everyone likes him. Before, he said he's loved me like I'm his daughter, and I love him like I love my Da. Now he wants me to wed with him. At least until I told him no." Honor looked at William with a girl's teasing twinkle. "Tis my Irish bad luck that I'm not English, and he's not Catholic." He gave her a little smile. "If it weren't so, I'd be knowin' what God wants, and I'd be goin' with Master Wiliam this very day."

"If he were Irish Catholic, would you wed with him?"

"Oh no, mum, but I'd be wantin' to go to his plantation."

"You would have to wed him before going with him. Anyway, tell me how you feel when you are with him?"

"Well, I know I'm safe when he's about. And sometimes I be wantin' to jump up and hug him," Honor paused for a second, "like I do with me own Da. Did you know, mum, Da often told me that I be as Irish as the shamrock and Catholic as the rose? Da told me that the Holy Mother is like a rose. That's why I want to be like her."

Clara took Honor's hand again. "Life is hard for everyone, and the greatest blessing a girl can have is to find a man who loves her and will keep her safe. If Master Logsdon had ill intentions, he wouldn't have left you with Mistress Skidmore, for he had every right to take you with him. And he didn't have to write a letter for you, nor did he have to bring you here to find you another place to live. Child, when the Lord presents you with blessings, perhaps you should accept them graciously."

Little Henry reached out and touched Honor's chin as the girl's eyes began to well up. She looked at William with a smile that sought his forgiveness. "Thank you for lovin' me. I'll not be sayin' evil things about you again." Turning back to Clara, she said, "but I am promised to the Church," pushing Henry's little hand back down.

"Eek," squeaked the ten-month-old, as if to indicate he liked his new friend.

Clara said, "I, too, came from another country — and when the parson courted me back home, I promised God to be a parson's wife, raise many children, and help the poor in my village. We've been married for eight years, and came to Maryland four years ago. Eight long years and Henry, whom you hold there on your lap, is my first child. Can you imagine how many times I promised to be a good mother if He would allow me to get pregnant? Since then, I have learned not to make such vows, but rather to listen for what God's will is as He sends me on my journey. Now, I'm a parson's wife, raising but one child and helping the poor in Annapolis."

"But, mum, he promised to help me get home." Honor looked back at William who had rested his chin on clasped hands and sat staring at the table. "Please," she said to him. "Da will send the money. I'm sure of it."

Clara turned her attention to William. "Sir, I can see that your love for Honor has grown deeper. What are your intentions today?"

"I want to make her happy, even if that means losing her, but my desire is to take a wife. I find Honor most desirable. She knows how to read and write and could teach my children. She is handsome, indeed, and speaks with a charming voice. But what I love most is the strength of her conviction."

Honor looked at him and simply said, "Thank you."

William continued, "I confess to being confused. When I dream of her and when we're together, I feel the desire to hold her close. If we were together every day at *Brotherly Love*, I fear my desires would overtake my commitment." William looked at Honor, sincerity and love clouding his features.

Clara rose from her chair, taking the baby from Honor. "This is not a difficult problem. I must feed the chickens and gather this morning's eggs. Let me leave you for a few minutes so that you can speak the truth to each other." She looked at William, "You may have to wed and remain celibate until the letter arrives." Then she turned to Honor and said, "You are fifteen and growing up. Perhaps it is time to move beyond your childish dreams and accept the new opportunities the Lord has given you." Clara walked out leaving them alone.

●●●

William looked at Honor across the table with a long, uncertain stare. In the light from the hearth, he searched her eyes for some sign of understanding, longing for any sign of acceptance.

She suggested a new plan for her eventual return to Ireland. "Master William, if we be wed in this church so that you can take me home to *Brotherly Love*, could you just wait three months more to see what Da will do?"

"What if we wed and then the money comes? Would you want to go back to Ireland and leave me wedded, but without a wife?"

"Yes, of course, for you could find another."

"It may be easy for a widower to find a new wife, but it is much harder for a married man whose wife has left him. The Church would not accept such an arrangement. Vows before God are not so easy to break."

"But we would only be wed in the Anglican Church. There would be no Catholic vows, and there would be no Mass."

"Only to you would such a distinction be important," frustrated with her selfish view of the situation. Honor swallowed hard and stared at him with the look of the lost. She needed to discover a compromise.

William offered another concern. "And what would you do if the money does not arrive, or if your father brings the rest of your family here instead? Would you leave me to become a nun here in Maryland?"

"I am sure Da will send the money," Honor said obstinately.

"But what if he doesn't send the money? We would be wed in the Church of England."

"If the money does not arrive, we would be findin' a priest to wed us a second time."

"So for three months, I would be your husband, but you would not be my wife?"

Honor pulled all her bright red hair forward and offered her most beguiling smile. "And I would be worth the waitin', don't you agree, Master Logsdon?" She dropped her chin and pursed her lips in a teenage tease.

William smiled, "If the money does not arrive, you would accept our Anglican wedding as binding?"

"Master Logsdon, this be very important to me. I will always be Catholic. And if we wed and have children, they will be Catholic, as well. If I nae go home to Dingle and wed you instead, you would have to accept this," she said, emphasizing the last word. "Or would you prefer a woman who would abandon her faith to become your wife?"

William looked at her. "I do not understand why I desire you, but I know my children will benefit from a mother as strong-willed as you are."

A new plan crept into Honor's thoughts, and she knew exactly how to convince William to accept it. "Sir, your desire is not enough." Honor rose from her bench and walked around the table. She stood close to him and lay her hand against his cheek, "As much as I love Da, I also love you. If Da's money does not come, I'll be needin' you all the more, but you must need me as well as desire me." She lifted his head and, for the first time, kissed him on the lips. It was like the kiss in his dream. Only in the dream had he ever known the pleasure of such an intimacy; the real thing took his breath away.

He pulled her into his arms and rested his head on her breasts. "Though I know not why, I need only you."

She held him to her chest and kissed the top of his head. "Then, you will wed me Catholic and let me raise the children Catholic. And if Da does not send the money, I will be everything you want."

●●●

Clara, who had been watching from a window, saw the embrace and came back inside. "I see you have made up your minds, and we shall have a wedding."

"Miss Clara, I have another problem," said William. "If we wed, and she leaves me, I cannot wed again, as I would have a living wife. Divorce might take years, and I am well past thirty."

"Perhaps I can be of further help. Unlike in the Roman Catholic Church, an Anglican wedding can be annulled if the union has not been consummated. It would take but a few weeks, if the girl can prove that she remains a virgin. All you would have to do is remain celibate until the letter comes, which you indicate should be within a few weeks. If it is God's will that Honor return to Ireland, you will be unattached and free to wed again. But, if it is His will that you, sir, be blessed with so great a gift as this young woman, then you must give Him thanks for the rest of your life. Remember, Master Logsdon, with Christ, all things work for the good."

Clara took Honor's hands in hers. "Shall we have a wedding then?"

"Yes!" said Honor. "I be wantin' to go to *Brotherly Love*. After we wed, he can take me with him. And if my being there be too much for him, I can stay with Comfort!"

"Who is Comfort?" asked Clara. "Is she the woman the parson wed when you were last here?"

"Yes. They are neighbors of mine, and she is a dear friend to Honor," William explained.

Clara looked at William, "If Honor could sleep at the neighbor's house, then Comfort could be her chaperone?"

"Perhaps, but when I last spoke of this to them, they mentioned how cramped it would be. They are already six, and their house is very small."

"Then remaining celibate for three months is the answer to both your problems."

William looked at Honor, feeling a bit like a new groom and a bit like a father. "Can I remain celibate? Yes, I'll have to.

As far as raising my children Catholic, we can leave that decision for another time. How could I reject such a woman?"

Clara put a hand on the shoulder of each of her guests. "Then all is settled," she smiled broadly. "Come the morrow, and Parson Blyth will wed you. And, God willing, if you want a priest this coming April or May, Parson Blyth and I will help you find one."

"This is a good plan, William," said Honor. "You always find a way to help me."

William hugged Honor again. Then he spoke for a moment of the letter they were expecting from Cillian, and how it would be addressed in care of Parson Blyth. Clara agreed to send someone to bring him the letter as soon as it arrived.

"No, I should prefer to come here and get it personally. Then if the news is not what she wants, I can bring it to her gently. Just send someone to fetch me.

●●●

After months of near enslavement and a wedding of a few minutes, Honor felt the joy of emancipation as she began her ride west, up the Patapsco River, toward *Brotherly Love* and William's backwoods cabin. She felt as though she had made a step or two of progress and she was grateful to be even a bit closer to her goal. Isaac and Obadiah rode in the back of the horse cart, and after a half-hour or so, began to tease their young mistress. "Perhaps she should be called Mistress Skinny-bones."

"Be that true, and I shall make her eat stones so she won't blow away come spring," William said. Sitting on the cart's bench next to William, Honor turned around to give them her most piercing look, the one she had used so often to challenge her brother Donavan.

Nonetheless, the boys went on with their game. "In summer, we should tie a hook to her toe and use her for fishing," Isaac said in a sing-songy voice.

"But, what if the fish swallows her whole foot?" Obadiah asked with mock concern.

"Then, I'll dive in and save it, 'cause good fishhooks are worth a lot." William listened and smiled, as Honor plotted a verbal comeback.

She grabbed William's arm and whispered to him, loudly enough for the boys to hear, "It be the luck of the Irish that God would be havin' me sit here with two such devilish lads. Starting tonight, I think they should both be sleepin' outside."

After a few more minutes, Honor began to reconsider a problem she had been considering since they left St Anne's. "Master Logsdon," she said. "I'm sorry for the trouble I've been bringin' you." Then she added, with a smirk, "and to those two unpleasant lads."

William just smiled at her. "You're no problem, Honor." He put his arm around her shoulder and tried to draw her to himself, but instead of sliding closer, she merely let her body bend in his direction. As soon as he let go of her shoulder, she straightened up again.

She turned to William. "Now then, where will Isaac and Obadiah be sleepin'?" she asked. "It would not be proper if they saw me in my sleepin' clothes."

"In winter, we all sleep up the ladder in the attic of the cabin, as it is warmer there. In summer, the boys sometimes like to sleep in the vegetable barn or out under the stars."

"And where would I be sleepin' tonight?" William didn't answer right away, so Honor went on, "I would be preferin' to live with you, but I am wonderin' if one of Master Rausch's daughters might be our chaperone?"

William understood the problem and had been working on a solution for some time. "That's a good idea. We shall ask if Petra or Anneliese would be willing to live with us until your letter arrives. We could bring some corn stalks in and make a place for you two girls near the hearth. You can sleep there until I can build a bed frame to hold the stalks."

"What if I be needin' a wee bath, Master William? It would be a sin if you or the boys were to be seein' me bathin'. And if I be givin' you impure thoughts, I would be guilty as well. Father Hannigan taught us all about David and Bathsheba."

"Child, how did you solve this problem in Ireland? My cabin is quite small, with just two rooms. We all bathe in the creek, but you could do so alone."

"Even in the winter? Where will I bathe in the winter?"

Unable to contain his frustrated, William said. "In winter, we use a bucket of water. The windows are closed tight, and we can leave the cabin if we must. Honor, where did you sleep and bathe in the winter back home in Ireland?"

"I slept with Donnie and Michael, but they were my brothers, and we had a room with a curtain for privacy."

Honor thought about her options and then spoke, "Perhaps we can wait to speak to Master Rausch about resolving these issues."

● ● ●

At eight that evening, the Logsdon crew arrived at *Brotherly Love*. Isaac fed the horses and put them in the barn while Obadiah fetched a bucket of water for tea. William set to work with a flint to start a fire in the fireplace, and Honor carried all the supplies from the cart into the cabin. After supper, the boys brought in armfuls of cornstalks to make a bed for Honor, and being boys, they played a few games of marbles before retiring.

However, the next morning, Honor was excited about visiting the Rausch family, who lived upstream a bit. As they arrived, Comfort ran out to greet her beloved shipmate with hugs of joy. She swung Honor around and around until the girl squealed with joy. "Oh, I have been hoping you would come to stay," said Comfort.

"I've been missin' you so much," answered Honor, as tears erupted in both women's eyes. When Comfort stopped spinning and Honor's feet touched the ground, the young girl smothered the elder with kisses.

Walter came out to greet the entourage with his sons and daughters. Shaking William's hand, he said, "*Willkommen*, Herr Logsdon. It *ist gut* to see you. *Kommen sie* in and warm yourself."

The Rausch boys greeted Isaac and Obadiah as boys have for centuries, with hard punches to the biceps. The promise of a meal of deer and turkey reflected in their smiles. And finally, the two Rausch girls, Petra and Anneliese, stood and waited for Comfort to introduce them to her friend from Ireland.

Inside, Walter put two logs on the fire to overcome the chill that the open door had left, and Comfort led Honor and the girls to the kitchen shelf to slice a loaf of fresh bread and pull pieces of deer jerky from a canvas bag. Comfort spoke to the grinning Honor, "So you agreed to wed with Master Logsdon and will be my new neighbor."

"Yes," said Honor. "We were wed in the English Church, but we agreed to remain apart until Da's letter comes. If Da is not able to send the money, the parson will find a priest to wed William and me again. William hasn't said whether I will be able to raise any children Catholic, but I am sure he will agree, if and when that time comes. He truly loves me. It is quite wonderful."

"Darling Honor, you are so stubborn and so foolish. When you learn more about this place, you will want to stay. There is food everywhere, and neighbors nearby who are always ready to help. If I had three times the money needed to return to England, I would never leave. I am happy beyond all my dreams."

"Well then, I'll be thankin' God for your happiness. And for the next three months, you will be makin' me happy, too, bein' so nearby. You can teach me all I need to know. After that time, though, I will still be returnin' home."

"Child, I will teach you all the things a woman needs to learn," Comfort assured her. Her eyes moved from her two new stepdaughters back to Honor. "We shall start this very day with the need to keep secrets. I have one to tell you now, a secret I've shared with my two new daughters and none else. So you can't tell anyone, either." Petra clasped her hands together and jumped up, in anticipation of sharing their secret with another girl. Comfort whispered, "I believe I am with child."

Honor squealed and reached up to kiss Comfort. Then all four women hugged in a circle, the younger three giggling. Honor whispered, "How wonderful. Sometimes I wish I weren't promised to God and I could be a mother."

"Can you imagine how I feel? One day soon, I will be able to give my husband a gift which only I can give him. Think how I will feel when I lay my baby in his arms for the first time," Comfort mused.

She then pointed a finger at Honor, "Walter doesn't know, as I am not sure yet, but I have many signs. Please don't tell anyone, not even William. Let Walter tell him later."

"How can you tell if you are with child?" Honor asked naively.

"Well, I've been tired, and I get upset with the girls too easily. Not to mention that I am two weeks past my time of the month. Those are good signs." Comfort watched as Honor's smile grew. "Little one," she said, "it will take eight more months before the baby comes, and I want you to be with me when it arrives. All three of you need to learn how to birth babies. Honor, you must stay at least until my child is born."

Chapter Seventeen

Life in the backcountry of colonial Maryland was like a Biblical experience, and being there was like living in Eden before sin had interfered. In spring, berries and mushrooms grew in the rich, fertile soil, while nuts grew abundantly on the big, old trees. Deer, elk and trout were plentiful. In spring, the rivers ran high, as though choreographed to some glorious rhythm of nature's awakening. In summer, the warm, sultry weather made the gentle rain refreshing. In fall the reds, oranges, and yellows painted every vista like a canvas from the Master. And in winter the snow pulled everything back to its beginnings, ready to sleep deeply and then begin life all over again. The land itself worked its way into Honor's heart, and she cherished her life at *Brotherly Love*.

One December morning, snow sugared the ground, but the stream was not yet completely frozen over. As Honor and William washed the plates, Honor spoke, "William, I be lovin' livin' here."

"It is beautiful indeed, more so with you here to grace its beauty."

"There be a question I want to ask of ye. Why do ye give me all that I want?"

"Perhaps because I truly love you. When I bought your contract, God moved me to do a good Christian deed. But since then, things have changed. You are so charming that I can't seem to help myself. When you ask for another deed, I want to do it. I'm not sure it's God alone who moves me when you smile."

"William, I must confess that when I lived with Mistress Skidmore, I often desired for you to come and hold me. You are strong, and I feel safe with you."

"I would have thought that you should want your father to come and hold you. Do you sometimes confuse me with him?"

She picked up a noggin and rinsed it out with winter cold creek water. "Every mornin' after breakfast, Da would be waitin' for me in the barn. He would pick me up and kiss me. In Annapolis, I desire for you to come and hold me. Once, when Mistress Skidmore punished me with her hickory branch, I asked Our Lady to bring you to me that very night. I did not pray for Da."

The dishes were cleaned, and they stood quietly next to each other. Holding a plate, Honor went on, "And I came to your plantation' not because you bought me free, but because I want to be with you until I return to Ireland. My feelings for you have changed, too. But, don't be worryin' yourself, for I know of your promise to send me home, and I shall not be temptin' you to forget that promise." She put the dishes down, stepped toward him, and put her arms around his chest to hug him. "Do you think Da might be bringin' my family here instead of sendin' for me?"

"Honor, your behavior is perverse. You say you'll not tempt me, then you hug me so that I wonder if you might stay here with me. I am a husband who wants you completely. Please don't tempt me unless you want me, too."

●●●

Later that week, Honor took a walk on her own. She wanted to be alone with God to pray. Her Catholic upbringing told her that she needed an intermediary, so she wanted to find a small tree branch she could ask one of the boys to carve into a rosary for her.

With crisp, cold air and a cover of snow, her trek over the landscape felt like a visit to a peaceful white paradise. Isaac had loaned her some of his winter clothes, and she was bundled up to keep warm and cozy. Honor felt free to enter a sanctuary to her God.

After walking a short distance into the forest, she came upon a magnificent sycamore. Three trunks from the tree rose like giant arms reaching into the air, each almost two feet in diameter. The few remaining leaves on the tree looked like brown fans hanging limp among round seed pods; they were motionless in the still air. The tree's bark rested loosely on its trunk, like half opened cocoons, and the new bark beneath appeared the pale green of her Dingle home. A yellow-breasted oriole swooped down to a low-hanging branch and greeted her like an usher seating a visiting parishioner.

In awe, Honor brushed the snow from a fallen log and sat to stare at the tree. The still magic of the place enveloped her, and her mind heard a voice in the still air. It might have been an angel, or perhaps Honor's inner voice speaking a variation of the new prayer Comfort had taught her on the ship. *Nothing can separate you from His love*. Honor had found the garden's cathedral.

She fell to her knees, picking up a brown leaf and putting it on her head. Then she said an Our Father, followed by her confession. She prayed, "Bless me Father, for I have sinned. Make this tree my confessor. I have disobeyed those over me, and I have angered those who love me. I have let boys lust for me and even see me naked. Please forgive me. Father, I've come to love this place and William and even the boys. I admit to be wantin' Your will for me to change so I could stay here, yet I want to be obedient. I'll try to say the rosary every day. Tell me what You want for me so I can do that." If the children of Dingle need me, why have You brought me here?" Honor sat and waited several minutes for an answer but sensed none coming, so she repeated her request differently. "Father, would it be pleasin' to You if I stayed here and did not go back to Ireland?"

She opened her eyes, still kneeling, and the bird hopped down between Honor and her tree, stopping to look at her. Honor bent forward and offered her hand to God's creature. The bird stepped toward her and pecked at her fingers. Then it hopped onto her hand and stood, like any bird would, before sin had entered the land. It looked lovingly at Honor, and cocked its head to one side. Having accomplished its holy assignment, the bird flew off, returning to its winter foraging in Maryland's Garden of Eden. Honor rose and walked slowly back to the cabin. She was very sad, almost crying, because she thought God had not released her from her promise.

● ● ●

After Honor had found her confession tree and Christmas was approaching, the Rausch family invited the Logsdons to their traditional German celebration. Although they were not very well established, the Rausches wanted to thank William and the boys for all the help they had offered over the past year. To enhance the special time, William would bring enough goodies to make the event a true feast, while Comfort would cook the main course of meat and boiled potatoes.

As he began to prepare the desserts, William asked Honor and the boys to help him make apple cobblers and walnut cakes, sweet dishes he had come to love years earlier, while he had been an indentured servant himself.

The boys went out to gather as many walnuts as they could find. Just like Honor and her brother Donovan, Isaac and Obadiah made a game out of the collection process. They knew where the walnut trees grew and raced from tree to tree picking up the nuts that had fallen. Isaac taught Obadiah that it is unwise to pick the still-green nut husks from the trees, but rather to harvest the fallen husks throughout the winter. Once they had two bagsful, they walked home, peeled away the husks, broke the nut shells and picked out the succulent meat. The happy chore took a couple of hours, during which they ate more walnuts than perhaps they should have.

While the boys hunted for nuts, Honor stayed home and milked the cow. Then she churned the fat-rich liquid. Up and down she worked the wooden plunger, agitating the cream in the milk and turning it into sweet butter. About the time the boys returned home, the butter was finished, so she scooped it out of the churn with a wooden paddle and poured the remaining buttermilk into a large pitcher.

From the vegetable cellar, William collected several bright red apples, along with some of the wheat flower, sugar, cinnamon, and yeast he had bought on his recent visit to Reisterstown. The pie baking made for great fun, and the family made an extra nut cake for their own supper that evening.

At the Rausch cabin, preparations for the holiday were also well underway. With his new flintlock rifle, Walter harvested a turkey. A processed deer already hung in the small smokehouse. For gifts, the boys, Christian and Hans, fashioned fishing poles for Isaac and Obadiah, while Anneliese and Petra made a pair of deer skin moccasins for William, and Comfort made a white cotton blouse for Honor.

Then, on the eve of the holiday, the Rausch women began to prepare the food and the men chopped down a beautiful pine tree. In German, the beautiful pine was called *der schöne tannenbaum*. They set the tree in the corner of the cabin and decorated it with strings of chestnuts, dried elderberries, and feathers from the turkey. Then they placed their gifts for the Logsdons and each other under a small blanket in front of the tree, the exciting climax to the celebration.

William and his crew arrived at about ten o'clock in the morning. Honor jumped off the cart and ran excitedly to speak with Comfort and find out whether her English friend was, in fact, pregnant. Amidst the glee of great Christmas tidings, Comfort took her aside, raised her eyebrows, and nodded in the affirmative. Honor jumped with joy. "Please be very quiet, Honor," whispered Comfort, "or you will spoil my Christmas surprise for Walter. He will learn of my gift after supper today, and then you and the girls can shout all you want. But let me tell him first."

Honor touched Comfort's belly and said, "All the love and protection St. Paddy can give be yours in abundance as long as you live." Then she turned her smile toward Comfort, "I am so happy and hope I can be here to help when your time comes." She hugged Comfort and smothered her with kisses. Anneliese and Petra who stood nearby hugged each other as well. Then the ladies walked into the Rausch cabin to set the scene for Comfort's Christmas announcement.

But first came the games. Walter had prepared several contests for both outdoors and indoors. The men got things underway, as each took turns trying to hit a small target with their flintlock rifles. Isaac won that event, hitting the piece of deerskin closest to the center circle. He took a deep bow to show his pride. Then the six men ran foot races down to the creek, over to the red oak tree, and back to the house. Christian won that event and took his victor's bow. The last outdoor game required each contestant to toss a small stone into a bucket twenty feet away. Honor came out to join the game and showed herself the winner, hitting the bucket twice in five tries. She smiled and thanked everyone for their applause.

"Let's go inside and play other games we brought from the old country," said Walter. They all went inside to play checkers and backgammon. William and Honor played checkers while enjoying noggins of hot apple cider and roasted chestnuts. After a while, Walter and Comfort brought out two wooden plates of sugar-covered treats. Walter offered Honor the first treat, and she took a bite, smiling with pleasure.

"Oh, I have never tasted anything so wonderful. What are they?" Honor looked at Walter, wide eyed.

"In Deutschland , we call them *plätzchen.*"

"In England," Comfort added, "we call them biscuits. Aren't they good?"

Walter passed the wooden plate to William, but Honor pulled it back and took a second cookie, setting it next to her half-eaten treat. They reset the board and played a third game of checkers. William stopped Honor several times to say, "No, that's not a good play," and then explained why she should do something else, which she did. Honor was a quick student and won the next game handily. Her half-eaten *plätzchen* tasted all the better after winning the game.

Inside, the women talked as they put the finishing touches on the dinner. The boys shared whispered jokes and laughed out loud while the men smoked their pipes and talked of anticipated crops and hunting exploits. As everyone enjoyed the opportunity to get caught up with news, a stew of venison, rabbit, onions, potatoes, and carrots, all seasoned with salt, boiled on the hearth, filling the room with a most wonderful spicy scent. The aroma of baking bread also wafted from the Dutch oven, as the pine boughs added their minty fragrance to the room. Like a well-tuned orchestra, the whole cabin seemed awash with happy sounds and smells. Honor felt a bittersweet pull, as she closed her eyes and recalled the many similar occasions with her family in Dingle.

At two o'clock, Comfort announced that the meal would be served and the games should be cleared away. The boys made no argument, and the table quickly filled with eager people and delicious food. Large pieces of hot bread were torn off the big round loaves and covered with butter and all kinds of preserves. Ladles full of piping hot meat and vegetables were dumped into the wooden plates and set before each hungry reveler. Noggins of cider and buttermilk were poured, and wooden spoons were set. Once every plate was full, the host said the blessing. Then the feast began, punctuated by "ums" and "ahs." Not in her entire life had Honor ever eaten so much or so well. "Sure as the saints are praised, I'm lovin' all this wonderful food," she confessed to William. He smiled broadly, because he loved it, as well, and thought it a testament to why Maryland might be the best garden spot in the whole world. He put an arm around Honor and drew her closer. Watching her lean into his shoulder, Comfort smiled.

After supper, the men turned around on the benches and leaned back into the table, where they sat sipping homemade applejack. The boys sat on the hearth and groaned like well-fed bears. They, too, had a bit of the juice, as did Honor and Comfort. All toasted to each family and to every blessing the year had brought them.

Sometime after three that afternoon, Walter announced that the performances were to begin, "*Und* now it *ist* the German way for Christmas. We must all enjoy the *tannenbaum, und* each will say a poem or sing a song." Anneliese clapped her hands with joy. She loved this part of Christmas. She stepped forward, volunteering to go first, and curtsied like a lady before a queen.

"I will sing, 'From Heaven I Come to You.' I try to sing in English, but it *ist* better in *Deutsch*." She curtsied again and sang her song.

From high in heaven, little angels come.
Come sing und jump, come pipe *und* drum.
Alleluia, alleluia.
Sing of Jesus und Mary.

Don't come mitout instruments.
Bring lutes, harps, *und* violins, too.
Alleluia, alleluia.
Sing of Jesus *und* Mary.

The lute must sound sweet;
From it, the little child must sleep.
Alleluia, alleluia.
Sing of Jesus *und* Mary.

Sing of peace to men, far *und* near.
Praise God und honor Him forever.
Alleluia, alleluia.
Sing of Jesus *und* Mary.

Having finished her song, little Anneliese curtsied for a third time. Then she sat next to her big sister, pulled up her knees, and much pleased, buried her head in her knees and wiggled. Everyone clapped their hands, and Walter said loudly,

"Wunderbar. Wunderbar."

Next came fifteen-year-old Petra's turn. She stood proud and ran her fingers through her hair, pushing it back, behind her shoulders. She shook her head like the beautiful young actress she was. "I *vill* say a poem," she announced and raised her left hand in a gesture of drama.

To you, today, is born a little child
From the virgin chosen,
A little child so tender und delicate
Which shall be your happiness and delight"

Then Petra put both hands on her knees and bowed low as she took her ovation. Her father told her the performance exceeded all expectations, saying, "*Sehr gut, wunderbar*." Isaac enjoyed that performance, especially because the beautiful girl had looked at him the whole time she made her recitation. He clapped longest when she was finished, so Petra sat down next to him.

Walter turned next to Comfort. "*Liebchen*," he said, "would you like to sing English song for us?"

"No. Let me perform last," she responded.

"*Das ist gut*," he said. "So, now the men will give a dance." He stood. "Come, boys." The two boys rose and stood with their father in front of the Christmas tree. "*Eins, zwei, drei*," said Walter, with three claps, and in true Bavarian fashion, the three men started to clap their hands on their legs, chest, and feet, all in rhythm. About halfway through, Hans lost his place and the unison of claps turned to chaos. So Walter stopped the dance, saying, "*Ve* do again, *und* this time *ve* do better." He tousled Hans' hair and sang out again, "*Eins, zwei, drei*." This time, everything went well. When they finished, they accepted yet another round of applause, and the boys sat down quickly. Christian sipped at his cider.

"And our guests," said Walter waving his hands toward William. "Have you to sing English Christmas song?"

"I recall but one," said William. "I learned it when a lad, and I cannot sing well, but I will say it like a poem." William stood in front of the tree and cleared his throat twice.

"That's a very short song, Master William" said Isaac, clapping. "But I liked it very well."

William smiled at all those gathered, then turned to look straight at Honor. "I will sing it for you, leap chin." William began his recite.

> On Christmas night, all Christians sing
> To hear the news the angels bring,
> News of great joy, news of great mirth
> News of our merciful Savior's birth."
>
> Then why should men on earth be sad
> Since our Redeemer made us glad
> When from our sin He set us free
> All for to gain our liberty

"*Wunderbar. Wunderbar,*" shouted Walter. "He has set us all free." Walter stood and shook William's hand. Imitating William's tune, Walter sang out. "And He has brought us to this land and given us new good friends."

"*Wonderbar,*" imitated William, in English-German.

"I have a song," said Honor. "It's from Ireland, and I want to sing it to you all." She stood as the two men returned to their seats. All fell silent as Honor walked over to stand in front of William. With a voice as sweet as any angel, she sang to him.

> Good people all, this Christmastime,
> Consider well and bear in mind
> What our good God for us has done
> In sending his beloved Son.
>
> With Mary holy we should pray
> To God with love this Christmas day;
> In Bethlehem upon that morn
> There was a blessed Messiah born.

With thankful heart and joyful mind,
The shepherds went the babe to find,
And as God's angel had foretold,
They did our savior Christ behold.

Within a manger, He was laid,
And by his side the virgin maid,
Attending on the Lord of life,
Who came on earth to end all strife.

When Honor finished, William stood. He took her in his arms and hugged her. She reached up and kissed his cheek. Then when he stood back to smile at his new bride in name only, Comfort stood and joined them. She took Honor's hand and turned to face her husband. Comfort spoke. "I want to give my gift now." She took Walter's hand and pulled him up to stand in front of her. "I have kept a tiny secret from you and wanted to save it for Christmas." She looked into Walter's eyes. "My good husband, sometime next summer, I will give you a new baby. You have made me very happy in this country, and I want to bring new life into my beautiful new family."

Walter took a moment to translate the words and grasp their meaning. Then he picked up his wife and spun her around. "This is being my big prayer, for a new baby in my new country. This is my best Christmas." The two Rausch girls ran up and started to clap with joy. Then the four boys rose to complete the cheer. When the clapping ended, Comfort spoke again. "Walter, I hope you approve, but if the baby is a girl, I want to name her after my dearest friend. We will name her Honor Rausch."

"*Ja,*" said Walter, "a good German-Irish name." They all laughed.

Chapter Eighteen

By year's end, Honor had been at *Brotherly Love* for three months. Conflicted as she was, she had made the place her own. Among the few animals William kept his homestead were two she-goats which Honor loved because they reminded her of making goat cheese back home in Dingle. Every day, she milked them and brought the fat-rich liquid into the cabin. Mostly, they drank the milk or used it for baking, but sometimes Honor used it to make cheese, which made a delicious treat in the winter. She would pour the milk into a kettle and put it in the fire to simmer for about fifteen minutes. She then let the milk cool and stirred in some apple vinegar to make it curdle. To separate the curds from the whey, she stirred it gently and then ladled the curds into a cotton pouch used precisely for that purpose, squeezing as much moisture from the curds as she could before ladling the remaining cottage cheese into a bowl. When the cheese had cooled, she often spiced it with salt and herbs. Finally, she set aside the low-fat whey for drinking or baking.

William and the boys loved to spread the cheese on their corn or pumpkin bread with a bit of honey for a delicious dessert. One Sunday after she had made cheese, she told the boys, "I've made biscuits tonight. I'll give you cheese and honey to go with them if you can recite the whole alphabet and also an Our Father. Say it correctly, as I taught you."

Obadiah replied, "I'll say the alphabet, sister Honor, but not the prayer. I'm not Catholic."

Honor turned, smiled, and replied, "And I nae be a sister to you. I'm your mistress. And we must all say a prayer before we eat; especially if we're having a treat. Perhaps I shall have to eat your biscuits, and you can go without."

Isaac joined in the banter, "Sister! The way you've been trying to teach us, I almost mistook you for our mother. If I say the Our Father twice, may I have his share?"

William laughed. Being a declared Anglican, he knew his biscuits were safe.

•••

It was warm for January, and the snow was not deep. One bright morning, William and the boys went hunting. Returning at midday, they were looking forward to a lunch of hot soup, fresh pumpkin bread and goat cheese. William went into the house, as the boys placed their catch on the ground near the smokehouse. He took a seat in front of the fire, where he unlaced the leather strips holding his rabbit skin moccasins tight to his legs and packed his corncob pipe with homegrown tobacco. He pointed his feet toward the roaring fire while Honor poured three noggins of milk. Handing one to him, she asked, "Did you men do well?"

Accepting the milk, he smiled at her. "I got only two rabbits, but Isaac shot a deer, God bless him." As if on cue, the boys walked in, beaming.

Honor watched Obadiah and Isaac as they hurried to the fire, turning to warm their backsides. "I'll nae be lettin' you boys eat until after you wash your hands," she said, smiling, "and recite the names of the twelve disciples. Use soap and speak clearly, so's I can hear ye and the Lord himself will be pleased."

"And who made you Queen of the Realm?" teased Isaac.

"Me ma did that. She always said a house without a queen is like a gander without a goose. Without a goose, ganders can nae tell north from south, in spring or in fall." She waited a moment for a smart response from either of the two, but the joke sailed right past them, so she walked off, smiling at her little victory. "Isaac, for bein' disrespectful, you'll be sayin' the twenty-third Psalm as well. I nae be takin' sass from either of you."

For the next few days, the family stayed busy smoking meat and tanning hides. The boys cut the meat into strips and soaked them in a barrel of salt water. After a day of curing, the strips were hung on racks in the smokehouse and a fire built to the side. They piled wet green wood on the fire to get the smoke going and closed the smokehouse door. After some time, the meat dried and could be stored for months in the food cellar below the tool shed on the far side of the cabin. Because the cellar remained temperate and didn't get too hot in summer or too cold in winter, the food remained fresh and free of vermin. The boys didn't need lunch on those days, as they ate smoked rabbit and venison while they worked.

As the boys prepared the meat for smoking, William and Honor tanned the hides, which would be used to make clothing and footwear. For the portion that would be used for moccasins, they left the fur on to add insulation to the boot. William showed Honor how to lay the rabbit skins, fur side down, on a smoothed log and scrape the fat and meat from them with a knife. They talked as they worked. Honor wondered aloud, "Do you think Adam and Eve made their own clothes after they ate the apple?"

"I wouldn't know." William answered. "Who would have taught them how to tan skins and make clothes?"

"Who taught you?"

"While I was a servant like the boys, my master taught me how to survive in the back country. Perhaps he learned from the Indians, who all wore animal skin clothes and rabbit fur moccasins. So I suppose the question one should ask is, who taught the Indians?"

"I be thinkin' I'm a good teacher. I've been here but a few weeks, and already the boys know their numbers and letters. I am most pleased that Isaac also knows the "Our Father" and the "Hail Mary." Now I can teach the Irish children how to make rabbit fur boots. Lord knows, we Irish have enough rabbits."

After a few minutes of scraping, Honor posed another question. "In Ireland, I heard stories that America is filled with naked savages who kill people. I've been here for many weeks and have seen a few Indians by the woods, but none without clothing. Where are they others?"

"They're close by, Honor. They live in the woods north and west of here."

"Do they really kill the men and steal the woman and children? Perhaps we must teach them to become Christians so they will no longer commit such sinful acts."

"Indians live very differently from us; our rules are not their rules. Some Indians get along well with us, but others don't want us here at all because we kill the animals they need for food. Mostly, they avoid us. But once in a while, small bands raid our farms to steal the things they need, and sometimes that includes women and children. They steal from other Indian tribes as well. Over the years, I've seen them raid several times. The men chase after them, and sometimes get their people back, but not always."

Honor stopped her scraping, "Do you think they will ever raid this plantation?"

"No. Our neighbors are the Susquehannock and Powhatan tribes. They are peaceable enough, but every so often I see one hiding among the trees. In fall, they sometimes take corn and squash from the garden, but other than that, I have not known them to hurt our people." William finished the last rabbit skin and reached for the much larger deer hide. "Did you know that most of the vegetables we grow and eat came from the Indians? They gave us our first seeds."

Honor worked at softening the rabbit skin before her, stretching it back and forth over a smooth birch log. "My friend told me that they run about with nothing but sunshine to cover them."

"I've never seen a naked Indian, and I doubt your friend has either." He pulled over a five-gallon barrel, half-full of warm water, and poured in some wood ash from the fireplace. He then added some lime, brought from the kiln in neighboring Reisterstown, and stirred the mixture with a stick. "My master taught me to plant more than I think I'll need, so the Indians can have some if they need it. Sometimes, when they take vegetables, they leave a fresh deer or a tanned hide in exchange." He stuffed the entire deer hide into the solution. "We must soak the hide for three or four days. Then we can scrape off the fur. After that, we will soak it for nine more days in a water-vinegar mix with a little salt to preserve it. Then we will make the leather as soft as the rabbit skin by rubbing it with whale oil I brought from Annapolis."

"I'm glad you know how to do so much. That way we will look like us, and not like the savages."

"Don't say bad things about Indians, Honor. Yes, they are different, but they are God's children, just like you and I."

● ● ●

Toward the end of January, Honor heard some noise from the food cellar while she was preparing supper. "There's a bear in the cellar!" she shouted. William and the boys were on the floor in the common room repairing the wood frame of a plow iron when they heard the sounds, too. Leaping to their feet, they ran outside and around to the side of the cabin. William took his gun with him for protection against the ferocious animal. When they reached the cellar, however, they saw three children running cross the snow-covered field that separated the cabin from the forest.

The runners' dress revealed their identities: they were Indians. The tallest, clad in buckskin leggings, a breechcloth, and a painted leather shirt, looked to be a teenage lad. He carried a heavy buckskin sack and took long strides, like a deer with its flag raised high. The second child appeared to be a girl who was wrapped in a bear skin and unable to swing her arms as she ran. The smallest child wore buckskin pants and shirt; a feather tied to a tress adorned his short hair. He lagged far behind the other two, struggling to run in the six-inches of snow.

Isaac and Obadiah lit out after the Indian children. Unencumbered, they were fast and closed the distance quickly. The taller Indian lad soon turned, taking up the bow he had slung over his shoulder in attempt to defend his smaller friends. But Isaac tackled him and pulled him down into the snow, spilling his sack with its cache of stolen vegetables. As Obadiah took hold of the girl's bearskin covering, the little boy ran toward him.

"They are a long way from home and are hungry," William explained to Honor as they followed the boys more slowly through the snow. "In their culture, no one owns the fruit of the land, and anyone can take what he needs." William and Honor closed the last fifty yards to where the two boys had control of the three Indian children. Honor looked at the girl, who could not have been more than eleven or twelve years old. Her mouth gaped open, her raven black eyes stark with fear. Her right eye was swollen, and she had contusions about her head. The sun had yet to set, but she trembled in the cold. Her feet and legs were bare, turning them a strange hue of Indian brown, dirt grey, and ice blue. When the little boy finally caught up to the group, he grabbed her legs, trying to get under the bearskin. When she opened the covering, William, Honor, Isaac, and Obadiah could see that she wore only a breechcloth, tied about her waist with a braided rope.

"William," Honor said. "She must be freezing."

"I can see that, Honor. I don't know why she is not better dressed for this weather."

Isaac brought the older Indian lad to the others, still struggling to release himself from the older boy's grip. Appearing to be perhaps fourteen or fifteen, the Indian lad had no marks on his face, indicating that he had not been beaten. Obadiah retrieved the lad's deerskin blanket, which served as the sack in which he carried the stolen foodstuffs.

The feisty lad screamed, "*Mahkakq, nir micon.*"[1] He looked at the food and then at the girl, who stared back with fear and guilt all over her face.

---

[1] Very few words of the Susquehannock language are known, and Powhatan is extinct. I have used phonetic Susquehannock here and provided the English translation s as footnotes. The names are fictional. "Mahkakq, nir micon" translates to "my squash."

"Honor, go and get some blankets for the girl," William said before turning back to the lad. Understanding some Powhatan, William handed the small squash back to the lad, saying, "*Micon.*"

The Indian lad stopped struggling, pointed toward the girl, and said, "*Nuhsimuhs* Tewan."[2]

He then he pointed to himself, saying, "*Nuturuwins* Miska."[3] Finally, he pointed to the small boy and said "*Numat* Neaque."[4]

"What is he saying?" asked Obadiah.

"I don't know," William shrugged. "I think he is telling us their names. Let him go, Isaac."

Now free, Indian lad spoke again, "*Numowán Powhatan pumitukew.*"[5]

Honor came running back from the house, carrying two wool blankets. William took them and offered one each to the lad and to the girl. The girl's arms were still wrapped in the bearskin, so the lad wrapped his blanket around her. She reached inside the bearskin to push the small boy out and then tried to pull the woolen blanket around her shoulders.

Honor looked at William, asking, "Are they savages? What were they going to do to us?"

William spoke calmly, "They mean us no harm. They're just hungry, and it's cold out here. Let's all go inside." William picked up the little boy, who kicked and twisted in violent protest. Guessing that the older two would not try to escape as long as he had the child, William held the struggling boy and nodded toward the cabin. Isaac pushed the lad and Honor motioned to the girl to follow. The small group hurried back to William's cabin as the darkness set in.

---

2 Sister named Tewan.
3 My name is Miska.
4 Younger brother named Neaque.
5 I am Powhatan, from the river tribe.

Once inside, William set the small boy down and pointed toward the blazing fire in the stone fireplace. The three natives moved toward the heat to warm themselves. They huddled together, pulling their animal skins more tightly around themselves.

Being concerned about the girl's modesty, Honor asked, "Should I be gettin' her something to wear?" Without waiting for an answer, she went to the shelf where she kept her own clothing and took pulled down some homemade buckskin britches, a blouse and a cotton chemise. When she returned to the hearth, she looked at Isaac. "You have to go outside for a few minutes."

William responded. "I don't think you should be alone with them. Take her to the sleeping attic." He smiled at Honor. "Take some water and soap with you so she can bathe."

Honor got the bathing items and stepped toward the girl. She handed the buckskin clothes to the girl and pointed to herself, saying, "Honor."

Then the girl dropped her bearskin and blanket and responded, "Tewan." Honor could see several welts on Tewan's back as the girl pulled the blanket back around herself. As the girls walked toward the ladder, the small boy tried to follow, but Tewan said something and the lad returned to the spot next to the older boy in front of the fire.

In the attic, Tewan understood why Honor had brought a bucket of water with her. Honor dipped the rag and started to wash Tewan's face, but the girl pushed Honor's hand away. Tewan dipped her hands into the water several times, splashing it over her body and rubbing it with her hands. Honor rubbed soap on the rag and handed it to Tewan, who washed her face and scrubbed parts of her dirt-encrusted body. When finished, she pointed at Honor, saying, "Tewan, *Arner, cheskchamay.*"[6]

Unable to understand what the girl said, Honor pointed and said, "You be cleaner." Honor pulled the front of her own blouse

---

[6] Tewan and Honor are friends.

away from her body and said, "Clothes." Then she pointed to Tewan, shaking her head, and said, "No clothes."

"Brrr," said Honor. Perhaps to the native girl, the lack of clothing meant nothing more than being cold. Honor was fairly certain the Indian would not appreciate her own Christian modesty. But in response, Tewan tried to repeat Honor's words, "No clo," shaking her own head. She then said, "*Susque tuche*," [7]before wrapping her arms about herself. She shook the remaining droplets of water from her body and said "*Tewan quat.*"[8]

Honor asked, "Why no clothes?" and raised her hands in a questioning gesture.

Tewan seemed somehow to understand what Honor was asking and used simple sign language to communicate. She held her hands like claws and made a face, pointing first to herself and then down to the boys. She made a grabbing gesture as though pulling something off of her chest and said, "Susque tuche Tewan Neaque lum."[9] She pointed downstairs and said "Miskasick."[10] Finally, the Indian girl pointed again to herself and then to the boys before circling away from Honor and back to her. "Tewan, Miska, Neaque ireh paspeen nonssamats."[11]

Honor had no idea what Tewan meant, but figured the Powhatan words must be an explanation for the girl's situation. Honor stood and hugged the Indian girl, much as Comfort had hugged Honor after covering the newly clean Irish girl on the ship, many months earlier. Tewan responded by not only hugging Honor, but clinging to her. When they finally broke the embrace, Honor handed the girl the cotton chemise, and Tewan pulled it over her head. It was much too large, covering the girl from her shoulders to her toes. Tewan smiled at the opportunity to wear the European girl's soft cotton garment. Honor then gave Tewan the more familiar buckskin blouse and britches,

---

[7] Susquehannock took them.
[8] Tewan is cold.
[9] Susquehannock devils stole Tewan and Neaque.
[10] Miska came (to Susquehannock village to rescue them
[11] Tewan, Miska, and Neaque escaped and are going home.

which also were much too big. She would definitely be needing a rope to hold them up. Remembering Comfort's comment on the ship, Honor leaned back and said, "Now there, aren't we the pretty one?" More bathing would be necessary, but in her new buckskin, the eleven-year-old girl looked indeed like a beautiful little Indian maiden, black hair, broad smile, and all.

Waiting on the girls to return, William headed to the pantry shelf to cut a large piece of cornbread and slather some goat cheese on it. He also scooped up a nogger full of water and took it to Miska. In stilted Powhatan, William said "Miska apon."[12] He pointed to the lad's bow and quiver, and the Indian handed them to the man in exchange for the food. William watched the hungry lad gobble the cornbread, unconcerned about the small hungry boy next to him, so he went to get another piece of bread for Neaque.

"Obadiah, fetch some onions, radishes, and squash from the cellar," William commanded. "Bring enough for everybody."

Obadiah looked uneasy with the whole idea. "Master, if you let them stay, they will kill us while we sleep," he said, the fear visible on his face. "They're just thieving savages. We should run them off."

"Come now, Obadiah. Don't you recall the golden rule? One day, you may need the help of an Indian. Do you want that person to ignore you because he thinks you a thieving Englishman?"

"I have never heard about that rule, Master Logsdon." Obadiah wagged his head in mock frustration.

William got more water and some dried venison for both Indian boys.

Listening from the attic room, Honor took the opportunity to teach another Bible lesson, "Our Lord is the God of the Indians, just as He is our God, and if his Indian children are hungry, He wants us to feed them."

---

[12] Miska's food.

Miska said, "*Vttapaantam.*"[13] He looked at Obadiah and held the dried meat out to teach his translation lesson.

"Okay, I'll get them some food, but we should make them sleep in the barn."

"That's not all, Obadiah," said William, smiling. "You're the same size as the older boy, and his moccasins are worn out. I'm pleased that you know how to love your new neighbors."

"No! If they're going to stay with us, we can give them some rabbit skin and let them make their own moccasins. Mine are almost new. Honor just made them for Christmas."

"Yes, and the boy's britches are good, but he needs another blouse."

With his hands held wide, Obadiah walked to the door in frustration, lamenting, "If you don't stop giving away my clothes, I'll be as naked as the other one."

Honor spoke up again, "Maybe you'll be lost and cold one day. You would surely hope an Indian comes along to help."

While Obadiah was gone, Honor and the girl came down the ladder. Tewan ran to Miska to show off her new clothes. She stared at her brother tearing into the venison strips. "*Micon.*" She said to him, "*Nir micis.*"[14]

The Indian lad gave his sister some of his dried meat, and she bit off a large piece.

Honor went to the cook shelf to get some more meat and handed some of it to Tewan, who grabbed it quickly. "Glory be, they be hungrier than ten dogs after a hunt."

Honor gave the rest of the meat to Neaque. She picked up the little boy and took him to the cook shelf where she poured some goat's milk into a noggin for him. Then she went to William, and said, "I love them, especially the baby." She handed the boy to William like a mother delivering her baby to his father. "Can we keep them for a while?" she asked.

---

[13] Deer (or venison).
[14] Me eat food.

"No, they're not pets for us to keep. In the meantime, you must make us all some supper." At that moment, Obadiah returned with an armful of vegetables, Isaac on his heel; the three European youths began preparing food for the lot of them.

Supper that evening was a cornucopia of different flavors: hot cornbread with goat cheese, dried and salted venison strips, onion slices, radishes, and hot acorn tea. William, Isaac, and Obadiah ate at the table, while Honor and the Indians ate on the floor in front of the fire. As was her habit, Honor insisted on a prayer before eating. The three Indians stared at her while she prayed and they gobbled down the food. William and the boys waited, having learned better than to suffer through Honor's displeasure. "No," said Honor as she pulled Miska's hand away from his mouth. The three Native Americans waited for the Irish nun-to-be to say grace.

Honor poured a second noggin of milk for Neaque, insisting on holding it as the boy drank. When the eating slowed, Honor pointed to the bruise on Tewan's face and the stripe on Miska's arm. "How happen?" she asked, holding out her hands and lifting her arms.

Tewan, the most comfortable of the three with the Indians' new acquaintances, tried to translate, saying, "*Susque.*" She touched her swollen black eye. Then she held her hand as though she was carrying a stick, swung it down hard, and wagged her head. "*Susque upeachi nis nummacha.*" [15]

Honor looked to William for help understanding. He asked her, "Do you remember why Mistress Skidmore said she beat you?" Honor nodded, considering the wickedness of human nature with regard to slavery. Then she focused her attention on the Indians, her eyes growing determined as the bad memories lowered her countenance and her sympathy increased.

William watched Honor grooming Neaque's hair with her fingers. When William looked back at Isaac, the young servant just smiled. "Are they going to stay for a while, Master Logsdon?" asked Isaac.

---

[15] Susquehannock beat us so we won't run away.

"Yes," answered Honor, "at least until they can make themselves some clothes and moccasins. Haven't you heard the story about feeding the hungry?"

"Of course," said Isaac. "I was here when the master told you about that."

Obadiah grinned, "Well, if I have to love my neighbor, so do you." He nodded toward Honor, who sat on the dirt floor. "She was already busy acting like a nun, ministering to the natives."

Looking to William, Isaac said, "After supper, I'll bring some corn stalks in from the crib and make a bed for them. We don't have enough blankets, so I'll put the stalks next to Honor and they'll be near the fire."

That night, after the boys climbed the ladder to their bunks, William sat at the supper table and watched the two older child visitors grow drowsy, while Honor cradled the small sleeping boy in her arms. After some time, Honor laid the boy down and came to sit beside William on the bench. She put her arm through his, snuggling up to him. "William, their situation is so much like my own, and praise be the saints, I'll be able to help them get home. I'm thankin' God for sendin' them, and you for lettin' them stay for a while."

"Do you know what I see when I watch you play with the baby?" he asked.

"Yes," she said. "At home, Michael has Ma to care for him, so he's just my brother. But here, they need me, and I'm like their ma." She hugged William's arm and kissed his cheek. "I've already talked to God about the possibility of becoming a mother, but he hasn't answered my prayer yet."

"You would be a wonderful mother, Honor."

"I think so, too, but what if God needs me to be a teacher to other people's children?"

William raised his eyes to communicate comic frustration. He lifted his arm from her grip and put it around Honor. Then, with his other hand, he pulled her toward himself and kissed her on top of the head. "Good night, Honor," he said, rising to go to bed.

The older lad slept in front of the fire. Honor took the little one under her blanket with her. A short while later, the young girl lifted the blanket and slipped in next to her surrogate mother. Silently, Honor kissed the girl's forehead, said an Our Father, and closed her eyes.

The next morning, the Indians woke first, and Miska put some wood on the fire to rebuild it. When William heard the lad working, he climbed down the ladder from the attic. The lad looked over at the bow and arrows which had been left next to the hearth but made no gesture to pick them up. Tewan climbed out from her warm place and lifted the still sleeping Neaque from Honor's arms. When the three siblings walked outside, William made no attempt to stop them. He simply put a kettle of water on the fire to brew some tea.

Honor awoke and immediately wondered where the Indians had gone. She asked William, "Have they run off?"

"I don't know," he answered. "They walked out just a few minutes ago."

Concerned, Honor put her moccasins on and followed them out. Just beyond the door, she could saw Tewan and the little boy relieving themselves next to the barn and Miska picking up pieces of firewood. Honor walked over to the girl, the snow crackling under her feet. It was bitter cold, and Tewan was still barefooted.

Honor motioned the children to come back inside the cabin. Tewan looked at Miska and took Neaque's hand. She smiled as she passed Honor to reenter the warm home. Honor went inside next, followed by Miska. By then, the two older boys had come down from their beds.

"Invite them to stay," Honor said to William as the native guests stood by the door.

"They're Indians," he answered. "We can ask, but we cannot make them stay if they want to go."

"They be needin' to make new moccasins before they leave," she pleaded. "And we need to give them some food for their journey." Honor picked up the little boy. "He needs a blanket or he'll be freezin' in the snow. Tell them, William."

William pointed to the girl and made an eating motion. Tewan looked at Miska and pulled him toward the hearth with his armful of firewood. He needed only to remain and wait for a break in the weather. The lad set the wood down and added two pieces to the fire going back out the door to get another load. Isaac and Obadiah followed.

The cold day included several necessary events. After eating, William gave the girl the four rabbit skins that he and Honor had prepared, and Honor gave her a heavy store-bought sewing awl and a spool of leather thread. Tewan sat in front of the fire and began to make herself a pair of winter moccasins. The Indian lad came back in, took up his bow and arrows, and went outside again. Honor heated some water and gave the little boy a thorough washing while the men of the Logsdon household returned to the task of preparing the plow for another spring's work.

That evening, Miska returned with a yearling doe, which he offered to William. In return, William offered the boy the tanned deer skin and a quantity of dried meat. That evening and the next day, the two girls made a new blouse for Miska, and the men processed the carcass.

Several days later, the cold weather broke, and the morning arrived warm and sunny. By the time Honor woke, the Indians had gone. That was the last William, Honor, or the boys ever saw of them.

Chapter Nineteen

March of 1702 dawned with signs of spring, meaning it would soon be time to return to Annapolis to collect the long-awaited letter from Honor's father. Several weeks had passed since the Indian children visited the plantation, and Honor took a growing interest in the need for a Catholic nun in the Maryland backcountry. She was enjoying her stay and several times expressed her mixed feelings about returning to Ireland. Nonetheless, God seemed to leave her prayers unanswered, His lack of response suggesting that He wanted her to leave before her growing desires tempted her into the sin of Bathsheba.

One Sunday morning, the temperature was 55 degrees, and William prepared to attempt what he thought might be his last chance to persuade Honor to stay. With breakfast out of the way, he released Isaac and Obadiah to enjoy a day of hunting. When Honor said she would like to go with them, he said, "No, Honor, I would prefer that we talk together. Perhaps we can go for a walk and look for deer." Then he suggested, "Put on your buckskin moccasins and britches. And I love the white blouse Comfort made for you. It is a beautiful morning, and you look so nice in buckskin." Honor smiled as she climbed the ladder to change her clothes. She had a plan of her own and thought the thin cotton blouse would help.

After the boys were gone, William and Honor made their way to the creek, enjoying the spring weather. The spot where they stopped was not unlike the place William had dreamt months earlier. Honor knew why he wanted her to dress in the backcountry clothes, and that the blouse showed off her budding breasts. She had noticed the wobble in his voice when she wore her buckskin pants and cotton blouse. Somewhere deep within her core, she enjoyed tempting him, even as she knew that she soon would be called to leave him forever. *I wish I didn't love him.*

They sat on a log at creek-side, and Honor kicked off her moccasins. She lay her head on William's shoulder. His hands started to shake, so he covered his nervousness by getting up and walking a short way downriver. He picked a handful of yellow and white crocuses, missing her smile as he added sprigs of spring green to cradle the blooms. "Here, Honor, I've picked some flowers for you," he said, handing them to her. "Aren't they beautiful?"

Honor rose, took the bouquet, and hugged William in a spontaneous display of affection. "I'm goin' to be missin' this place," she said. Then she graced him with one of her dimpled smiles, touched the flowers to her chin, and teased, "William, you are always so good to me. I'm wishin' I could stay longer."

"I picked them for your hair," he said, taking one of the yellow flowers and weaving it into her auburn tresses, using a few strands to wrap around the stem and hold it in place.

Honor sensed that he was prepared to give her everything she wanted, and she rewarded his goodness with a taste of her charms. She felt his hands quivering. "You're always so good." Deep inside, however, she experienced a new sensation, her heart racing and her skin becoming sensitive under her blouse. William bit his lip, sensing that his impossible dream might come true. He held his breath, thinking it better to say nothing for the moment and to risk saying the wrong thing.

Honor tilted her head to the side and began her maneuver to get him to agree to her plan. "I be so glad the saints have given you to me. It makes my time of trial and temptation so much easier when you be helpin' me remember how good you are."

William pursed his yet unfulfilled lips. "Come now, have these months really been a time of trial? Look about you. The trees, the grass, the creek. This land is a paradise. How can you call such beauty a place of trial?" Then he added, "Honor, has anyone ever put flowers in your hair?"

"You know that I love it here, and I know you think me beautiful. I'd like you to be puttin' flowers in my hair every day, but Da's letter should have arrived and I may soon have to return to Ireland. William, I don't want to leave here, but it may well be that God needs me to teach Ireland's children. I can't do what you want."

He smiled. "Would you like to walk along the creek?"

"That would be grand." She handed him the flowers and slipped back into her moccasins. Taking her hand, William gave the flowers back to her and they walked down to the path beside the water. For several minutes, they continued in silence. Two young rabbits hopped across their path as if they weren't even there. She exclaimed, "Oh, look." Then a robin, with its beak full of fresh grass, sprang from the riverbank and flew to a nearby tree.

William turned to Honor and asked, "What makes you so sure that God wants you to leave? Perhaps He wants you to build a nest here with me. Perhaps we're like those rabbits, except more blessed. You could be a teacher to the Indian children." In silent reply, she tucked her shirt deeper into her britches and stood erect to stretch the blouse tight over her new figure. He smiled, captivated by her beauty. "You've grown into a wonderful young woman," he said softly.

Honor blushed a bit, but enjoyed his response. She bumped his hip with hers. "Ye have a wee bit of the devil in ye this morning, Master Logsdon," she said, "and ye should be keepin' your eyes where they belong." The situation seemed perfect to Honor. She released his hand and skipped ahead enjoying the effect she knew she'd had on him. In her mind's eye, she could envision her life outside the seclusion of a cloister. She remembered the dream she had several days earlier. Glancing over her shoulder, she said, "How much do you love me? I think if we were wed in a Catholic ceremony, God might let me stay."

"Maybe He wants you to stay here with me. I would certainly wed you Catholic."

"I would like that. Perhaps He brought me here so I could spread the faith to the Indian children. That way, when I'm teachin' them, I can tell them why it is so important for them to say their prayers every day."

"Maybe God just wants you to enjoy His creation. This New World is a gift, not a schoolgirl's lesson. Perhaps I could be your priest?"

To Honor, William's comment sounded vaguely heretical and she remembered telling Sean about becoming a priest so they could serve together. She said, "But you're Anglican." She took off her moccasins again, stepped down to the river, and waded into the cold water. Just as in his dream, her hands were stretched out for balance. William began to follow her, but then remembered his dream and sat down on a log to await her long, naked kiss. He put his trembling hands on his knees and watched as she bent over to roll the legs of her deer-skin britches almost up to her knees, stood, and danced for him in the water. When she had finished her dance, she came back to sit next to him on the log. "Brrr, the water's a wee bit cold for me today," she said. Honor knew exactly what was on William's mind. She picked up his hand and kissed his fingers. "What about our children?"

"As you say, Honor, I'm Anglican. My children should be Anglican, as well."

"If you will permit me to bring my faith to our children, God might let me stay here with you."

Hearing only the last part of her thought, he pulled her in and kissed her on the mouth, the delicious fruit of his long desire. Though she was caught off-guard, Honor put her arms around William and pulled him closer. She pressed her lips to his, enraptured by the glorious new sensation that overtook her whole body. But after the kiss ended, she looked at him and asked, "Why did you do that?" She pulled herself away, jumping to her feet, and made the sign of the cross. She shouted, "Please, William. God wants me to do something grand, and I must not be sinnin'. To do what you want would be a sin." She stood, insisting, "You must agree to this!" She circled him impatiently while he remained sitting, facing the creek. "Why can't you understand?" She cried, tears of frustration stinging her eyes. For her, the delicious kiss had tasted like an apple freshly picked from a tree — sweet, tingling, and sinful.

William put his head in his hands and, after a long pause, spoke with obvious frustration in his voice, "If God wants you in Ireland, then why are you here? I don't understand why you reject happiness for yourself?"

"It would please me to have devout children."

William said, "Honor, I want you to stay and bear my children, but you ask too much."

"You want your children to be raised Anglican."

"As their father, it would be my right to choose how they are brought up."

"Yes, *master*. That would be *your right*. But if they were *my* children, they would have to be baptized and raised in the Catholic faith."

The air emptied from his lungs and his conversational tone turned to pleading. "When I first saw you, I had come looking for a wife, but there were none I favored. You were just a skinny rag of a girl. It seemed right to purchase your contract and help get you home. But over the time you've been here, you have changed, and so have I. You are a grown woman, and you should put away these childish thoughts. You must learn that the man is the head of his household."

His words had gone too far and too fast for her inner conflict to abide. She knew that she wanted to be his wife and the mother to his children. She wanted to teach Isaac and Obadiah about God. She wanted to minister to the neighboring Indians. She had even dreamt of being completely his. But she could not, would not, sacrifice her faith for any of those things.

"Master Logsdon," she said, searching for a response, "I am not the slave girl you seek. Sometimes you act like the ugly butcher in Annapolis. I knew why you asked me to wear these clothes, and I wore them to please you — but I know now that was a mistake." She took a step back, committed to her present path. "I know a little about the things men desire, and it has been unfair for me to give you a taste of what you want when I cannot give you all of it. If I have misled you, I am sorry. I'm not perfect." She walked a few steps up the path toward the cabin, and then turned around. "It's not been easy for me, either. Can you understand that I want what you want, but I must return to Annapolis and wait for Da's letter there. You must take me there at once!"

She immediately regretted the finality of her response, recognizing that she had worn the buckskins and blouse to feed her own ego. Honor knew she didn't want William to take her to the city and leave her forever. The remarks hurt her soul, and she regretted delivering such a cold rebuff to a man she loved so much. She walked back to him, putting her hand on his shoulder and coming around the log to kneel before him, just as the red-haired woman in his dream had done months earlier. "I'm so sorry, William. I didn't mean that. I want you always to be a part of me." She touched his hand. "But I've promised Da, and it is my sacrifice to remain pure for the Church. Please don't take that from me. You must find another to be your wife."

The next morning, after a night of sleepless tears, Honor rose with the sun and walked out to her confession tree. As she made her way down the path and out between the rows of tobacco seedlings, the sun topped the horizon, its rays offering warm hope to her dilemma. Noticing new leaf buds as she approached the tree, she saw a rabbit hop away and watched a turkey hen resume her search for food. Perhaps nature told Honor that the rest of the earth was not so confused. Or perhaps the world had sent an answer to her prayer. "Why is this so hard?" she asked.

Honor knelt down and began to pray before the beautiful old sycamore. "Father, I am so sorry. William says he's lovin' me, and I know I am lovin' him, too. It is so beautiful here, and I would stay – except that I promised you. Why would You allow me to be so tempted? Am I to be like Bathsheba or the Holy mother?" She sat back on her heels, opened her eyes, and looked at the tree in front of her. Everything came to a silent stop in anticipation of God's answer. There was no breeze wafting, no birds singing, and no rabbits sniffing the air. She went on. "I am sorry that I wore the deerskins and danced for him. I shouldn't have worn my blouse without a chemise. It was evil of me to make him want me, and I am truly sorry for wantin' him to touch me. But I really liked it when he saw me naked in my dream. I wanted to be like Bathsheba. Please God, I'm so sorry. Tell me what to do."

Then Honor prayed the first set of "Glorious Mysteries," using the rosary Isaac had carved for her. But, she perceived no answer. Frustrated, she began to cry. Once she finished, she walked back toward the small cabin.

By the time Honor emerged from the forest, the sun had risen higher and warmed her face. It would be another glorious day in Maryland's paradise.

Chapter Twenty

Brotherly Love sat beside Gwynn Falls Creek, a tributary of the Patapsco River between Owings Mills and Reisterstown, communities of English and German settlers. The communities were neighbors to the Susquehannock and Powhatan Indians who lived in nearby villages. Relations with the Indians were peaceful, for the most part; the Indians were the settlers' allies against the more militant Iroquois. But as the Europeans moved westward, they competed with the native population for the game that fed them. Additionally, the demand for furs and leather in Europe made trapping a profitable way of life for the European settlers. Finally, the Indians had little immunity to the white man's diseases. Understandably, these conflicts angered the Native Americans and could sometimes make life on the frontier dangerous. One Sunday in March of 1702, the Susquehannocks raided the community at Reisterstown, burning homes, murdering the citizens, and taking five women and children captive.

Survivors of the raid gathered nearby settlers into a militia that would go after the raiders and retrieve the kidnapped. One survivor came on horseback to the Logsdon cabin. William walked outside to greet the rider. "Sir," said the young man, "the hostiles have raided Reisterstown and taken our women and children. Get your muskets and join our militia."

Joining such militias when needed was an accepted aspect of life in Colonial America. "Where will the militia rendezvous?" asked William.

"A mile north of Reisterstown, in the big meadow. The hostiles took our people to the north."

"Ride upriver," advised William. "A family of Germans lives there with more men. Tell the women there to come here and stay with my family. I will leave one of my servants to protect them. Tell the Germans that we will meet them at the south edge of the cedar swamp in an hour. That's about all the fighters we have in this area, so you should meet us there as well to take us to the rendezvous spot." The lad rode off to inform the Rausch men, and William went inside the cabin.

To the boys he said, "Isaac, you stay here and protect the women. Comfort and the Rausch girls will be arriving shortly. Obadiah, you come with me. I'll get the muskets, oilcloths, and blankets. We will each need a bottle of water, enough rations for three days, hatchets and knives. Make up shot pouches with enough patches, balls and powder as the pouch will carry. Then put bridles on both horses and take them out."

William turned to Honor. "Please go to the vegetable barn and bring in enough food for five people for three days. Fill all the buckets with water. When we're gone, bolt the door and windows shut and push the table against the door. I'll leave muskets for you and Isaac. Comfort will have a musket, as well. I doubt the Indians will come here, but if they do, there won't be many. If they try to come in, shoot one and use the muskets as clubs." Terrified at the sudden development, Honor listened, mouth agape, and did exactly as William had instructed.

●●●

Some time later, William and Obadiah met up with Walter, his two boys, and the militia recruiter from Reisterstown. Each had a horse, which would make it easy for them to reach the rendezvous in time. When they arrived, they met twelve other men and teen boys, each with their own horses. William learned that six others would be following on foot. William guessed that the Indians had a dozen or more warriors but figured some might be wounded, all were on foot, and they were busy controlling the six captured women and children.

They elected a German blacksmith as their captain because he had the most experience with Indian fighting. The smith had his dog with him. William calculated that they could travel twice as fast as the Indians, who were already more than five to six miles ahead. Captain Schmidt said, "We should meet with them after dark, *und* we can fight at sunrise on the morrow. Make twos, *wiz* one man and one lad. Ride east and west and look for their trail. When you find the trail, fire two shots to bring the rest of us to you."

William and Obadiah formed a team and rode east, looking for evidence that a large number of people had recently walked through an area. They examined the ground for broken twigs and fallen leaves that had been kicked up. About twenty minutes into the search, Obadiah heard two shots to the west, and all the men turned to ride in that direction. At about twelve-thirty, several of the pursuers met at the newly found foot trail and started to follow it. Within an hour, the entire mounted militia of seventeen had been reunited and made good progress in the chase.

Fifteen minutes later, the lead man shouted, "Up here! Blood drops."

Another man to the side shouted, "There's more over here."

Captain Schmidt spoke up in a low voice. "Okay, so two Indians are wounded. This is for us *sehr gut, ya?* But from now on, only talk in whispers."

A bit later, they found a pair of colonial shoes on the side of the path. The Indians knew the tracks from white man's shoes would indicate the presence of captives. One of the militiamen dismounted his horse to put the shoes in his rucksack.

At three, the militia came upon a grisly sight. The body of the Reiserstown housewife whose husband had been murdered that morning lay thirty yards off to the left. She had been killed with a tomahawk blow to the neck. From what they could make out from the tracks, it looked as though she must have panicked and tried to run. The couple's three children were now orphans. The captain dispatched the youngest of the militiamen to take the body back to the village for burial.

As sundown approached, the troop came to a creek, about four feet across and six inches deep. It was too wide to jump over, meaning the Indians and their prisoners would have had to cross it; they would now have wet feet and would be very cold when the nighttime temperature dropped to into the 30s. Captain

Schmidt decided to stop for the night, so the men climbed a small hill near the creek and set up camp.

The captain asked William to continue up the escape route on foot to see if he could learn whether or not the Indians and their captives were close at hand. "Walk slowly on the trail so they will not see you. But watch for spies left behind to see if we follow. When you find the main party, count them *und* come back. If they are close, we go around them tonight and set the ambush, j*a*?"

William left his horse and rucksack with Obadiah and went to perform his mission. He walked close to the Indians' trail, always keeping their tracks in view. In the light of the full moon, he could see that the virgin forest had little undergrowth and the trees let in enough moonlight for William to make his way. He ate two johnnycakes and an apple as he headed north. An hour into his search, William heard voices up ahead and concluded that the Indian party had also stopped for the night. Although it was cold and dark, no campfires burned, so he had to feel his way toward the sounds. He would crouch down and clear the dried leaves and twigs away from the place where his next step would fall. Then he would take another step and search the darkness for any signs of life. Every so often, he heard voices, and he listened intently to determine whether any were speaking English or German.

Step by step, William worked his way to a place so close that going any farther meant to risk being seen. He could make out shapes in the dark. From behind a tree, he searched for sounds and movements that would identify any of the people. After about thirty minutes, he thought he counted ten warriors around the encampment. Then he backed away, step by step. He had duck-walked about forty yards when his leg muscles started to burn from the strain, and he knew they would no longer support creeping, so he stood to walk upright. At that moment, an Indian sentry standing about sixty feet away let out a fierce war cry.

Like a spooked rabbit, William began to run, burning muscles or not, his heart pounding violently in his chest. He had one thought: *My life is in danger and I must escape.* Quickly, he made the decision to run in the same direction from which he had come because he was somewhat familiar with that path. The Indian running behind him couldn't see William and had to stop periodically to listen for his enemy. William calculated that his pursuer had come alone but figured other warriors were close behind, running toward his war whoop.

The first order was to deal with the one enemy before the others caught up. He remembered a huge fallen tree he had walked around during his approach. The trunk had seemed too big to jump over. He decided this would be the best place to make a stand. When he came to it he leaped on top, jumped down to the other side, and took ten giant steps away before circling back. Leaving a wide space with no broken twigs or overturned leaves, he returned to the tree and crouched down three feet from where his tracks indicated he had jumped over. Hoping that a cloud would further darken the moonlight he kept himself hidden from the Indian.

His plan worked. When his pursuer came to the tree, he stopped to listen for his foe. Then the Indian walked up to the log and leaned over to search for footprints on the other side. William was counting on that mistake. He took a deep breath and jumped up, swinging his hatchet and burying it deep in his adversary's neck.

Instantly, the warrior's eyes grew wide and he stared at William. For a few long seconds, those eyes stared at him in silence. Then they went dead as the Indian fell across the tree trunk. William retrieved his bloody weapon and took three giant steps backwards while staying as close to the tree trunk as he could. His heart pounded, never before having killed a human being. He jumped on the tree trunk and walked away from the bloody mess he had made. He came to a place where many branches reached out from the fallen log and leaped as far as he could toward safety. Then he went back to his normal pace. He walked for at least twenty feet before he started running again, hoping his trackers would take some time to find his new trail so that he would be able to elude them.

In a half-hour, William returned to the colonialists' fireless encampment, hearing no further signs of the pursuers. He walked over to the captain and gasped out his message. "Their camp is over a mile out, toward the top of that rise," he whispered, pointing uphill to the north. "They saw me, and I had to kill one of them. They know we are close, and my guess is that they've already broken camp and are moving away." Captain Schmidt handed William his own water bottle, telling him to sit down and catch his breath. After a few seconds, William continued his report. "I counted ten or so Indians in their camp. They had only one sentry posted."

"*Ja*, did you see any English or Germans?"

"I couldn't see any of the captives, but I heard their voices."

The captain thought for a few minutes and called several men over, "The men will post guards near the river. The boys will build three or four campfires. Make as much smoke as possible. Maybe the Indians will attack us or they think we stay here, *ya*. But we go around to the side und try to put the sneak on them. Make haste, we leave in ten minutes."

William sat and ate another apple and a strip of venison jerky. Obadiah came over and shook William's hand, "Master Logsdon, I'm proud to be here with you. What was it like to kill that Indian."

"And I'm glad you're here, as well," William responded. "Just remember, when the fighting begins, don't fire your musket. Let me do the shooting. Killing people is not for boys. You just keep loading the muskets. If they get too close, stay low and use your musket as a club." The boy just walked away, never having experienced anything as exciting as preparing for war with the hostiles.

By the time William had regained his strength, the fires were ablaze and the men were ready to move out to flank the Indian camp.

At about eight o'clock, the party came upon the raiders' abandoned campsite. They found a crying ten-year-old girl tied to a tree, left by the Indians in an attempt to slow down the pursuers. The daughter of one of the militiamen, the child and her father cried with joy as they hugged and kissed each other.

The captain spoke, "The hostiles were slowed down by the girl, but they left her alive so we be slowed too. We can fool them. Instead of taking the girl along, we send one of the young boys to take her back to the men following behind us." Captain Schmidt insisted that the escort return to the pursuers on horseback as soon as he was able.

Experienced at fighting the Indians, the captain demonstrated his leadership skills to William. He sent the men out in groups to look for enemy scouts who might have been left behind to harass the colonials while the other Indians marched toward their home with their captives. Hearing that his men had detected no Indian scouts, the captain said, "We bed down here. If the Indians run all night, they will be very tired in the morning and we can overtake them quickly. This, too, *ist gut* for us, *ja*? We camp here and rest. Everyone stay close together and we will have two stay with the horses all night. Take the dog, for he will bark if someone comes."

The Indians made no attempt to attack the camp that night, and the rescue militia awoke afresh at first light. "Eat *gut*, men," said Captain Schmidt, "because we will fight them today."

He explained his new plan after breakfast. "Look," he said, pointing to the tracks in the fallen leaves. "They don't go over the hill. They go around it. They expect we follow their trail. Every mile or so they will post a scout up the hill to watch. When we ride by, that one will shoot our horses *mit* his arrows. Then he will run up the hill and hide. If we follow him, the others will shoot more horses until we are all on foot. Then they will be shooting at us."

William nodded his head, knowing that such a guerilla battle tactic would be likely. The captain however, had a counter measure in mind. "Here is what we do. Half will ride ten yards downhill from the trail, *und* half will ride fifty yards above the trail. That way, when they see us they will have longer be shooting and we have them in cross fire, *ya*. Remember there may be at least two of them, so don't let any escape."

William and Obadiah were in the squad that rode below the trail. "Obadiah," said William, "when we come on the Indians, ride away from them and get behind a tree. I will come and give

you my horse. Tie the horses and follow me, but do not shoot
your musket. Remember, I shoot and you load."

"Yes, sir."

The troop wasn't out an hour when the captain's prediction
of the Indians' strategy proved accurate. Two arrows flew down
from above, one of them hitting a colonial horse in the rear
flank. The horse reared with a loud whinny and started to run off
out of control, with its rider still on its back. The other men rode
their horses to safety and dismounted. They formed a skirmish
line and started up the hill, moving from tree to tree. The uphill
riders also jumped down from their mounts and formed a line to
move down toward the Indians' rear. The forest was quiet until
one of the warriors bolted like a spooked deer. Several shots
rang out, and the young brave tumbled forward and dropped to
the ground.

After five minutes of silent hunting, one of Schmidt's men
shouted, "I found one!" He pointed his musket at another brave,
perhaps sixteen or seventeen years old, hiding under a bush. The
man was the father of the girl who had been tied to the tree.
Before the whole company swarmed around them, the man
pulled his hatchet and dispatched the young Indian.

"No!" shouted Captain Schmidt, running up to the man's
side. "This *ist nicht gut*. If we kill our captives, they kills theirs.
We keep them alive and maybe we can trade."

"They killed my wife with a tomahawk and left my
daughter to die. I want them all dead."

"No," repeated the captain. "They just do what they always
do. They make raid and steal what they need. We must show
them better way."

"Well, I aim to kill every damn one of them," said the man
with angry obstinacy.

The captain grabbed the man's musket from his hands.
"Then you go back to Reisterstown. We don't use you. I keep
gun *und* give it back when this is over."

After a few more minutes of angry gesturing and arguing,
the man walked down the hill to pick up his horse and headed
home. The rest of the party resumed its guerilla fighting

countermeasure in pursuit of the remaining Indians and their captives.

A half-hour later, the colonials attacked again, this time capturing two Indians alive. The leg of one young native was wounded in the skirmish. The colonials wrapped the man's wound and left both prisoners with a guard who would follow the main party on foot. The wounded Indian rode his guard's horse with his hands tied behind him. The colonials who had been taking up the rear caught up and resumed the chase again. At William's estimate, the Indians were now down to five or six warriors.

Forty-five minutes farther up the trail, the colonials came upon the main party: six braves and four captives, three adult women and a twelve-year-old girl. The Indians had no muskets and no horses, putting them at a great disadvantage. Captain Schmidt sent four troopers to ride around the enemy's flank and cut off their escape. William and Obadiah were among them. Within fifteen minutes, they had surrounded the enemy and hunkered down, ready for a fight. The remaining men moved to within a hundred feet of the Indians and took up their positions. They snuck from tree to tree, closer and closer to the Indians.

Tensions on both sides rose to a heart-pounding pitch. A hostile rose up to shoot an arrow but was easily felled by a musket shot. A number of arrows began to fly, met by the boom of the colonials' muskets. Hit in the arm, William sustained the only casualty on the colonial side. A second Indian fell dead, and three more were wounded, leaving just one Indian to continue the battle, obviously well outmatched. That warrior grabbed one of the women, raising his tomahawk to kill her. Another shot rang out, and the hostile spun around and fell. The woman, hands tied behind her, ran toward the colonials screaming and shrieking. Once they silenced her, the forest again grew quiet, save the pounding in every chest.

"Stop shooting!" shouted Captain Schmidt. In one motion, the three wounded Indians each grabbed a captive around the neck, using the women to form a circle and shield their group. Their bows were useless in such a tight group. The captain barked an order, "Don't shoot! We wait for our two prisoners to catch up and try to trade. As long as they do not harm their prisoners, we don't shoot." He stood, resting the butt of his musket on the ground, leaning the muzzle against a tree.

"Stand up men," he shouted. "Do as I do." Everyone obeyed the order, and the fighting ended. Fifteen minutes later, the guard walked up with his two warrior captives. The captain went around to each of his men, collecting all the jerky and johnnycakes they had. Then, with loaded muskets pointed at the enemy, he and a lieutenant walked the two prisoners toward the remaining hostiles, the natives carrying the food. About twenty feet from the enemy, the captain stopped and pointed at the three women. One of the Indians pointed up the path toward William and his three companions.

"Get on your horses and come back," the captain shouted to William. The wounded William, Obadiah, and two others obeyed and rode back around the way they had come. "Come over here," Captain Schmidt said to the captive women, pulling them away from their captors. The two Indian prisoners walked toward their kinsmen, food in hand. With the trade completed, the Susquehannock raid to replace lost women was over.

Though both sides had suffered deaths and injuries, Obadiah had seen the other side of paradise. The four captives returned home, and William, who had by now lost a lot of blood, was in need of help as quickly as possible.

Chapter Twenty-One

Walter and Obadiah transported William home to *Brotherly Love*, finding Comfort waiting with Isaac and the girls. As the men rode up, Obadiah shouted, "Open the door! Master Logsdon is wounded."

An arrow had hit William in the upper arm, cutting a gash all the way to the bone. The arrow had been removed and a bandage applied, but he had lost a great deal of blood and could barely stay on his horse. With only primitive forms of trauma care available, William's simple wound put him in grave danger.

Walter helped William down from his horse, and supported him for the difficult walk to the cabin. As he lay William on the supper table, Comfort removed his buckskin shirt to examine the wound. His shoulder had swollen and appeared bright red. As soon as the bandage was removed the wound began bleeding again, the blood pooling in a puddle that stained the tabletop. Comfort brought a bucket of water and a piece of cloth. Dipping the cloth in the water, Comfort cleaned the dried blood from William's arm. Honor and the others looked on with fear for the fate of their benefactor and master. Honor sat next to him and took up his hand, her eyes wide with anxiety at his ashen coloring. William smiled at her and closed his eyes.

Honor stood and leaned over to cover his chest with her body. "Mother of God," she prayed loudly, "don't let the Lord do this. I need him!" Loud wails wracked her body.

Walter looked at Honor, then at Comfort. The older woman understood his unspoken message. She gently pulled Honor up and took her outside, sitting her down on the haystack in the barn. "Honor, child, you must be strong, for it is William who needs you now. Instead of praying to Mary, pray to God himself." Comfort hurried to return to William's side.

Approaching the table, she said sternly, "Isaac, go sit with Honor in the barn."

Walter piped up, "We should burn the wound *mit* hot metal to stop the blood." "I know nothing about such things," said Comfort. "Perhaps we should take him to Annapolis?"

"*Nein.* He has lost too much blood. He would die on the way. Is a lady doctor in Reisterstown. She could help?" He answered his own question, "I will go and find help if I can." Though near exhaustion himself, Walter headed out to seek help in Reisterstown.

Comfort removed William's dirty wet breeches, shoes, and stockings. With soft soap, she cleaned the area around William's wound, keeping the soap away from the infected gash in his arm. When she finished, she wrapped the wound with a clean cloth. The three remaining boys carried William to Honor's bed next to the hearth and laid him on the bottom cover. Comfort sent Obadiah to get the blankets from the sleeping attic, while Walter's two boys went to get more wood to build up the fire. When Obadiah returned, she covered William with two wool blankets.

William woke up and smiled at Comfort. He whispered, "Now she will have to take care of me."

Comfort smiled back. "We will all take care of you," she reassured him, stroking his hair.

"Where's Honor?" he asked, struggling to look around the cabin.

Trying to calm the ailing man, Comfort knew better than to let on the truth. "She's getting more water. She'll be back soon."

"I want her near me," William said in a voice so low she could barely hear him. Then his eyes closed and he lapsed into a coma. Moments later, Honor came back inside, sliding into Comfort's place next to her Anglican husband. Comfort and the Rausch children stayed over to keep vigil that night, each taking a turn to sit watch over William. Knowing she must keep up her strength, eventually Honor agreed to join Comfort in William's attic bed.

●●●

Early the next morning, Honor had recovered her composure and returned to William's side, though he remained unconscious. Walter arrived with an old German woman from Reisterstown. Though very tired, the old woman knelt beside William's bed and went right to work, unwrapping his injured arm. The ugly gash was swollen and red with infection. Comfort asked, "How bad is it?"

Honor didn't panic again, but asked straightforwardly, "Please, Can you help him?"

The German woman smiled at Honor, "Your Husband *ist* not in *gut* place."

"I'm not bein' his true wife. We are wed, but I am more like his servant. " said Honor, feeling the need to clarify her position.

The old woman looked at her inquisitively. "Sometimes I see wound which looks very bad, *und* the person lives. Other times, a small wound festers and kills. I don't think the arrow was poisoned with snake spit," said the woman. "If it had been, the flesh around the wound would be black and dead. So I won't have to bleed him. But the wound is poisoned with his blood, *und* he has high fever." The woman squeezed William's arm hard, causing a bloody white discharge to ooze out. William groaned. The old lady wiped his arm with the old bandage and squeezed it again.

Honor knelt next to the German woman and wiped William's head with a wet cloth. The woman went on, as if speaking to herself. "I should cut away the infected meat. *Nein.* There *ist* too much. The whole arm might need to must come off. I never have such a thing done."

She looked at Honor. "Do you have salt?" Honor nodded. "Get meat and pound in as much salt as you can," the woman continued. "Fresh meat *ist besser.* Cook in the ashes in your hearth to kill poisons in the meat. I will show you how to wrap the arm with the hot meat *und* the salt can draw poison from wound. *Ist* best I can do. He needs much care, and still might die. That *ist* up to *Gott.*"

Obadiah stood up to go to the smokehouse and fetch the meat. Walter spoke up, "*Wat* about using hot metal? Would that kill the poison?"

"No. That is done only for stopping the bleeding. I no think he needs here." Then she looked at Honor. "You must change the wrapping every day *mit* clean cloth."

The German woman stood. "I will show her how to apply the salted meat *und* change the wrapping. I also leave some Dittany flower petals to rub on the wound when wrapping she changes. Then I go."

Obadiah returned with a piece of raw meat and a bag of salt. The German woman said, "*Frau* Logsdon, wash him *mit* cool *wasser und* change his wrapping four times every day. Change also salted meat every day until the swelling goes down. There *ist nussing* more we can do."

The nurse left in the late morning and returned to Reisterstown to tend to several others who had been wounded during the Indian raid. "How is it you are wedded and not his wife?"

Honor just smiled.

A bit later, the Rausch family set out for home, leaving Honor and the two boys to care for William and manage the plantation.

"What do you want us to do, Mistress Honor?" asked Isaac, eager to please and awaiting her instructions.

Honor simply stared back at Isaac, never having been responsible for more than herself and perhaps her younger brothers. Isaac continued to wait, meeting her gaze steadily. Finally Honor spoke, "Mother of God, I don't know what to do. Maybe you could get some fresh meat. Go kill a rabbit." She thought for a few moments before adding, "Get some fresh water, too, and help Obadiah bring more firewood inside."

After the boys left, Honor knelt down in front of William and began to pray. Obadiah soon returned with an armful of firewood. He stopped just inside the door, out of respect for Honor and her prayer. She turned to look at him. "Put the wood by the hearth and come over here." When he had done as she asked, she spoke again. "Kneel down. If he is to live, you must pray, too."

"Mistress Honor, I don't know how to pray," Obadiah said uncomfortably. "I'm just a beggar and a street urchin. God would never hear or respond to my words. The Master and Isaac take care of that for me."

"Obadiah," Honor said sternly. "The Master is very sick — he might die. We must all pray. So come here and kneel down next to me." Obadiah saw her demanding stare and did as she asked. Honor took his hand and instructed gently, "Just say what I say." The boy nodded. Honor began her prayer, with Obadiah repeating after her, "Our Father, who art in Heaven…"

When they finished, she leaned over and hugged Obadiah. "On the ship, I acted very poorly toward you. You deserved better, and I am sorry." She got to her feet, and Obadiah stood as well. Seeing his teary face, she reached out to hug him again, saying, "Thank you, my brother. There's a sayin' the sisters taught me, and I now give it to you: "May Christ and His saints stand between you and all harm, and may God always hold you in His strong right hand." Obadiah smiled as he walked out the door to get another armload of firewood. He was starting to appreciate what it meant to be Irish.

●●●

Isaac returned with a rabbit. Honor took it from him, then salted and cooked it, as instructed by the old German woman. When she unwrapped William's wound, she saw that the gash had turned an even uglier color. She tried to copy the nurse, squeezing out more poisonous ooze, which caused William to groan. Otherwise, he remained unconscious. She remembered Comfort's suggestion, washing the pus and blood away with soap and water. With no more cloth scraps to use as bandages, Honor tore a strip from her chemise to make a new bandage. Silently, Isaac and Obadiah watched the entire procedure.

Honor stood and turned to the boys. "What are we going to do? I have been praying since the moment he returned, but… what… what if he dies?" Her eyes searched theirs for the answer, but they did not appear to have any more ideas than she did.

"Obadiah and I will do whatever you ask," Isaac finally responded.

"But, I'm not knowin' what to do. I'm only fifteen!" Honor wailed.

"Ma'am," replied Isaac emphatically. "You're the mistress of the cabin, and you always know exactly what you are going to do. So it is you who must decide. Obadiah and I will do whatever you ask of us."

"Isaac, I'm not your ma'am and I nae be knowin' what to do. So don't be askin' me!"

●●●

At mid-morning of the next day Comfort returned to the Logsdon cabin to find Honor sitting on some hay in the barn, staring off in the distance. Concerned, Comfort went to her friend and asked, "Has William turned for the worst?"

It was only then that Honor became aware of her guest. "Oh Comfort, I'm so glad you came. He's still asleep and I'm nae be knowin' what to do. The boys want me to tell them what they should do. But what if I should do something wrong and he dies? What will I do then? Why do these things always happen to me? All I wanted was to grow up and become a nun."

Comfort said with necessary sternness, "Honor O'Flynn Logsdon, this is not about you! Stop acting like a spoiled child and grow up. If God wanted you to be a nun in Ireland, where would you be right now?"

Honor had not seen such a stern look since arriving at *Brotherly Love*. "I suppose I would be at home in Dingle, mum," Honor said, hanging her head.

"And if He wanted you to help William right here in Maryland, where would he put you?" Comfort chided.

"He would put me here."

"Then what is wrong with you? You are exactly where He wants you to be. Master Logsdon needs you now, more than you ever needed him. Doing nothing is never the answer. If you don't want to lose Master William, you must stop acting like a child and care for him. He needs you to save his life."

Honor stepped outside the barn and dropped to her knees, praying, "Lord, the boys and I be needin' him, and now he be needin' us. He needs me something special. If I go home, what will happen to the boys? Please, God, tell me what to do."

Comfort came outside and stood beside Honor. "Honor," she said, "no one ever promised you an easy life. You must worry about William today, and let the morrow come when it comes." She stepped forward, taking Honor's hand and rubbing it over her growing belly. "This is a new place and a new life."

They went back inside the cabin. Comfort pulled the blanket from William to reveal his sweat-covered chest. She took the soft soap and one of several clean washcloths she had brought from the Rausch home and began to bathe William. She took special care to wash William's wound with the soap, though she knew nothing of infections and hygiene. "I remember when my Tommy scraped his knee, and the wound was filled with dirt," she explained to Honor. "My neighbor scrubbed his wound with soap until all the blood stopped coming. It healed quickly, and he had no scar. Maybe that will work with Master William." Honor nodded. "Rinse the soap away, my dear," Comfort gently instructed the girl.

From the other side of the bed, Honor picked up two more washcloths. She dipped one in the water and, reaching across his body, wiped away the soap from William's chest, shoulder, and arm. She washed both the wounded arm and the healthy one. Comfort watched as Honor nursed William. She smiled, "That is much better, Honor. The loving touch of a woman is often the best way to heal a wound. Even when he's asleep, your gentle attention shows him that he is not alone, that someone cares. That is all God would ask of you." Honor smiled as she continued her nursing touch.

The time had come for Comfort to point out another reality. "Honor, dearest, do you remember on the ship, when you told me about Sean?"

Honor continued to dab at William's arm, resting her free hand on his bare chest. "That happened when I was a foolish girl. I told you that he pulled me down, and I had to confess to Father Hannigan."

"Yes. And you said you liked him because he was so strong that it took two hands to go around his arm. You told me you didn't mention that part to the priest, do you remember?"

Honor smiled. "I thought I loved Sean, but I wasn't sure and didn't want Father to know."

"Right. You told Sean that he could become a priest and you could serve beside him, teaching the children of his parish. Was that because you wanted to be near Sean?"

"Yes, I suppose it was."

"You're not a foolish girl anymore, Honor. Look at Master William's arms. Is he not much stronger than Sean? And aren't your feelings for William stronger, as well?" Honor's face reddened, and she pulled her nursing hand away from William's body. "Honor," Comfort continued, "Don't take your hand away. William needs your loving touch right here at *Brotherly Love* more than Sean needs a nun." Comfort smiled. "You know as well as I that William loves and needs you. Don't you see that you've come to love and need him every bit as much?"

"But if I forsake the Church to wed William, it would be a sin. He's much older, and so sick now. What if he dies? I would have nothing."

"You'll not have to forsake the Church to love William. What if God's plan for you is to give him children and teach them to love the Lord? They will need you as much as any children in Ireland, and you'll be doing everything you ever promised God."

Honor looked from Comfort down at William and put her hands back on his chest. "I do love him, so," she said, bending to kiss his mouth. "And I do want to touch him."

"Honor, child, God often uses difficult times to teach us what He wants."

Honor stared at Comfort, her eyes beginning to tear up. Finally, she had to look away, so she got up and walked to the other side of the room.

●●●

Comfort's words stayed with Honor, playing over again and again in her head. Unable to find peace, she decided to visit her sycamore tree. A delightful breeze blew through the fields of spring corn sprouts, while the sunlight and the budding forest seemed to sing Hosannas to God's glory. New green leaves were opening on every plant, and countless wildflowers stood like tiny buttery yellow and sunset orange statues. Honor ran to her tree, knelt down, and pleaded, "Please don't take him from me." Then, in a calm voice, she confessed, "I am sayin' true, I love him, and I want him so. But I love You too, and will do as You desire of me." The air became warmer and her soul quieter. Honor closed her eyes and continued to pray, "Help me save William from the poison, and let me give him children and teach them to serve You, no matter where you send them."

Suddenly everything around Honor, including her breath itself, seemed to stop, as if listening. An inaudible voice came to her soul, and she perceived the sound not meant for mortal ears. It was a peaceful thought, like a gentle spring breeze whispering secrets to the rustling leaves. It was a warm thought, like sunshine on one's face. It was a purposeful thought, like a tiny bird in search of seeds, or perhaps a gently buzzing insect. And it was unmistakably clear: *Take up your blessing, and plant your garden where you are. Then, give the Lord all the glory for your increase.*

As quickly as it came, the thought changed Honor's world. Opening her eyes, she no longer felt confused or afraid. The birds and the insects, the wind and the sun returned to their duties, and time began again. Honor was no longer conflicted about her future; her soul was free of all its burdens. Honor offered a whispered prayer, "I am the Lord's servant."

Remaining on her knees, she took her beaded rosary and began to recite the Our Father. Just as she noticed the coolness of the approaching sunset, she turned to see Obadiah bringing her a cloak. As she got to her feet and crossed herself, Obadiah asked, "Mistress Honor, are you all right?"

Honor smiled at Obadiah, "Yes. I be fine, thank you." She paused and looked at the young man, allowing him to drape the cloak around her shoulders.

Honor's next words signaled a profound change that would carry her forward into the rest of her life. "I love you, Obadiah, and I will be needin' to teach you all about our gracious God."

Chapter Twenty-Two

Obadiah and Honor returned to the cabin to find William still laying unconscious in the downstairs bed with Isaac watching over him. "Comfort left for home," he told them on their arrival. Honor moved to William's side, while Obadiah put new logs on the fire to warm and light the cabin, as nightfall was approaching, and Isaac set about to prepare the evening meal. The room was comfortably cool, but soon the shadows would grow long and the temperature would drop. Isaac had become an accomplished cook; supper that night would be rabbit stew with onions and turnips, as well as biscuits with cheese and apple jelly.

Honor knelt beside William and removed his shoulder bandage to inspect the wound. It had improved greatly in the last day, but she washed it and changed the wrap anyway. "Obadiah, could you be bringin' some clean water? Bring some soft soap and a clean bandage, as well." She leaned over and kissed William's cheek, stroking his hair and whispering in his ear, "I've a wee bit of good news for ye. An angel has told me that I'm to wed with ye and I'm to be makin' my place here at Brotherly Love. Come back to me and I'll be tellin' ye all about it."

Obadiah brought the water, soap, and bandages, kneeling down beside Honor, ready to help. She leaned toward the boy and said, "Thank ye, brother, but I'm wantin' to do this on my own." Honor slipped her arm around Obadiah and went on, "I think our prayers have been answered. God has brought healing to Master Logsdon. Perhaps ye should be prayin' a bit more often."

"Do you think my prayers could ever heal anyone?"

"I'm sure of it. God likes it when He hears from someone who's not been knowin' Him well. Perhaps ye will become a grand prayer-maker." Obadiah smiled, and she returned the favor. "Obadiah," she said. "After supper, I should like to read you a story from Master Logsdon's Bible. Would you like to hear about the Baby Jesus getting' born?"

"Oh, yes," Obadiah nodded, "I'd like that." He got up to go help Isaac with the cooking.

Honor washed William's wound and wrapped his shoulder in the new bandage. She closed her eyes, and felt at home for the first time in many months. Her search to find the will of God had come to an end.

●●●

Two days later, William's fever broke and he awoke. When he opened his eyes, he saw Obadiah feeding the fire and Isaac helping Honor make cornbread. With a weak voice he said, "Tis a welcome sight, the three of you, all at work."

Honor turned and rushed to his side, with both boys close behind. She kissed his hand, long and soft. "I knew you would come back today. Thanks be to Mary and Joseph, and to all the saints," she said, crossing herself and looking upward in grateful praise.

William stared at her for several stunned seconds. He needed time to catch his breath at the new experience of receiving such a loving kiss. Then, like any dumbstruck man, he said the first words that came to his mind. "I'm thirsty. Can you bring me some water?"

Isaac rushed off obediently, while Honor took William's hand and pressed it to her dimpled cheek. Obadiah, the recent unbeliever, simply looked up and said, "Thank you."

"You've been gone for several days and we've been some worried," said Obadiah.

William looked at him and Honor. "Help me up so I can sit in a chair." As weak as his knees were, it took all three of them some effort to move him to the chair Honor had brought to the bedside. Honor stood next to William, brushing his hair with her hand. When Isaac brought the water, she held the noggin as he drank a few sips. Then she poured some water in her hand to refresh his face.

William looked at Honor with a quizzical expression. "You kissed me?"

She offered up her best dimpled smile. "I've been a-kissin' ye quite a bit these past few days, and I'll be doin' lots more of that from now on." Isaac and Obadiah took that as their cue to get back to fixing supper.

William answered, "If that is true, something has changed. You've long been good at the praying part, but ... "

She covered her smile with a handful of orange-red hair, using her eyes to tell him what was in her heart. "William, what do my eyes tell you? I've been practicin' with the hand mirror you gave me." She leaned over so he could see her loving stare.

"I don't know, Honor. You're somehow different."

"I'm hopin' you can see that I be wantin' somethin'. I'm hopin' you're seein' that I'm no longer a child. Are you seein' how I feel about this place?"

"I don't know, little-one. I have never been good at understanding what's in your eyes."

"Then I've much to teach you. You are supposed to be seein' that I want to give you everything you've asked of me. Surely you are seein' a mountain of love in my eyes?"

William's eyes grew wide and he stared at her. She watched as his eyes became just like her own, each one looking into the eyes of love.

Honor dropped her mask of hair and moved her head close to his, putting one hand on the back of his chair. "I think it be your turn to kiss me," she said, shutting her eyes. He put out his hand to touch her hip, working it upward to the back of her head. He pulled her into an embrace that warmed every corner of his being. Then he released his hold and she move back a bit. He was surprised to find tears stinging his eyes.

After supper, Honor went for a walk while Isaac and Obadiah bathed their master, changed his clothes, and helped William back to his bed. A short while later, Honor returned and asked, "Would you both leave us, so we can talk without fillin' your anxious ears?"

Obadiah chided her, "Aw, we know what you're going to say anyway."

"Leave now, or I'll bring down an angel to strike ye deaf," William heard Honor say.

The boys obliged and went up the ladder to their own beds. Alone with her husband, Honor knelt down next to his bed. "I'm so glad ye have come back to me."

"I would have returned sooner, had I known I would be greeted with such a lovely reception." His eyes lit up and he stared at her like a puppy looking for a table scrap. "Would you bless me with another kiss?"

She bent over, taking his head in her hands, and kissed him again, but this time just to the side of his eager lips. "I have something to tell you," she said, stroking his hair again. "While ye were asleep, I went to pray for ye. I told the Lord how much I love ye — and this place. Then a thought came to my mind, from an angel, I am sure. The angel told me that I'm to be makin' a garden here with ye. William, if ye still want me, I am to be your wife completely."

William said nothing, but she felt him reach out with his good arm to draw her in. But one thing more needed to be made clear. "I'm sorry, William, but we've not yet had our weddin' blessed with a Catholic mass. You must wait a wee bit longer, and we'll need to be goin' to town soon so we can find a priest." Trusting him completely, she had no need to wiggle out of his strong protecting arm. Then she added one last thought, "And, of course, you must agree that our children be raised Catholic."

"You're as stubborn as you are wonderful, Honor, but let me think about the children."

He looked up. The fire in the hearth gave off the room's only light, soft and flickering, the hues of yellow and gold bouncing off the ceiling like shadows of cherubim. Crackling sounds from the flames and his own steady heartbeat provided a rhythm the cherubs seemed to need. Honor's presence provided all the warmth necessary.

"Get well soon," she said, "for we will need to go to town soon."

"All I need is you," he whispered. "I will get well as fast as I am able, and then we will go to Annapolis to find a priest."

She sat up but didn't leave his chair. "I've been askin' myself, 'What if Da sends the money?' What will we be doin' then.

Chapter Twenty-Three

Afew weeks later, in May of 1702, William was well enough to travel. The boys harnessed a horse to the cart and prepared it for the trip to Annapolis. They loaded several bundles of deer hides, along with beaver, fox, and other pelts they had harvested during the winter, which would bring in the cash needed to purchase imported necessities. On this trip, Honor wore her best dress and sat close to William, while the two boys stayed at home to continue the spring planting.

It was a balmy morning, and soon the cart approached the unincorporated community which would one day become Baltimore. Wildflowers in full bloom gave off a sweet scent and created a colorful vista. Songbirds preened their breast feathers, singing for mates. It was a grand day for a wedding.

Honor listened as William suggested that they stop for food and to rest the horse.

"As you think best, William. I'm a wee bit hungry myself." She then changed the subject to share one of her more consuming thoughts. "I'm so grateful to Mistress Comfort for all she's done for us. Do you think we could name our first daughter after her? Ann Comfort Logsdon, how does that sound?" With the coyness of a spoiled young girl and the wisdom of a long-married lady, Honor stared at the ground, awaiting William's answer.

"Yes, of course. We are certainly in her debt, and I would like that very much." He teased her with an added thought, "If it pleases you, we'll add Comfort to the names of all ten of our daughters."

Building on his afterthought, Honor asked another question. "Sir, have mercy. How many children do you think we should have?"

"Am I not still young?" he asked. "And if you call me sir, must I call you 'Madam?'" He paused before answering her question. "Honor, I want no more children than you desire. Nor one less than God will grant us." Several minutes passed before she spoke again. *She needs to think about my answer,* he thought.

"Permit me to ask, then. What should I be callin' you? If we have ten daughters and ten sons, will you be known as the man with twenty Catholic children?" He looked at her and saw a smile, brighter than he thought possible. They both laughed at the absurd thought.

"You're no longer the young girl I met last summer. You're to be my wife, who needs only to tell me whatever she wants. If I can, I will give you all that you ask because I want to love you completely."

"And I love you completely, as well." Honor formed her next thought as the announcement of her wishes. "Comfort's baby will be born in a few months, and she wants me to be with her when she gives birth. I also would like to give birth soon, so that she can help me."

His next comment proved that they were in agreement about their married future. "I am so thrilled that you are happy about being a wife and mother," he said.

"Oh, yes," she said, "I want lots of babies, too, but not quite twenty."

●●●

They ate chicken soup with fresh hot bread in a Baltimore tavern and drank rum mixed with honey, the first time Honor had tasted such spirits. She flashed her dimples, and she and William carried on with their courting conversation. "What do you think, William? Should a back-country lady wear gloves at her wedding, if they're not too expensive, of course? Do you love me that much?"

She saw him smile again at her, "That would be wonderful. I think white lace groves will look most appropriate with your Sunday dress."

"And, if I want a new dress to go with my new gloves?"

"That, too," he said.

"And a horse and carriage, if I said I wanted that too, would you give it to me?" She gave him a love tap under the table. "Are you going to give me everything I ask for?"

"Perhaps – if you will give me everything I ask for."

"And then some. We Irish be good at kissin'. You should know that by now. We're also good at makin' babies," she said with a wink.

"Then, if I am able, I shall give you everything you ask for, and more."

"William, you do understand that I must raise my children in the Church? You have not answered me about this, but we must discuss it, or it could become a problem."

"Well, if I remain Anglican and you are Catholic, will that be a problem for you?"

"You are a grand man, William, strong and courageous." They both smiled, and she touched his cheek. "If you have but that one wee flaw, I suppose I can make allowance."

"Thank you, Honor. And you are a grand lady, as well – stubborn and devout. If the children are to be raised Catholic, I am thinking I, too, can make an allowance."

After lunch, they followed the road south around Severn Bay and then east toward Annapolis. The road they took had been hewn from the forest and was much smoother than the creek bed they had driven through earlier. Honor asked, "William, have you ever considered a regular bed which sits up off the floor, one with a feather mattress? Ma and Da have a bed like that."

"That would depend on how much we can get for the skins. We still need other supplies, like salt and tea. I will need lead for shot and gunpowder, too. And you'll need yard goods for sewing. After we pay Mistress Skidmore and buy our necessities, we can look into the cost of a feather bed."

As the two approached Annapolis, William asked, "Honor, will you be upset if we stay tonight at the Skidmore boarding house?"

"Of course I'll do as you wish, William, but I'd be preferin' a room at a tavern. Mistress Winifred is not a happy woman, and stayin' there while we wed could cast a dark cloud over our beautiful new day."

"You are right," he said. "A tavern it will be, but I will first need to sell the furs and stop at the boarding house to settle your bill. I still owe Mistress Skidmore two pounds-six, and she owes me four shillings. Owing money would not make for a good start to our new life."

"That brings up another question," he said. "What about the letter? What will you do if the letter arrives and your father has sent the money for your return to Dingle?"

Honor didn't answer. He looked at her in time to see her troubled countenance.

Chapter Twenty-Four

The next morning, their first stop was the furrier where they sold their skins. With coins in his pocket, William and Honor went to meet with Parson Blyth and his wife Clara. Unlike their last visit, William was all smiles as the two knocked on the parsonage door. Clara opened the door, looked at their faces and clapped her hands together. "Child," she said, "I've been praying for the Lord to bless you with peace and joy, and your face tells me that He has done just that."

"Yes, Mum, I'll be havin' much to tell you about God's blessings."

William shook Samuel Blyth's hand as the parson invited the couple into the house. The Blyths' fourteen-month-old son wobbled his way toward Clara, who picked him up. "Would you like to hold Henry?" she asked Honor.

"Oh, yes," said Honor. "Our good news is that William and I are to wed, and I will soon be a mother myself. I've come to believe that bein' a mother is God's very best blessin'."

Clara said, "Pray, are you with child now?"

"Oh, no. We must have a Catholic wedding with a Mass first. After that, we can be quick about makin' a baby."

"Darling child," asked Clara, approaching the delicate subject, "has your mother spoken to you about being married and making babies?"

"She has, a little. I am a bit worried about that part of things."

"Then I shall keep you over for tea this very day and tell everything you will need to know." Honor smiled over at William, who nodded his approval.

Samuel Blyth brought a freshly baked nut cake from the pantry shelf and they all sat at the supper table. Clara inquired, "Then you've discovered God's will? I'm so pleased. He tells us what He's doing and what our part is, you know, when you ask Him. So what do you think God is doing and what does He want of you?"

"I believe He wants someone to minister to the people on our plantation and to our neighbors, especially to minister to the Indians who live north of us."

As she spoke, Honor sat very close to William and played with the little boy. Samuel sliced several pieces of cake. "Won't you join us for a little treat?" invited Samuel, putting four slices on pewter plates. "I'm sorry I wasn't here when you last visited, but I'm anxious to learn about your winter months."

Honor pulled a plate toward herself and pinched off a little bite for Henry.

William spoke up. "We were visited by some Powhatan children, and Honor learned that she has a gift for being a mother. Then the Susquehanna raided a neighboring village, and I helped rescue our captives. I was wounded in the shoulder, and Honor proved also to have the gift of healing. I think she has fallen in love with the way we all need her."

Honor broke in, "I have always been lovin' William, but I didn't know how to serve God here in Maryland. He fell into a deep sleep after he was wounded, and when he wouldn't awake, I was sore afraid of losin' him. So, I prayed. I told God that I love William and asked Him if I could stay here and wed with him."

William added, "Before I was wounded, I told her of my feelings, and she rejected me. But when I awoke after the injury, she kissed me and said she wanted to live here with me." He grinned and touched Henry's shoulder.

Honor, continued, "I believe God wants me to be a mother and raise my children for His honor and glory. He has set me free from my promise to become a nun in Ireland."

William lifted his wounded shoulder and continued. "That's one of the reasons we have come to visit. We wish to find a priest, and also to ask if you've received a letter from Honor's father."

Clara turned to Honor, "Do you like how Henry has grown?"

"Oh, yes. He's a strong lad."

She paused for a moment. "It's something we Irish do, you know. We're always sayin' nice things to the children. The girls are always pretty and the boys are always strong." Honor fed another small bit of cake to Henry.

"I've another wee saying for the baby," she said, looking at Henry. "May God grant you always a sunbeam to warm you, a moonbeam to charm you, and a shelterin' angel so nothin' can harm you." She looked up at Clara and grinned, "I like that about being Irish — we all love children."

Clara stared at Honor with a smile that only a loving mother can manage. "Your spirit is like the brightest sunshine. When we last talked, you were a frightened little girl in need of help. Now you're a charming young woman wanting to help others. What a joy it is to see you again."

Honor lifted and kissed the baby, cuddling and tickling him. The baby responded by kicking his feet and taking hold of Honor's bright-red hair.

Parson Blyth wanted to answer William's questions. "I will speak to a man I know who secretly holds services here in Annapolis. He is not a priest but will know of one who can wed you. As to a letter, I remember you speaking of it, but I've received nothing from Ireland."

"I be knowin' of a Catholic gentleman," said Honor. "Master John — he makes barrels at a shop near Mistress Skidmore. I am thinkin' that he might come to the weddin'."

"That's the same man," the parson confirmed. "John Connolly be his name. He holds services in his home every Sunday. And once a month, a priest comes from Port Tobacco to say the Mass. He could say your wedding Mass for you. Why don't you speak to Master Connolly yourself this very day? If the travelling priest is coming this week, he can say the Mass in our church. Clara and I would be proud to be your witnesses.

William spoke up, "Thank you so much. But I'm surprised that you've seen no letter from Dingle. It's been more than seven months, surely enough time for a ship to get to Ireland and another to come back here. I asked for the response to be sent to St. Anne's, in your care. I doubt that Honor's father would not respond as quickly as he was able. Could it be that my letter did not arrive?"

Clara rose and suggested to Honor that they visit the sanctuary to discuss the wedding. Happily, the two took Henry and left the men to talk.

Parson Blyth went on, "I've seen no such letter. Perhaps you should speak with the postmaster. Ship Captains are required to list in their logbooks all letters they carry across the ocean and our postmaster keeps copies of the records for all the mail to and from Annapolis. He would know if a letter was sent and another received."

"I will do that this very afternoon," said William.

"You did, of course, pay the postage tax for the letter?" asked the parson.

"I gave the money to Mistress Skidmore with instructions to post it on the day I left for home. I will speak with the postmaster before I settle my debt with Mistress Skidmore."

Later that morning, William and Honor found John Connolly at work making barrels. "Master John," shouted Honor, like a long lost friend. As he turned, she struck her best teasing pose. "How much have you been missing me these last few months?"

The cooper immediately recognized Honor and lifted his arms. "Aye, if it isn't the most charmin' red-haired lass in all of Maryland. I've been lookin' out for you and hopin' we would be drinkin' some tea sooner than this. I've stocked up on honey, don't ye know, just for an occasion like this. So, where have you been, lass?"

"Well, you see, I had a wee bit of bad Irish luck with Mistress Skidmore, but praise the saints, all is well now. I'd be tellin' you me story, if you have a day or two to hear it all?"

John laughed. "At the risk of askin' a leprechaun to tell a wee bit of truth, can you give me the shortest version possible?" The cooper looked at William. "Good day to you, sir. I am the cooper, John Connolly."

"And I am your humble servant, William Logsdon, of *Brotherly Love*."

"Aye, the true Christian gentleman who saved this precious Irish lass."

With a grin that offered to join the Irish chorus, William bowed and said, "Aye, sir, I am the same, and I am also the lucky Englishman who will wed this lovely Irish lass."

"Praise be to Saint Paddy himself!" The cooper returned his attention to Honor. "And is that the wonderful tale you want to be tellin' me, girl?"

Honor's face glowed in all its Irish glory, and she recapped her tale in brief. Her countenance then shifted to a serious one, as she explained, "We've come to you to ask if your priest might say a Mass for us."

John smiled, and asked simply, "And who would be tellin' ye that I know of a priest in Maryland?"

William spoke up, "Parson Blyth told us that you know a travelling priest from Port Tobacco, and that we could use St. Anne's church for the Mass."

John walked over and shook William's hand. "And what is your desire, sir?"

"I have grown so fond of Honor that it would seem impossible not to have her near me for the rest of my days. I shall remain Anglican, but we have agreed that our children will be raised Catholic."

"Of such families comes the better part of heaven," answered Cooper John. "Honor would, of course, have to say her confession first, but after that the Priest from Fort Tobacco would be most happy to say a wedding Mass for you. He should be here on Wednesday. How does the day after tomorrow sound?" The cooper smiled broadly, turning to look at Honor. "Are ye prepared for a wedding day?"

She beamed beatifically. "I need first to buy a dress and speak with Mistress Clara, but after that, as soon as possible would be my desire."

"Then if Parson Blyth is willing, we shall have the Mass on Wednesday." He looked at Honor, quizzically. "Child, do ye know the tradition of the horseshoe and the handkerchief?"

"No, sir," she shook her head.

"Aye, 'tis an old Irish tradition for the bride to carry a horseshoe on her wedding day to ward off bad luck. Ye should also use a white kerchief as your head covering. Then, save the kerchief to be used as a christening bonnet for your first babe. Save it still longer, so that when your daughters are wedded, they can carry it with them to the altar. It's nae a wink of truth in the idea but it's a good old tradition, and ye should keep it."

"I would gladly do that," she said, looking at William.

William responded to her with a smile. "Why don't you walk to the milliner and get what you need. I'll go to the blacksmith for a horseshoe, then to the postmaster, and on to Sister Skidmore's. We can meet later at the Parson's house and discuss our plans for this evening."

William left Honor with the cooper and went to the blacksmith's shop and on to the postmaster near the Annapolis docks.

"Good sir," said William said to the postmaster. "I have a concern to discuss with you."

"Yes. How can I help you, sir?"

Last August, I posted a letter to Cillian O'Flynn of Dingle, Ireland. The letter requested that a reply be sent to Parson Blyth at St. Anne's Church. It has been more than six months, and no return letter has arrived. Can you help me?"

"I can try," said the postmaster as he walked to a shelf with several large logbooks.

"We are seeking a letter from the father of my betrothed, Cillian O'Flynn."

The postmaster smiled and said, "I shall help if I can. What is your name, sir?"

"I, sir, am William Logsdon of *Brotherly Love*, near Reisterstown."

"Let me look at my log. You say you posted the letter in mid-August?" The postmaster pulled a book off the shelf and shuffled through its pages. "Master Logsdon, I have no record of any posting from you at any time in August."

"I did not post it myself, but asked Mistress Skidmore to pay the tax and post the letter. Was there something posted by her to Ireland?"

Again, the postmaster searched his book. "Yes, I've found it, sent via the *Blissful Lady* to Cillian O'Flynn in Dingle, Ireland."

William inquired further, "Has any letter arrived from Dingle in the past few weeks, or any communication to Parson Blyth from Britain?"

The official searched another book. "The Parson has received two letters, both from England, but neither was from an O'Flynn" He continued to search. "Ah," he said, "come and look at this." The postmaster turned the book so that William could read another entry. He read it, and reread it again to make sure he understood. Dropping his head, he frowned, thanked the postmaster, and walked out the front door.

● ● ●

A short time later, William arrived at the Skidmore boarding house to find Winifred toiling in her garden, preparing it for a new crop. "Good day to you, madam. I see that you are, as usual, hard at work."

Winifred looked around and dropped her hoe, wiping her hands with her apron before taking a few steps toward William's cart. Her countenance was, however, one of anxiety. "Master Logsdon, what brings you to Annapolis? Are you sending the young woman back to Ireland? If I remember correctly, I warned you that she would be a vexing problem." Her eyebrows lifted, as though she were seeking affirmation of her earlier prediction.

William climbed down from his cart. "She can be vexing, to be sure, but her stubborn mind has changed and we will wed in two days thus."

"That is most interesting news," said Winifred, her demeanor changing from anxiety to relief. "I had hoped her stay with me might yield a good woman. Perhaps my efforts served you well."

"If that be the case, I owe you a debt of gratitude, for I am certain I shall have a most delightful and resourceful wife."

With an ever-growing look of relief, Winifred smiled and invited William to come inside for some refreshment. "And why have you need to visit me? Have you come with her father's money to pay the remainder of her debt? That is what I would expect from a gentleman such as yourself."

William removed his tri-cornered hat and stooped under the door lintel. "In part, I have come to settle her debt, but no letter has arrived. I am sore surprised that Honor's father has not sent a response to my letter. Are you quite sure you posted it with the outbound ship's captain?"

"As sure as I know you are here with me today, I gave your post to the captain. Please sit and have some refreshment, Master Logsdon."

"Did you send it to Ireland aboard the same ship upon which Mistress Honor arrived?" asked William, as he sat.

Winifred replied, "Could it be that the captain did not deliver your letter? His ship would have been bound for England — maybe he decided that a stop in Ireland was too inconvenient to bother. Perhaps he feared going back to the place where he had so recently kidnapped women and children."

"In such case, he could have gone to Dover or Liverpool and transferred the letter to another vessel bound for Dingle."

"Could have, yes, but perhaps he did not. Judging by the cut of his jib, he was not much of a sea captain," she said.

"Aye. But his log would have listed it and, were an inquiry launched, he would risk losing his captain's license. No, his livelihood would require him to mark in his log that he either delivered the letter or forwarded it."

Winifred ladled two noggins of water and set them on the table. She quickly stepped away and returned, carrying a loaf of fresh-baked bread and a knife. "Well, then I believe I prophesied correctly. Her family had no desire to pay for her return and chose not to respond. As I said, I am a good judge of a woman's character, and that girl's character could be most unpleasant. It is entirely likely that her family had no need of her and did not want her back."

At that response, William's countenance shifted from pleasant inquiry to angry interrogation. He knew Honor's character, and took personal affront at Mistress Skidmore's disparaging comments. "Madam, I ask you directly, have you received a letter from Honor's father?"

"Of course not. Why ever would I have received a letter from Master O'Flynn?"

William's face grew redder and his voice grew louder. "That is precisely what I seek to determine." He folded his arms, setting a prosecutor's stare on his face. "The postmaster's log indicates that you received a letter from Dingle, Ireland less than a month past. How do you explain such an entry?"

Befuddled and without sufficient time to conjure a good response, Winifred proved herself to be a poor liar. "Perhaps because Honor was in my care, her father preferred to communicate with me."

"Aye. Then you have received a letter from Cillian O'Flynn. I wish to see it immediately."

Again scrambling to protect her web of lies, Winifred said, "Perhaps I received it and have already discarded it."

William's voice turned accusative, "How could O'Flynn have known with whom Honor was living if I did not mention it in my letter? Where would he have learned your name?" Then he rose to his feet, pointing at the old matron. "Did you alter my letter, or substitute one of your own?"

Winifred assumed an attitude of indignation, "You insult my integrity, sir. I will not speak further of this with you. Leave my house this instant!" Her faux indignation failed her.

"If you do not satisfy my query, I shall visit the constable, and you will have to face his consequences. Produce that letter at once, or suffer public humiliation." The glare in his eyes and grit of his teeth left no doubt in the old woman's mind that he would do as he said.

Winifred swallowed hard, and switched her tactic to pleading. "Sir, I tried to help by following your desires. You said you had no interest in her, save that she return home, and I did not know that you would take her to your plantation. I thought to save you the trouble and send her home myself. Or, if her family did not wish to pay for her return, to find another man who would wed her. I meant no harm by altering your letter."

"And how exactly did you alter it?"

Winifred put her hands together in a motion of false piety and paused before responding. "I had another letter written," she explained, looking at the ground as she spoke. "Please sir, with God as my witness, I meant no harm. My letter explained the truth as I knew it. The girl was sickly when she arrived, and you put her in my care. She might not survive a return passage and could join a convent here in the Colonies. She needed money to repay you for the purchase of her contract, for her keep with me, and for her entry into a religious teaching order."

"I would never have approved such a letter!" He set his hat down on the table. "And what was her father's response?"

"Would you let me go and get the letter?"

"Do that promptly!"

Winifred climbed the ladder and returned with Cillian's letter. She handed it to William to read.

My dear Madam Skidmore, I am grieved by your letter regarding my daughter, Honor. Pray this letter finds her in better health. When she was kidnapped, she promised to return, and I would rather she do so, if that be at all possible. Her whole family wishes for her safe return. But if the journey is too dangerous and she can find her way in the Colonies, I will accept such a fate.

This letter arrives with fifty pounds, which I put in the ship captain's keeping. Please use it to cover her debts and give her whatever funds remain. If she wills to return, we would be most grateful. Tell her my prayers – and those of her dear mother – will always include mention of her, and that she remains my Irish shamrock and my Catholic rose. If she remains in Maryland, please tell her to write often so that we can know of her success in the New World.

I am your unhappy servant, Cillian O'Flynn.

William read the letter twice and stared at Winifred. He looked up to see Winifred looking sheepishly at him. "Bring me the fifty pounds."

"I have expenses," said Winifred when she returned with the coins. "The remainder of Honor's boarding bill is still unpaid. Will you go to the constable?"

"I will let Honor decide that. It is her money."

"If you accuse me, I will tell the constable that I held the money until your return." She handed him several coins.

"Madam, you are truly a scoundrel." William picked up the letter, paid the boarding house bill, and made his way to Saint Anne's Church.

●●●

What should I do, William wondered. Two days before his wedding to the beautiful red-haired girl, he learned that her father had spoken, would prefer her to return to Ireland, and had sent the money to pay for the journey.

At St. Anne's manse, William was greeted by Samuel Blyth and Cooper John. "Good day to you," said the parson. "We are all much excited about the wedding next Wednesday." Four festive folk turned to see the groom come through the door, all smiling at his return. None seemed to notice his apprehensive look. The cooper shook William's hand. Honor skipped over to the table and picked up her new dress, white gloves, and kerchief. She laid the dress across her body, and twirled for William. "I am so happy!" she exclaimed.

William continued to smile, but it was not the smile of a groom before his wedding.

Parson Blyth sensed that something was amiss. "Your bride and Clara have much to discuss," said Blyth. "Come, let us retire to the sanctuary." The three men left the manse, heading inside the church building.

"Are you having second thoughts, Master Logsdon?" asked Parson Blyth kindly as he sat down. "It is often true that men so close to their wedding become nervous."

Cooper John put his hand on William's shoulder, "I have never seen another so charming as your young bride."

"She is far more than charming. She is all I desire in this world. Alas, perhaps it is she who will have second thoughts. Truly, that would put an arrow through me heart."

"I can assure you, sir, she is more than ready to wed you," said Connolly.

William reached into the pocket of his waistcoat and removed a folded piece of paper. He looked at John Connolly, "Sir, do you know of my arrangement with Honor when she came to live at my plantation?"

"No, sir, I do not."

"Honor agreed to wed with me in an Anglican ceremony so that she could stay with me at *Brotherly Love*, and I agreed not to be with her as her husband until a letter arrived from her father in Ireland."

"Yes, I do know of the letter. Is that it in your hand?"

"My Lord," said Blyth. "You agreed to allow the girl to return to Ireland if that was her father's wish. Does he say that in his letter?"

"Yes, and he sent the money to pay for her voyage. We agreed that the letter would determine her fate. In my letter, I asked that he consider moving his family to Maryland and join us. That letter was never sent. In its place, he received a letter indicating that she did not wish to go home. In his response, he wrote... William unfolded the letter and read, 'When she was kidnapped, she promised to return, and I would rather she do so, if that be at all possible.' "

"And you fear those words will put doubt in her mind?" asked Connolly. "May I please see the letter?" William handed the letter to the cooper, who read it through.

"My son, her father also writes: 'But if the journey is too dangerous and she can find her way in the Colonies, I will accept that.' She has already accepted her wedding to you. Surely, you're not thinking of keeping this from her?"

"No, I must tell her, but I fear that she will be transported back into a state of confusion and forever doubt whichever decision she makes. I could not hide the letter because she would eventually ask about it. And she would likely write another letter, eventually learning that I had been dishonest and wedded her with a lie. I must show her this before we wed."

John went on, "So you know the right thing is to show her the letter, but you are fearful of losing her if you do so."

"I might lose her this very day, but if I lie, I will lose her love soon and for certain."

Parson Blyth asked, "Master Logsdon, why do you think she changed her mind and decided to wed with you?"

"It was while I was unconscious from my wound. When I awoke, she told me she had learned from an angel that God wanted her to wed with me. It is my thought that she came to understand how much I needed her — still need her. I will always need her. I would have died without her, and she learned she was truly needed as well as loved."

Blyth said, "Then, I would suggest that I ask her two questions before you present the letter. I will ask her why she wants to wed you. Her answer will focus her decision on you. Then I will ask what she would do if the letter arrived and she could go home if she chose to. It is my belief that God truly has spoken to her, and she will choose to stay."

William nodded in understanding. "After that, I will show her the letter and speak my love to her."

Blyth smiled, and Cooper John spoke in agreement. "I believe that is a good way to proceed. I will suggest that she write a letter to her family, telling them about you. Also, that she return the money and suggest that her family try to join you here."

● ● ●

On Thursday, the newlywed couple sent the fifty pound note back to Cillian, along with a long letter explaining her decision. Next, they began their day-long journey back to *Brotherly Love*, Honor holding onto her husband's good arm as they rode out of town. Although they'd had many weeks to grasp the meaning of their new situation, a long drive to town to enjoy it, and a balmy night to consummate it, they still had much to talk over. Periodically, Honor turned to William, not as a daughter, but as his wife, saying something like, "Husband, I would rather choose a life with you and all the children God blesses us with, than all the children in Dingle. So, let us gather our neighbors and hold feast in our royal castle."

Honor could see that he was giddy about being wedded, because he acted like a love-struck boy. He put the reins in his injured hand and waved his good hand like a sovereign greeting his loyal subjects. "Wife, I believe we should do that. I will speak to the servants in the morning," he said, sitting up tall like a king holding court, acting as though his new role was to grant his royal magnanimity.

Playing along, Honor bowed her head. "I confess, my King, I believe the Lord has crowned you my king and I be your queen."

Instantly, he changed personas to speak like a simple Irish subject. "Darlin', I'm not a king, but I've grown a wee bit more Irish."

She giggled at his attempt to speak in her tongue. "Praise be to Saint Paddy!" She leaned to the side so she could look at his face. "We been wedded but a day, and I believe you've already become an Irish Catholic."

William summarized the last many months. He put his arm around her and hugged her, declaring, "One day! It seems like just a moment."

Addendum

William Logsdon and Honor O'Flynn were real people; they are the author's seventh great-grandparents. They are the likely immigrant ancestors of nearly all the Durbins and Logsdons in Maryland, Kentucky, Ohio, Indiana, Illinois, and Missouri, including one United States Senator. Documented details about their lives are few, but what follows is, at least, one interpretation of the available data.

William was born in Bedfordshire, England, in 1664. At the age of 10, he came to Annapolis in January 1674 where he was sold as an indentured servant. He is listed on the tax rolls as owning a farm called "*Brotherly Love*" from 1692 through 1703. He married Honor O'Flynn in 1702 when he was 38, and died in Carroll County, Maryland, in 1742 at the age of 78.

Honor was born somewhere in Kerry County, Ireland, in about 1685. I chose the seaside town of Dingle in Kerry County as her fictional childhood home. Some suggest that she came from a wealthy family and was, possibly, a princess. She was kidnapped in 1701 and brought to Annapolis. She died in Carroll County in about 1740, at the age of 55.

Ann (Comfort) Logsdon was born to William and Honor in 1703. She married Samuel Durbin and had sixteen children with him. William and Honor's second child, William Logsdon, Jr., was born in 1705. He married Ann Davis, and the couple had five children. Two of William and Honor's grandchildren, born to either Ann or William, were Christopher Durbin (1742-1825) and Elisha Logsdon (1735-1815), and one of their great-grandchildren, Samuel Durbin, Jr. (1726-1817), are significant in history. All three immigrated to Madison County, Kentucky, in about 1788.

From the Honorable Benjamin Webb's 1844 book, entitled *Centennial of Catholicity in Kentucky*, we learn that these three families were among the very first to bring Catholicism across the mountains into Kentucky. Several chapters of that book are devoted to the efforts of Honor and William's great-great grandson, Father Elisha Durbin, who planted the seeds for many of Kentucky's Catholic churches. For example, on page 364, we read:

"Catholicity in Union County, and in all Southwestern Kentucky, indeed, is to the present hour so intimately connected with the name and personal labors of Rev. Elisha J. Durbin, that the writer regards it here necessary, and as a preliminary to his account of that important mission, to present to his readers a short sketch of the life of this venerable and most meritorious priest: Elisha J. Durbin was born in Madison County, Kentucky, about sixteen miles from Boonesboro, on the 1st of February, 1800. His parents were John D. Durbin and Patience Logsdon."

Further, we read:

"Neither were the Durbins nor the Logsdons descended from stock that was known to be Catholic beyond a couple of generations previous to the appearance in Kentucky of the families spoken of in the text. An ancestor of one of the families — I am uncertain as to which — intermarried with one Honor O'Flynn, an Irish girl of great piety, and it was through her, no doubt, that is to be traced the faith that has distinguished one or the other of the Kentucky families referred to, both of which have for generations been consistent exponents of its teachings."

And thus did Honor O'Flynn accomplish the will of God.

What follows is a list of William and Honor's children and partial family tree of William and Honor's descendants, leading to the three families mentioned in the 1844 Webb book.

According to The World Family Tree, Vol. 5, Ed. 1, August 1996, Honor and William had, at least, six children:

1. ANN COMFORT LOGSDON. Born about 1703, Annapolis Co., MD; married Samuel Durbin on July 4, 1723; died in about 1770.

2. WILLIAM LOGSDON, JR. Born about 1705, Annapolis Co., MD; married Ann Davis; died between 1754 and 1798.

3. PRUDENCE LOGSDON. Born 1707, Annapolis Co., MD; married James Kelly; died after 1737.

4. EDWARD LOGSDON, SR. Born about 1709, Annapolis Co., MD; died about 1793.

5. HONOR LOGSDON. Born 1711, Annapolis Co., Maryland; married Richard Fowler, September 13, 1730, Annapolis Co., Maryland; died bef. 1802.

6. JOHN LOGSDON. Born 1716, Annapolis Co., Maryland; died about 1797.

Other Books by James Bailey

Bailey's Blood
Moonshine, Murder and Wild Women

"With masterful storytelling, Dr. James Bailey breathes life into the violent characters of his Eastern Kentucky heritage. We are drawn into the infamous Bailey-White Feud as Bill and Martha Bailey's sons exact revenge to preserve their family's mountain pride. Bailey's Blood will hold you spellbound to discover who will survive hot tempers and moonshine madness."—Edwina A. Doyle, author of From the Fort to the Future: Educating the Children of Kentucky and The Bless Mark.

"Moonshine, wild women and murder! James Bailey takes a hard look at the roots of clan feuds and violence in this tragic historical family saga set in rural Kentucky."—Kris Neri, author of High Crimes on the Magical Plane.

Based on actual events, the book is a fictionalization of violent lives of three Bailey brothers in southeast Kentucky between 1907 and 1931. Jim Bailey is the youngest son in a proud, violent and fearful family. To escape his family's deadly lifestyle, Jim needs to commit himself to his sweetheart Sarah, the daughter of a Baptist deacon. Again and again, he tries to satisfy Sarah's requests, but he is repeatedly unable to separate himself from his mother's demands for loyalty and his brother's murders. Disgusted, Sarah finally leaves Jim and he spirals down the evil path of his family. In the end, Jim is murdered by one of those brothers in an argument over a still that he sold to one of them.

Should you wish to be apprised of future Christian Romance novels by James Bailey, request your complimentary copy of the SAMPLE CHAPTER of Bailey's Blood at:

http://bit.ly/SAMPLEBaileysBlood

Made in the USA
Monee, IL
26 November 2023

47411661R00155